THE SCARLET THIEF

THE SCARLET THIEF

PAUL FRASER COLLARD

ISIS
LARGE PRINT
Oxford

Copyright © Paul Fraser Collard, 2013

First published in Great Britain 2013
by
Headline Publishing Group
an Hachette UK Company

Published in Large Print 2014 by ISIS Publishing Ltd.,
7 Centremead, Osney Mead, Oxford OX2 0ES
by arrangement with
Headline Publishing Group
an Hachette UK Company

CIP data is available for this title from the British Library

ISBN 978-0-7531-9240-5 (hb)
ISBN 978-0-7531-9241-2 (pb)

Printed and bound in Great Britain by
T. J. International Ltd., Padstow, Cornwall

To Debbie, Lily, William and Emily

Glossary

Aut vincere aut mori	Either to conquer or to die
Deficit omne quod nasciture	Everything that is born passes away (Quintilian)
Qui audit adipiscitur	He who dares wins
Per aspera ad astra	Through difficulties to the stars
Cave quid dicis, quando et cui	Beware of what you say, when, and to whom
Nulli secondus	Second to none
Aut viam inveniam aut faciam	I'll either find a way or make one
Absit invidia	Let there be no ill will
blagging	lying
bye-blow	bastard child
chokey	cholera
cove	fellow, chap
Crapauds	the French (the toads)
Jack Puddings	British officers
Jack Shephard	infamous thief from the eighteenth century
kick up a shine	making a fuss, causing a ruction
muzzle	mouth

pannie	burglary
passing queer screens	passing counterfeit notes
rhino	money, cash
rummy	odd, strange
same kidney	alike, resembling
slating	beating
walk the chalk	withdraw, go away

CHAPTER
ONE

*20 September 1854. The banks of the Alma River,
Crimean Peninsula*

The redcoats staggered to a bloody halt. The men of
the King's Royal Fusiliers crouched at the edge of the
vineyard, ducking and twisting as the storm of shot,
shell and bullet tore through their ranks. Dozens of
fusiliers went down under the Russian barrage, the men
falling silently, their passing unremarked. Those still
living pressed close to their comrades, the desperate
need to be near to another human being overwhelming
the rational thought that to be grouped together was to
present a larger target for the enemy to hit.

Beyond the shattered vineyard there was no cover for
the frightened fusiliers; a dozen yards of open scrub
separated the last of the vines from the shallow banks of
the Alma River. The bloodied redcoats clung to what
little shelter they could find, stubbornly refusing to
advance, no one willing to dare the killing ground
to their front.

On their right, the men of the 2nd Division were
going to ground, the heavy fire driving its battered
battalions to seek cover in the ruined walls and burning
buildings that were all that remained of the village of
Burliuk. All along the line, the redcoats milled in

confusion and fear, still yards short of the river they had been ordered to cross. The Russians poured on the fire ruthlessly, striking redcoat after redcoat to the ground, their bodies forming a tide line, a high-water mark for the advance.

General Raglan's army was paying in blood for the simplicity of his plan. His decision to fling two of his divisions against the strongest point on the Russians' right flank was the cause of the suffering being endured by the men who had been ordered forward. It was a plan devoid of all subtlety. A plan that now looked destined to fail.

Jack Lark forced a path through his men. He saw the terror on the faces of the fusiliers, a fear that he knew well as it seared through his own veins. It threatened to drive him screaming to the ground. It begged him to do anything to get out of the merciless fire that swept along the stalled line, yet he made himself move, even though his body flinched at every bullet that whipped past.

"Fusiliers!" Jack's voice was huge. "Advance, damn you! Move! Move!"

Still the fusiliers refused to advance. Jack shoved at the men closest to him, trying to force them forward. But they ignored him, their eyes flashing in anger as he tried to bully them. The fusiliers were not advancing for anyone.

The men started to edge backwards, the movement fluttering through the packed ranks. The battalion was moments away from turning to flee from the unrelenting Russian fire that was flaying their ranks.

They had reached breaking point.

Jack cringed as a bullet cracked into the ground at his feet. The fear was paralysing him, ravaging his guts like a caged beast. Every part of him shrank away from what he was about to do. His mind pleaded with him to let someone else carry the burden of responsibility. Yet he had chosen to become an officer and now he would have to repay the debt that came with the gold epaulets and the respect that came from being addressed as "Sir".

He shouldered his way through the snug pocket of men to his front, ignoring the oaths and the insults directed at him. He strode out of the vineyard and into the cauldron of fire.

"King's Royal Fusiliers!"

He turned to his men, his fury building, the anger driving out the last of his uncertainty. He might have stolen the right to command these men but now he would prove he could lead them. He goaded the enemy fire, prowling in front of his company, showing them he was bigger than the storm of fire that had bludgeoned the slow, steady advance to a standstill.

"King's Royal Fusiliers! Look at me!" Jack demanded attention even as the Russian fire cracked and whipped through the air around him.

"We will advance. You hear me? We will advance!" His voice faltered, his throat half closed. Yet he forced the order out, screaming the words at his men who watched him as if they were staring at an inmate of Bedlam let loose on the field of battle.

Jack turned his back on his men and bounded across the few open yards between the vineyard and the river. It felt as if every Russian skirmisher was firing at him but by some miracle he made it to the shallow bank of the river without coming to harm. As he slipped and slithered down the bank, he turned to glare in accusation at his men.

The fusiliers were stationary, as if petrified.

Then, finally, they moved. Prompted by a secret signal the battalion surged forward. The open ground that had caused such fear was crossed in moments, the fusiliers streaming forward to slide down to join Jack in the shallow water of the Alma. The Russian fire doubled in its intensity the moment the fusiliers abandoned the shelter of the vineyard, striking dozens from their ranks. Yet the redcoats ignored the casualties, storming forward, their paralysing fear forgotten.

They had crossed the line.

In the melee, Jack was pitched unceremoniously forward. The river flowed over the tops of his boots, the water icy cold where it splashed against his legs. The fusiliers careered through the water, the ordered line forgotten, the men moving together in one amorphous mass. The wiser heads among the redcoats lifted their ammunition pouches and rifles away from a soaking in the river but they were few in number amidst the crazed, adrenalin-fuelled mob.

The gravel bed of the river was treacherous, the weeds and slime making the footing uncertain and twice Jack slipped and would have fallen if he had not been so tightly pressed into the pack of redcoats.

Around him, his men cursed angrily as they forced their way across the river, elbows working furiously, fighting each other to reach the relative safety of the south side of the Alma. The south bank was far steeper than the north side, rising three to four feet before levelling out and forming a shelf above the river. The redcoats threw themselves up the slope with abandon, churning the ground to slick mud as they tried to find purchase with their wet boots.

On the ledge the fusiliers were screened from much of the Russian fire. Above their heads, the awful barrage continued. To move forward would mean walking straight into the enemy roundshot and musket fire.

For a second time, the advance halted. The wet, mud-splattered fusiliers caught their breath after the wild scramble through the river and steeled themselves for what was still to come.

"You bloody idiot!" Jack's orderly, Tommy Smith, thumped into the ground beside his officer, ducking away from a flurry of musket fire that whistled past less than a foot above their heads. "You'll get yourself killed if you carry on like that, Jack."

"It had to be done." The shock of walking into the open ground still coursed through Jack's body and he shivered at the memory. He felt the cold hand of near death.

"But not by you, you damn fool." Smith had to shout to be heard above the din. "You might be dressed as a bloody Rupert but that doesn't mean you have to do it all by yourself!"

A flurry of activity prevented Jack from replying. Another officer was indeed taking control, showing his men what he expected of them.

General William John Codrington was fifty years old. He had joined the army thirty-three years previously, yet this was his first taste of action, the only time he had heard guns fired in anger. Codrington commanded the 1st Fusilier Brigade, part of the once famous Light Division. Although it was no longer made up from the same regiments that had marched to such renown and fame in the battles Wellington had fought in Portugal and Spain forty years earlier, Codrington was determined his command would live up to their high standards. He had watched his brigade march into the violent storm of the Russian barrage and he had witnessed their desperate plunge into the Alma. Now he had to show his men what he expected them to do next.

Mounted on a small white Arab mare, Codrington spurred his way across the river, encouraging the young horse up the far bank. The men of his command watched the grey-haired general charge straight into the terrible fire that was raging above them.

Jack looked on in astonishment. He flashed a smile at Tommy Smith and then, saying a silent prayer, he pushed himself up over the lip of the shelf, determined to be at the head of the attack.

With a huge cheer, the redcoats followed.

The steep undulating slope led up to the four-foot-high wall of the great redoubt, the fortified position that was the key to the Russian general's right flank. The Russian skirmishers had moved back up the slope and were already re-forming on the crest around the guns hidden in the redoubt. It was up this slope that Codrington's brigade would have to advance, into the mouths of the guns that waited to sweep the attackers away.

"Forward the fusiliers!" Jack screamed, leading his men up the slope. Around him, the fusiliers were horribly disordered, the different companies now hopelessly intertwined after the mad scramble across the river. The precise two-man line was gone and the redcoats moved forward bunched up in groups. The angle of the slope pulled at their already aching muscles. In the middle of the disorganised crush the young ensigns carrying the colours found the strength to wave their heavy ash staffs from side to side, forcing movement into the lifeless silk that refused to stir in the still, breathless air.

As the three battalions of Codrington's brigade erupted from the confines of the river, the attack snarled back into life.

CHAPTER
TWO

Six months earlier. Aldershot Barracks, England

The officer groaned with relief as he eased his heavy scarlet coat off his shoulders, the thick bullion epaulets jangling as he tossed it on to the iron bed that dominated the small room. He let out a sigh of tired exasperation.

"Lark!" the officer barked. He listened for any sound that showed his servant was rushing to answer the summons. To his annoyance, he heard nothing.

"Lark!" the tall officer bellowed for a second time, his voice rising in anger.

"Sir?"

The officer's servant half ran, half stumbled into the small bedroom, wiping his hands furiously on a stained lint cloth as he entered.

"You don't have time for that now, Lark." The officer's face betrayed his annoyance despite his best attempts to keep it under control. "Where is my best uniform?"

"In your cupboard, sir." Jack Lark was new to the ways of being an orderly. He still had much to learn.

"What good is it there?" Captain Arthur Sloames ran a hand over his thick, black, mutton-chop whiskers and through the mop of unruly hair that he would soon spend some time attempting to subdue. "You should have it out and ready."

"Sorry, sir." Jack looked around for a convenient spot to dump the stained cloth he was carrying. Seeing nowhere suitable he stuffed it into the waistband of his grey fatigues before making towards the tall, mahogany wardrobe that stood in the corner of the small room.

"You cannot do it now, you fool. I have no intention of attending on the dowager countess this evening stinking like a damn navvy. Go and wash your hands thoroughly. I'll do it myself."

"Yes, sir." Jack muttered a curse under his breath. He had forgotten to have his master's finest uniform ready. The list of chores to be done in a single day was taking him too long. He knew he would have to work harder if he were to remain in his new position. He turned to hurry from the room, determined to wash quickly and make up for his error. He would not throw away the chance he had been given. An orderly was a step up from being an ordinary redcoat and Jack was desperate to succeed.

"Wait." Sloames snapped the curt command. "You can help me with my boots before you go."

The young captain turned his back and offered up his foot for Jack to hold. The two men were of a similar height, both a shade under six feet tall, yet their faces betrayed their relative status as eloquently as the badges of rank that adorned their uniforms. Sloames's fleshy face and thick waistline betrayed his privileged lifestyle, his blue Oxford uniform trousers straining across his generous backside. Where Sloames was portly, Jack Lark was gaunt, his hard face and wiry physique the result of a youth spent in London's slums. His ill-fitting fatigues may have hung from his sparse frame but his rolled shirtsleeves revealed a pair of finely muscled forearms. Jack may have lacked his officer's bulk but there was strength in his sinewy build, strength that he needed as he strained to pull the tight, calf-length boots from his master's feet.

"You must try to improve, Lark," Sloames grunted as the first boot was tugged free. "I'd have thought you would've begun to get the hang of things by now."

"Sorry, sir." Jack bit his lip as he took a firm hold on the second boot. "I lost track of time."

"What were you doing?" Sloames sighed with pleasure as his right foot found freedom.

"I was polishing your sword, sir. Coxy, I mean Private Cox, told me you would be likely to inspect it to make sure I was keeping on top of everything."

Sloames chuckled. "He was right. You would do well to listen to Cox. He is a good man. Major Hume is fortunate indeed to have him. Let us hope you are as good one day."

"I'll try my best, sir." Jack stood up and looked his officer in the eye. "Sorry about the uniform."

Sloames dismissed Jack's apology with a wave of his hand. "Quick now. Wash up and hurry back to help me get dressed. The colonel hates to be late and I cannot risk keeping him waiting." He fixed Jack with a warm smile. "Even us captains have to do as we are told."

"You'll throw this chance away if you're not careful."

Jack twisted away from Molly, his pleasure at seeing her waning in the face of her criticism.

"I know, Molly. I'm not soft in the head."

"Well, you will be if you mess this up." Molly stepped back into Jack's arms, ignoring his churlish response. "You have to make something of yourself or we'll never get anywhere."

She and Jack had been together for nearly three months. He came to visit her in the garrison laundry often, his new life as an officer's orderly giving him a freedom he could have only dreamt of as a simple redcoat.

"I won't mess it up." Jack's pride had been stung. He knew he had forgotten his master's instructions and Captain Sloames was well within his rights to admonish him but he had hoped Molly would be more sympathetic.

"You'd better not. I can't waste my time on a redcoat. I want to make something of my life, even if you don't."

"I'm not a waste of time. Sloames picked me to be his orderly, didn't he?"

"Well, just don't make him regret it." Molly moved back and brushed at his lapel where a few of her hairs lay. "I know you like being a servant but it's not that much of a step up, is it? It's not like being a corporal, or a sergeant."

"I'm not a servant. I'm an orderly. It's different." Jack's fragile pride was offended. "It keeps me away from Colour Sergeant Slater and that is good enough for me."

"I don't know why you're so frightened of Slater. He's not that bad. I think he's a fine figure of a man and he's always nice to me when he comes in here. And *he's* a sergeant." Molly reached for Jack's face, her finger sliding over Jack's smooth and unfashionably hair-free cheeks.

"Slater's not a fine figure of a man." Jack looked at Molly warily, sensing she was showing more than a passing interest in his company's colour sergeant. "He's a bastard. If that's what it takes to become a sergeant then it's not for me, thank you very much." Jack's words belied the ambition that burned brightly inside him. To be a sergeant would be the pinnacle of his time as a soldier. It was a position he was determined to achieve, his role as an orderly merely a stepping stone on his climb up the ranks.

"Well, I can just see you with them stripes. Why, you could even become an officer and have your own servant."

"Orderly," Jack rebuked her. "I'm not about to become an officer. It's not for the likes of me. You have to be born with a silver spoon in your muzzle to become an officer. If you have the money, you can become an officer. If you don't then forget it."

"Some do it."

"Some do. But they never go far. Quartermaster is about all they're good for. And even that's as rare as finding gold in horseshit."

"You give up too easy. You'll never get anywhere if you don't try. I can see it even if you can't — you this big handsome officer and me your lady," Molly giggled at the wild fancy.

Jack smiled at the notion. "It's never going to happen."

Molly's hands disappeared behind her back, untying the knots that held her apron in place, her teasing smile making Jack's heart race as he began to hope the afternoon's visit would not be completely wasted.

"My mam says you lot are going to be posted."

"What?" Molly's darting train of thought often left Jack lumbering to keep up with her.

"You lot is going to be posted. Mam says that Billy who looks after Major Dansen told her." Molly tossed her apron to one side and started to undo the buttons of her blouse.

"Billy Burton don't know shit." Jack tore his eyes from the glimpse of flesh and took hold of Molly's hands to stop her undoing any more buttons. Her words had changed the focus of his thoughts. It was exciting news if it was true. The battalion had been stationed in Aldershot on garrison duty ever since he joined it four years previously. It was dull and Jack chafed at the routine life that ground out through the days and months. A posting would mean going abroad, seeing the world and, with any luck, doing some proper soldiering.

"Well, my mam says he said it, so there. You don't have to believe me." Molly pouted.

Against his tanned skin the red rawness of her hands stood out vividly, the countless hours spent in hot water dealing with the battalion's laundry taking its toll even on her young, seventeen-year-old skin.

"I believe you. It's that fool Billy I don't trust."

"I hope you don't get posted. I wouldn't know what to do if you up and left." Tears welled in Molly's eyes.

Jack brushed the tears from Molly's cheeks. "Don't fret. There's always talk. Nothing is going to happen. It never does." Molly nestled into his arms, consoled and safe in his embrace. Jack rested his chin on the unruly curls pinned on top of her head. His heart raced, his hopes coming alive at the idea of leaving. For a posting might mean facing the harshest test a soldier could imagine: battle.

CHAPTER
THREE

Jack paused at the door to the barrack room, the stench emanating from the confined space like a physical wall barring his progress. The smell was always worse when he had stayed away for a while. The small box room Sloames allowed Jack to use in his suite was a palace compared to the confines of the rank barrack rooms the other redcoats were forced to live in.

The air was thick with the smell of pipe clay, boot blacking, damp clothing, and lamp oil. The forty redcoats who called this their home ate, slept, cleaned their kit, cussed, complained, drank, pissed and farted in the one small area. In summer they boiled, sweating and stinking through the warmer months, the meagre windows firmly shut and barred no matter how hot the room became. In winter, they froze; a single stove and limited ration of fuel left the accommodation cold, damp and inhospitable. But no matter what the season the room still stank, the smell of forty unwashed bodies and the sour smell of urine from the single piss pot ever present.

"Have you boys been eating dead dog again? It smells like Satan's arse in here." Jack pushed his way into the room, greeting his former messmates with a warm smile. He missed being with his fellow soldiers. The long hours he spent with his officer took away the companionship of his brother redcoats. Despite his best efforts, his new role had created a barrier between them, something he regretted.

The soldier closest to the door looked up briefly then returned his attention to the cross-belts of his uniform, which were laid carefully on his bed as he applied the thick layer of pipe clay that gave them their smart, white colour. A few other members of the mess greeted Jack's arrival with a brief comment before they carried on with the serious task of preparing their uniforms for the parade their captain had ordered.

One burly redcoat ambled towards Jack, a wide smile spread on his face.

"Hello, Mud. Come to check up on us?"

"I couldn't stay away." Jack took the meaty hand thrust towards him and shook it vigorously. He had been known as Mud ever since joining the regiment, a reference to the mudlarks of the River Thames that more than one of the redcoats had been before they had taken the Queen's shilling.

"You're looking good. Being Sloames's orderly is obviously good for you. I wish I'd taken the chance when he offered it to me."

"You had a lucky escape. Just think of all the extra bull, and Sloames can be a hard taskmaster."

Private Jonathan Pike nodded his agreement. Of all the redcoats in the company, Pike had been Jack's closest friend, the one who had looked after him in his earliest days in the battalion, saving him more than once from falling foul of Colour Sergeant Slater, who ran the company with an iron fist. "You got that right. Making us go through this bloody malarkey just because it takes his damn fancy."

Jack slid the tall, black shako off his head, careful not to touch any of the polished brasswork. He ran his hand over the stubby red and white plume on its crown, picking away imaginary tufts of fluff. "You have it easy. What time did you start this morning?"

"Four o'clock."

"See! I was up at three. Not only have I got to get my uniform ready, I also have to do his."

"All right. You win. Is it still raining?"

"Only a little."

"It'll still make everything get rusty. Which means more bloody work. So, Sloames didn't need you to button his breeches this morning then?"

"I don't button his breeches, you daft clot. And no, he doesn't. He spent the night at the Horse and Hounds in town. It was Lady Catherine's ball last night which means he probably got boozed up."

"The lucky bugger. I expect he spent the night with that barmaid, Sally."

"Probably. He's going to be knackered." Jack laughed at the notion. He was enjoying being back with his friend. The camaraderie the common soldiers enjoyed was the best thing he had discovered since joining the army. The bond that was formed from shared hardships and from surviving everything their officers and sergeants demanded of them tied the men together, creating friendships that many would never have experienced in their former lives.

The door to the barrack room was flung open. "Stand by your beds!"

The shout of command had an instant effect on the barrack room. The bustle of quiet industry evaporated, replaced with a palpable tension. The men stood rigidly to attention at the foot of their iron bedsteads, their eyes fixed, and staring forward.

A finely dressed redcoat with the golden chevrons of a sergeant on his sleeve strode into the room, his two black, beady eyes sweeping the room above a mass of moustache.

"Attention!"

The forty redcoats tensed their already stretched muscles even further, striving to attain the perfect position of attention. Jack pressed himself into the tiny space between two of the closely packed bedsteads, forcing his shoulders back, his heart sinking as he realised his rare presence was sure to attract attention.

The sergeant snapped to attention as he held the door wide open. There was a moment of complete silence, broken by the sound of heavy boots thumping along the short corridor to the barrack room. Tension rippled through the air, barely a single redcoat daring to breathe as they awaited the tempest that was surely about to break over their heads.

Colour Sergeant Slater loomed large in the doorway. The man who ran the company had arrived to inspect his charges.

Slater strode down the narrow aisle that ran between the feet of the iron beds. He was a bear of a man and dominated the enclosed space. He was easily the tallest in the company and every man lived in fear of him. It was a fear based on bitter experience and in the cold silence that followed his arrival, the men felt it flutter and stir in their bellies as Slater stalked the room.

"You should be ready. That means dressed and booted." Slater did not raise his voice as he rebuked them; his icy tone betrayed his anger more effectively than if he had been screaming with rage. When he reached the far end of the barrack room, he swung round to face the soldiers whose lives he ruled, his thick moustache twitching. Above the sergeant's chevrons, the badge denoting the rank of colour sergeant flashed in a beam of sunlight, its crowned Union flag and crossed swords reminding the redcoats that they faced their company's most senior noncommissioned officer.

"Captain Sloames has asked you to parade and you should be honoured to have been asked. Is that not so, Sergeant Attwood?"

The first sergeant to have entered the room slammed the door shut, taking up position as if blocking any of the redcoats from bolting from the room, an idea many entertained but would never act upon.

"That is correct, Colour Sergeant. These miserable bastards should be honoured."

Despite his ready agreement, Attwood was no stooge or lickspittle. He was as brutal and as uncompromising as his colour sergeant. Together they abused those under their command at will, punishing any who

19

showed even the remotest sign of disobedience. Beatings were commonplace and it was rare for a redcoat to avoid being on the receiving end of the two sergeants' wrath for long. If a simple slating was not enough, then the two had a long list of other ways to break a man's spirit. They were not shy of framing an innocent soldier, forcing them to face the more formal list of army punishments that could be administered by the battalion's officers, and more than one man in the company had been flogged at their instigation. To take a stand against the pair was to court disaster.

"Hello, hello," Attwood shouted. "Why, it is us who should be honoured. Look here, Colour Sergeant. Mr Lark has condescended to join us this morning." Attwood offered Jack a mock bow; Slater narrowed his eyes.

Jack had been one of the very few men in the company foolish enough to stand up to the two sergeants. His independent spirit had cost him dear, the last beating the sergeants administered one of the most brutal they had ever inflicted. Had Jack not escaped their clutches by becoming Sloames's orderly, it was almost certain that he would have been up before the colonel on a trumped-up charge of theft or insubordination, the result of which would have been a brutal flogging. Instead, Slater and Attwood had been cheated of their victim. Neither had been quick to forget.

"My, oh my. To what do we owe the pleasure, Lark? Have you had enough of wiping the captain's arse?" Attwood sneered as Slater came close. Jack could not help but cringe. He had the sense to remain silent, fixing his eyes on a rusty nail head that stuck out of the wall opposite.

"Cat got your tongue?" Slater whispered.

"Beg your pardon, sir?"

Slater stood in front of his former charge, his head thrust forward so it was a matter of inches from Jack's own. "Dear, oh dear. I can see your time spent away from me has done little to improve your manners. You are still beholden to me. You would do well to remember that." The menace contained in his quiet words and the warning they gave was clear.

"Yes, Colour Sergeant."

"Do you miss me, Lark?"

Jack lowered his eyes so he met Slater's. The colour sergeant's eyes were a soft, moist brown. On a woman, they would be beautiful. On Slater, they were pure evil.

"No, Colour Sergeant."

A very faint ripple of laughter went round the room. It was enough for Slater to twist on the spot, his eyes roaming over the men, his fierce stare silencing the redcoats in an instant. He turned back to Lark.

"You should miss me. Because if I am not looking after you then who is?" Slater smiled as he spoke. He turned and looked quickly around the room of silent redcoats. Each man stared into space. The silence seemed to please the huge man and he let out a bark of laughter. "You all need me looking after you. Because without me you'd be nothing. Now, as soon as the bugle calls you get yourselves out on that square. Do not let me down."

With that Slater stalked from the room, Attwood following closely in his wake.

The room stayed silent until the sound of heavy footsteps had faded.

Then the redcoats grudgingly returned to their preparations. Slater's presence was still heavy in the confined room. None of the men would risk not being ready for the parade. A few shot Jack a reprimanding glare, the men painfully aware that his presence had contributed to Slater's mood. Their disapproval saddened him. He had once counted many in the room amongst his closest friends. His desire to better himself had come at a heavy price.

CHAPTER
FOUR

Jack checked Captain Sloames's washstand for a third time. The carefully arranged toiletries were all in their allocated place, the pots of pills and the jars of potions and creams ordered and precise. He had stropped the razor, cleaned the brushes and combs, picked the stray hairs from the towel, filled one porcelain jug with hot water and another with cold. He made sure the washbowl was without stains or watermarks and the sheet on the floor was laid out evenly and blemish-free. He was certain that Sloames would have no cause to find fault this morning.

"Good morning, sir." Jack took a deep breath and pulled back the thin curtains that had been fighting an uneven battle against the early-morning sunlight. It was past ten yet Jack had delayed waking his master, knowing full well that he had not struggled home until the small hours of the morning after another heavy night of drinking in the officers' mess. However, a meeting with the battalion adjutant had been arranged for noon and despite Jack's silent prayers, Sloames had not stirred of his own volition.

A groan came from deep under the bed's tousled coverings.

"Coffee, sir?" Jack stood dutifully at the foot of the bed, a cup of the first medicinal coffee of the morning in his hand.

"Good morning, Lark." Sloames's muffled voice was feeble. "What time is it?"

"Past ten, sir."

"Good God." Sloames pushed his way clear of the covers, emerging into the sunlight blinking furiously. "You mentioned coffee?"

"Sir." Jack stepped forward and carefully placed the china cup of steaming black coffee in Sloames's trembling hand.

Sloames peered at him over the brim of the scalding liquid. "You look like an overeager hound, Lark. Whatever is the matter? Goodness, my head."

"You'll soon feel better, sir." Jack did his best to sound composed. He did not want Sloames to think he was anxious. "I have prepared your second-best uniform for your meeting with Captain Ramsay."

"Very good." The coffee worked its restorative power and colour returned to Sloames's cheeks, warming his former deathly pallor. "Good coffee."

"Thank you, sir. The mess had fresh beans this morning."

Sloames handed the empty cup back to his orderly before taking his head in both hands and ruffling his hair vigorously. "God, I feel awful." He stopped and looked up. "By God, that was a night. I suppose I should've learnt my lesson by now!" Sloames smiled ruefully at his orderly, abashed yet obviously proud of his own fecklessness.

24

Jack smiled back at his officer, his charm impossible to ignore. Like all officers, Sloames was a hard drinker, the officers' mess famous for its riotous nights. More often than not these evenings ended with some horseplay or mischief that would have the colonel wondering at his officers' sanity. Only the other week a precious teapot had been smashed in an impromptu game of indoor cricket, much to the delight of the officers and to the despair of the colonel's wife.

With a loud groan, Sloames pushed himself up from the bed. He staggered to the washstand and Jack leant backwards to make enough room for Sloames to pass without their bodies touching.

Sloames made a quick appraisal of his toiletries. "Damn you, Lark! Can you do nothing right?" He spat a thick wad of phlegm into the washbowl.

"Sir?" Jack stepped forward, his heart pounding as he tried to work out what he had done wrong.

Sloames laughed at Jack's horrified expression. "Just jesting, Lark. Just jesting. Everything is perfectly in order." He turned and threw two handfuls of water over his face. "You really are a hopeless cove."

Jack did his best to smile. He helped his officer through his morning wash routine, passing and taking items as they were needed or discarded.

"Have you heard the rumours?" Sloames lifted his chin high and started to scrape away the unwanted hairs, carefully trimming round his thick mutton-chop whiskers.

"Rumours, sir?" Jack was immediately interested. For the officers' orderlies, gossip and tittle-tattle were the common currency of their lives, sought as eagerly as the scattering of forgotten coins that could be slipped unnoticed into a diligent servant's pocket — and as jealously husbanded.

"Do not play the innocent with me." Sloames looked at his orderly from the corner of his eye. "The rumour that we are to be posted."

"I'd heard something about that, sir."

"That doesn't surprise me. Would it astonish you if it were true?"

"I suppose so, sir. I thought we'd be stuck here forever."

"Would that suit you? Or have you the taste for adventure?"

"I've never given it much thought, sir, if I'm honest."

"Truly? I must confess that I think of little else. What could be worse than stagnating in this Godforsaken place? What glory is there to be won in Aldershot? What legacy will be left if I languish here and waste the prime years of my life?"

"There's plenty of time, sir."

"You're wrong there." Sloames waved the razor at Jack to emphasise his point. "I'm fast approaching thirty years of age. Thirty! My life is slipping away. My father had fought a dozen battles in Spain and faced down the damn Frogs at Waterloo by the time he was my age. Whereas what have I done?" Sloames gave Jack no time to answer, not that he would ever be unwise enough to offer a suggestion. "Nothing! I crave glory, Lark. Glory."

Jack was keen to steer the conversation away from his master's frustrated ambition and back towards the news that the battalion could be about to move. "So is the battalion to be posted overseas?"

Sloames nodded. "We are bound for the West Indies. To Jamaica, in fact."

"The Indies!" Jack could not contain his dismay. All soldiers dreaded this posting. Duty in the West Indies would be a death sentence to many. Yellow fever, dysentery and all manner of other Devil-inspired illnesses waited to strike down a newly arrived redcoat. Jack craved going overseas. But, dear God, not to the Indies. To go there was to die.

Sloames paused in his shaving to stare at his orderly. "Your face betrays you. You no more want that destiny than I do."

"No, sir." Jack met Sloames's stare as evenly as he could while his soul screamed at the injustice of the cursed news.

"All is not lost. There is hope. I have written to Horseguards expressing my willingness to exchange. I am sanguine of my chances. In my letter, I expressed a keen intention to serve my country on the field of battle. There is talk of a war in the East and I am hopeful there will be a less martially inspired soul who feels their talents would be best employed by remaining away from the rigours of a campaign."

"I wish you luck, sir."

"There is no need for you'll be coming with me. We'll journey to the fields of battle together. What say you to that?" Sloames tossed his razor into the bowl with a flourish and turned to face his orderly, his face alive with the prospect of going to war. "Can you see the future unravelling before us? We shall leave this mundane existence behind us and go to war."

Jack swallowed hard. Molly's rumours had proved to be true.

CHAPTER
FIVE

"To war? Why on earth do you want to go to war?" Molly stamped her foot in frustration. "What's wrong with going to the Indies?"

"Well, for starters, I don't fancy puking my guts out every day for a year before they shove me in a box." Jack's frustration matched Molly's. He had come to deliver the momentous news only to find it had reached the garrison laundry before him.

"Who says it's like that? I heard the sun shines every day. And there are servants, even for the likes of us. And you can swim in the sea that's as warm as a bathtub!"

"You can't even swim, you ninny. Who's filled your head with all his nonsense?"

"It's not nonsense. Mam says."

Jack snorted with laughter. "And what does she know? She's never even been to London!"

"She knew you lot were getting posted before you did, didn't she?"

"But that doesn't mean she knows anything about life in the Indies."

"Oh, and you do, I suppose."

"I know a damn sight more than your mam."

"You're just being your usual cantankerous self just to slight me. I'd do anything to get out of here. I want us to go."

"Us? Since when do they send the laundry girls with the battalion?"

"They send wives!"

"You're not a wife."

"And whose fault is that?"

"It's not mine. Besides, even the wives get left behind."

"Not all of them."

"And I'd need permission."

"Who said anything about you?"

"Do you have someone in mind then?"

"Maybe I do."

"Oh, there's others, is there? Can't you keep your legs shut for more than a bloody second!"

Molly's arms had been strengthened by countless hours of dollying, stirring wet clothes with a heavy wooden paddle, and she delivered a punch any prizefighter would have been proud of, a rising blow that connected spectacularly with Jack's chin. With teeth-juddering force, his jaws snapped together, his head knocked sideways by the force of the blow, and he staggered back.

"Don't you dare talk to me like that! I'm not some common doxy. If you think so badly of me, what on earth are you doing here?" Molly stepped closer. She looked ready to continue her assault.

Jack lifted his hands to ward off further blows. "What do you want, Molly?"

Jack saw the anger leave her eyes. It was replaced by a look of such sadness and longing that he forgot the pain of her right hook and took her in his arms, pressing her close.

They stood in silence for a moment, quiet in each other's embrace.

"What I want . . ." Molly sounded uncertain as she began to speak. "What I want is a future, one that doesn't mean spending my years toiling away in a laundry. I want a different life."

"It's not that simple, is it? Wanting is one thing. Getting is another."

"I know that, Jack. I'm not a fool. But don't you ever feel trapped? Stuck in a life not of your choosing but which has wrapped itself around you so tightly that you can never get out. I know I do."

Jack kept quiet. Molly could have been expressing his own feelings. He knew exactly what it was to feel trapped. It had taken him years to pluck up the courage to leave his mother and take the Queen's shilling. All in an attempt to better himself, to find a life far away from the one into which he had been born.

"So are you going to take me away? Like one of those knights in those stories my mam told me when I was a girl."

Jack laughed at the image. "I'm no knight in shining armour. I can't even ride a bloody horse."

"But will you? Will you take me away? I'd follow you anywhere if it meant leaving this behind."

"If I ever get the chance, I will." Jack pulled Molly tight against him. "I promise."

★ ★ ★

"You wanted to see me, sir?"

"I did indeed. Give me a moment."

Sloames turned back to his desk, his attention focused on a thick pile of documents. The thick, creamy parchment looked official and Jack did his best to peer past his officer's shoulder and read the neat, copperplate writing.

It was a fortnight since the momentous news that the battalion was to be posted had broken. Two weeks for the battalion's mood to go from high excitement to sombre contemplation as the reality of moving to the far reaches of the empire left the redcoats wondering what their new future would be like. After so long on garrison duties, they had put down strong ties with the local community, ties that would be brutally severed when the battalion marched through the barrack gates for the last time.

The spring sunshine spread across the desk. It warmed the dreary room, the soft yellow light meandering over the stained, peeling wallpaper that had once been deep red but now looked blotchy and discoloured. Sloames had obviously been working on these papers for some time; his fingers were stained with blue ink. With a flourish, he scratched his name on the uppermost paper and threw his steel pen to one side. The rickety chair he used at his desk creaked loudly as he twisted round to face his orderly once again.

"There, it is done." Sloames stood, brandishing the paper he had just signed, waving it imperiously under Jack's nose. Sloames seemed well satisfied with his work; he smiled widely and brushed his wayward hair from his face, oblivious of the inky streak he left on his forehead.

Dressed in civilian clothes and with the warm sunlight playing on the red and yellows in his brightly coloured waistcoat, Sloames looked much younger than he did when encased in the scarlet shell of an officer.

"It, sir?"

"It, my dear Lark, is our ticket out of here. This beautiful missive is the final document that confirms that I am to purchase a captaincy in the King's Royal Fusiliers! Fusiliers, Lark! We are to be fusiliers!"

"Us, sir?"

"Of course. I told you I couldn't do without your services. We shall face this new adventure together. I shan't know a soul in the new regiment so it will be good to have a familiar face around."

Jack took a moment to digest Sloames's sudden announcement. He felt an absurd surge of pride that Sloames had made the effort to arrange to take him.

"I shall have to go to London for a few days to finalise the affair with the agent handling the transaction. I've hired a coach and driver to collect us tomorrow morning."

"Very good, sir. I'll start preparing your things."

"That is not all." Sloames brushed past his servant, the small sitting room not allowing for easy movement when two people occupied it. "Have you heard of the events unravelling in the East?"

"A little. Something about the Russians and the Ottomans."

"You have it exactly. For too long, Tsar Nicolas has been trying to exert pressure on the Ottomans with an eye to increasing Russian influence on their southern borders. Ever since that shameful episode at Sinope when those Russian blackguards massacred those poor Turkish sailors, the papers have been calling for something to be done. And I for one am in full agreement! Even as we speak, Lord Raglan is putting his command to readiness and I have it on good authority that the King's Royal Fusiliers are to be a part of his force. They expect to sail shortly and although I shall not be there to join them before they are despatched, I expect to be able to follow them without much delay. Indeed, time is of the essence. I would not have anyone say we dallied and I am keen for us to arrive and take command of my new company before the campaign starts properly."

"But the government hasn't declared war yet, has it, sir?"

"No, it hasn't, but the papers have been demanding nothing less for months and I fully expect war to be declared before the end of the month. The Turks and the Russians have been battering at each other for an age now so the stage is set for us to remind the world that the British army is still to be feared, even if we are to be allied with the damned French."

"Doesn't that strike you as queer, sir? Us fighting alongside the Crapauds."

"It is war." Sloames looked suitably grave, an expression at odds with his obvious excitement about his new commission. "It is not pleasant but I am sure the government knows what it is about. If I am ordered to fight alongside the French then I shall do so with pride. My own misgivings cannot be placed above the needs of the country."

Jack nodded in agreement, doing his best to match his officer's gravity. It shamed him that he did not know more about the situation that would soon lead his country to declare war. He had free access to Sloames's newspapers but had never bothered to take the trouble to read them.

"So where will we be sent exactly, sir?"

"Here, let me show you." Sloames reached for that day's paper which was on his desk. "*The Times* has an excellent representation. Yes, here it is." Sloames folded the paper so that a half-page map appeared uppermost. He made space on his desk's blotter and smoothed *The Times* flat. Jack moved forward and leant over his officer's shoulder to see. The two men shared a moment's companionable silence as they gave the map their fullest attention.

"Here is Moldova." Sloames's finger moved over the map. "The Russians invaded back in June last year. This here is Wallachia. The Turks have been fighting the Russians in these parts since October. It is a nasty business but if the reports are to be believed, the Turks have given the Russians a bloody nose or two. As yet it is not clear where our army is to find work but I would not be surprised if we were to join the Turkish army here, near the Danubian principalities. However, there is some pressure for us to do something a little more dramatic and some observers are calling for a campaign here on the Crimean Peninsular with a view to seizing the Russian naval port at Sevastopol. That would make Tsar Nicolas sit up and take note."

Jack listened to the exotic names and tried to work out exactly where these strange foreign places might be in relation to England. His knowledge of geography was scant, to say the least. As Sloames spoke of the protracted series of events that had led Britain to contemplate going to war for the first time in nearly forty years, Jack did his best to read the article that accompanied the simple map. He was so engrossed that he didn't notice that Sloames had stopped talking and was staring at him.

"You find this interesting, don't you, Lark?"

Jack pulled himself upright and took a respectful step away from the desk. For a few minutes the social gulf between the two men had been bridged by their shared interest in the wider events of the world.

"Yes, sir." Jack's use of the honorific broke the spell, reestablishing their respective ranks.

"You may take the paper with you, if you wish. I have read enough for today. I didn't know you could read, Lark."

"My mother taught me. I don't get much chance to practise though so I'm a little slow." The admission brought back some of their earlier closeness and Sloames handed the newspaper over with pleasure.

"Here, take it. I would be perfectly content if you were to take the daily paper with you at the end of the day. *The Times* is a little long-winded but at least you will learn something of the campaign we are shortly to join."

Jack nodded his thanks.

To go on campaign with Sloames was everything Jack had ever dreamt of since he had first taken the Queen's shilling. But it would mean leaving Molly.

CHAPTER
SIX

The street was dark. A few gaslights lit the main streets in town but in the long rows of terraced housing behind the new train station the darkness was left to smother the backstreets in an impenetrable gloom. The days had finally started to draw out but the evenings still pressed in quickly. In the poorer areas of town, little spare money could be wasted even on the cheapest tallow candles, so the darkness was left to rule unchallenged.

Jack dawdled his way closer to the house where Molly lived with her mother. He was smartly dressed in his best uniform, as was required to pass the guard and be allowed into town. He did his best to avoid stepping in any of the unsavoury mess that littered the ground. He wished he had had the foresight to bring a lantern and he prayed he would arrive at Molly's house without his well-polished boots smeared with some noxious substance.

There were few people around now darkness had set in, the people crammed into these small terraced houses seeking whatever rest they could get before returning to their work in the morning. Occasional raised voices echoed down the street as people vented their anger and frustration on one another, and in the house next door to Molly's a baby wailed, its plaintive cry reverberating through the gloomy street.

With a determination he did not feel, Jack rapped on the scarred front door of number twenty-seven. The house behind its sturdy door was silent.

The sound of bolts scraping gave Jack just enough time to pull one last time at his uniform before the door was cautiously opened and an anxious eye peered round its edge.

"Jack!" The relief in the familiar voice was clear. Few respectable people welcomed visitors once night had fallen and Jack had expected to waste half the night on the doorstep persuading those inside to lower their guard and unbar the door. "What are you doing here at this time of night?"

Molly opened the door wide, quickly ushering Jack into the narrow hallway while nervously looking down the quiet street to see how many of the neighbours' curtains were twitching.

The house stank of boiled cabbage and the harsh carbolic soap the family borrowed from the laundry for use at home. Molly held a single candle in a holder and in its flickering flame Jack thought she had never looked so lovely. She had discarded the linen cap that contained her unruly locks during the day and she wore her hair down. In the dim light she looked almost angelic, her face now devoid of the constant red flush he was so used to seeing in the heat of the laundry.

"You shouldn't really be here this late. It isn't proper."

Jack removed his shako and held it awkwardly in front of him. "It's a bit late to worry about that now." He smiled as he saw a flush of crimson on Molly's cheeks.

She turned to call up the stairs. "It's alright, Mam. It's just Jack. He won't be staying long." She fixed Jack with a challenging glare, daring him to try any more of his ribald humour.

But Jack was there on a more serious errand. He looked at Molly as earnestly as he could. "I haven't come for anything untoward, Molly. I just want to talk."

"Then you'd better come through to the kitchen. We can't use the parlour, not just the two of us."

Molly edged carefully round Jack and led him through the door at the end of the hall into the kitchen at the back of the house. The room was warm to the point of being stuffy, with a small fire in the grate adding its heat to that emanating from the cast-iron range that dominated the room. Two mismatched wooden chairs sat in front of the fireplace, one for each of the women in the household and Molly pointed to the largest one for Jack to sit on.

"You'll be wanting tea, I expect."

"About time you offered. I've been here ages." He thought he caught a flash of anger in her eyes so he resolved to be more serious. "Thank you."

Molly used a cloth to pull the large iron kettle on to the range and busied herself wiping clean two tin mugs she pulled from the narrow dresser in the corner. Jack watched her move around the kitchen, enjoying seeing her in such a domestic setting. It led his thoughts to what it would be like if they were to become man and wife, what it would be like to have Molly in his own kitchen, looking after him as only his wife would. He was surprised to find the notion did not sit badly in his mind.

"You'll go blind if you keep staring." Molly delivered the warning with a smile.

"At least you know your place, woman. Now, where's my tea?"

Molly stuck out her tongue. "I'll throw it over you if you don't take care, fancy fig of a uniform or not."

"I'm glad you noticed my fine turnout."

"I couldn't miss it. I've never seen you looking so smart. Are you out to impress the ladies?"

"There's only one lady I'm trying to impress but she's a bit daft. She can't see what's right in front of her face."

Molly laughed and handed him his tea. "So what brings you to my door. Did you get lost?"

Jack stared at the dark liquid in his mug as if he could read his future in it. Molly saw his serious expression and had the sense to remain quiet as she took the seat next to him, reaching her hand out so that it rested lightly on his arm.

"It's Sloames." Jack spoke at last, his voice quiet.

"Sloames?"

"He's managed to exchange his commission. He'll be leaving the regiment."

"And you?"

"I can go with him."

"Oh." Molly's hand withdrew.

"That's what I'm here to tell you."

Molly studied her hands for a long while before she spoke again. "What are you going to do?" Her voice was small now, the question asked hesitantly as if she did not really want to know the answer.

Jack looked deep into Molly's eyes. "I don't know."

"You could stay with the regiment."

"And go to the Indies? No thanks."

"So you'll go with Captain Sloames."

"I don't know, Molly. Sloames wants me with him. He wants us to go on campaign."

"Of course he does. He wants you there to clean his boots and wipe his backside."

"He's not so bad. He took time to tell me about the news. I've got to go with him to London for a few days so he can finish all the paperwork. It'll give me a chance to think."

"Bully for you." Some of Molly's normal sharpness was returning.

"I could always volunteer for another regiment."

"What good would that do? You'd still be leaving and you could end up going to war all the same. Besides, you like being an orderly. You're always telling me that it's the first step to getting somewhere."

"Sometimes I wonder if I'll ever amount to anything."

"You won't if you go around with that kind of attitude. You were born poor and you'll die poor same as me if you don't get a grip and shift yourself somewhere. You make your own future. It doesn't get neatly delivered on a silver platter. You have to go and find it."

They were both silent for a moment.

"So what happens to me when you swan off with Sloames and go and fight your war?"

"You could wait for me. I'll come back for you."

"And when would that be? A year? Two years? And all the while I sit here like a nun and work in the bloody laundry waiting for my hero to return."

It was the first time Jack had heard Molly swear. "What would you have me do, Molly?"

"What is it to me what you do?" Molly crossed her arms. "You'll make your mind up with or without my two pennyworth."

"So be it." Jack stood up quickly. "I'll see myself out."

His heavy boots were loud on the wooden floor as he made to leave. But Molly would not let him go without having the final word.

"That's it. You bugger off as soon as the going gets hard. Well, you listen to me, Jack Lark. I'm not some little milksop who'll sit on her backside waiting for some cove who may or may not come back some day. So you think hard on what you are going to do. Because I won't wait forever, you hear me? I won't damn well wait forever."

Jack closed the door, shutting off the angry tirade.

He had to decide what he was going to do. He did not want to lose Molly, but nor did he want to pass up the chance to prove himself as a soldier. Somehow he had to square the circle.

CHAPTER
SEVEN

Jack had just begun unpacking Sloames's travelling trunk when Major Hume's orderly barged into the room. As he served one of the senior officers, Cox felt obliged to look down on the orderlies of the lower ranking officers, passing critical judgements on their lack of diligence and on what he judged to be their less than satisfactory ability to care for their officers.

Cox looked over Jack's shoulder at his attempts to lay out Sloames's clothes. "You're a clumsy bugger, Lark. You should've got the hang of this by now."

Cox shook out each item of clothing from the pile Jack had already started. He smoothed his palms over the fabric in an attempt to tease away the worst of the creases and then refolded the garments neatly.

Jack smiled. "You can always do it for me, Coxy."

"You lazy sod. I'll help you but I'll not do your work for you." Cox pulled a soiled shirt from the trunk, his face showing his distaste at the muck streaked down its front. "So, how was London? Did Sloames let you off the leash?"

"We were only there for two days. There wasn't time." Jack tried to copy the movements of Cox's deft hands which made the art of folding clothes look effortless. Cox had a sharp tongue and was never shy of criticising his fellow orderlies but he had gone out of his way to help Jack on too many occasions to count, teaching him the skills he had needed in order to adapt from soldier to orderly.

"That's what they all say. Martyrs, we are, Jack. Martyrs." Cox tutted in rebuke as Jack twisted another of Sloames's shirts into a rumpled mess. "Take your time, those shirts are expensive. Have you heard the news?"

Jack scowled in frustration at his own clumsiness. "No. What news?"

"Well." Cox obviously relished revealing a juicy bit of gossip. "You know young Tom Black? He's in your company."

"Of course I know him. He's full of himself. A real barrack-room lawyer."

"He has got himself into trouble. Nothing good ever comes from being a gobshite."

Jack stopped folding the clothes and looked at his fellow orderly with interest. "What the hell happened?"

Cox grinned. "Listen to you. You should learn to speak like an officer. A foul mouth will do you no good."

"Just tell me what happened, will you?" Jack replied before correcting himself. "If you would be so kind."

"That's better." Cox perched his skinny shanks on the edge of Sloames's bed. "Manners cost nothing, young Jack. If you want to get on in this world of ours you are going to have to face facts and learn to speak with some decorum and not like you just barged in straight from the gutter."

Jack grinned at the lecture, enjoying Cox's company despite his prissiness.

"Now, then," said Cox. "Sunday night, Colour Sergeant Slater was assaulted. He was on his way back to the sergeants' mess when some cowardly cove set about him."

"That could be anyone in the damn company! Why do they reckon it was Tom?"

"Patience, Jack. I'm coming to that. So this rascal comes at Slater out of the dark, trying to take him unawares."

"Sounds like a good idea to me."

"Hush! But of course our valiant hero is not one to be beaten so easily. Not only does he fearlessly beat off the dastardly ambush but he also manages to capture his assailant. And who does that turn out to be?"

"Tom." Even as Jack spoke the name, he knew what had happened. Slater had not been assaulted. The mouthy young soldier must have fallen foul of Slater and this was simply the sergeant's way of exerting his authority.

"So you do have some brains after all, Jack. Yes, it was Tom and he's been in the clink ever since."

"And I suppose no one else saw what happened."

"I told you. It was dark. Anyway, Slater caught him so he's bang to rights."

"We both know that is not necessarily so. Just because Slater says something doesn't mean it's true."

"What are you saying, Jack? That Slater would stoop to blagging? Anyway, Tom Black is going to be flogged in the morning. He's been sentenced to fifty lashes'"

"Bloody hell! Fifty! He must really have upset Slater to get a flogging like that."

"Listen to you. Tom has only himself to blame, the fool. Fifty lashes should learn him right. If it doesn't kill him."

Jack closed his eyes as he absorbed the horrid tale. Tom had had no chance. No one, especially not an officer, would take the word of a young private over that of an experienced noncommissioned officer.

It was a vivid example of the power a colour sergeant wielded and the price that had to be paid for daring to flout Slater's will.

In the quiet stillness of dawn, the ten companies of the battalion marched on to the parade ground. The only sound that marked their entrance was the slow, mesmeric beat from the battalion drummers. Like a heartbeat, the sound never faltered, each ponderous strike of the drummers' sticks sending another beat to echo around the barrack blocks.

The redcoats marched to their allotted place and then stood in grim silence.

The whole battalion was on parade, the ten companies arranged to form three sides of a square, with the side closest to the gatehouse left open. The men faced the open space in the centre where the punishment triangle stood. Fashioned from the fearsome half-pikes that the battalion's colour guard wielded in battle, it waited impassively for its victim, the apex of the triangle thrusting up towards the dull, lifeless sky, the base resting on the ground, the whole held up by a pair of supports pushed hard into the clay soil. Thick ropes had been tied to the uppermost pikes, their ends left dangling, ready to tie Tom Black's wrists to the thick staffs of ash. Two more sets of rope lay coiled on the ground, ready to lash his ankles to the sides. Held fast by the ropes, Tom would be unable to move, his back presented to the whip, open and exposed.

The soldiers stood in their ranks, eyes fixed facing forwards, waiting for the arrival of their officers and for the signal that the punishment parade was to begin. A punishment they knew to be unjust.

The redcoats bore a strict sense of fairness. They did not shirk from punishment. Indeed, a flogging broke the monotony of garrison duty. They understood the rules, they knew that to break the army's regulations was to risk dire punishment and if anyone was foolish or slow-witted enough to do so and, worse, be caught, then they had to damn well live with the consequences.

Yet the redcoats knew there was no justice on parade this day.

The battalion knew Colour Sergeant Slater just as they knew Private Tom Black. The knew the mouthy soldier had fallen foul of Slater but that alone should not merit the infliction of fifty lashes, the heaviest sentence the colonel could order on his own authority.

The officers' arrival was announced by the jangle of horse tackle, the damp soil deadening the sound of the horses' hooves. To the solemn beat of the drum, the officers rode to their allotted places. If they sensed the men's tension, there was no sign of it in their languid pace and in the easy way they sat their chargers. Barely a glance was given to the stationary ranks of redcoats.

"Carry on, Sergeant Major." Colonel Stimpson gave the order to the regimental sergeant major in a low tone. Still, the words sent a ripple of tension through the battalion, as if the hundreds of men had drawn breath as one. Stimpson looked around him warily, suddenly becoming aware of the strange mood gripping his battalion.

To the words of command, the prisoner detail left the guardroom and made their way on to the parade ground. Tom Black marched between the men charged with bringing him to his place of punishment, his head low, his eyes fixed on the ground, unable to look at the formed ranks of the battalion assembled to witness his shame.

Tom marched without his musket, his scarlet coat bereft of the cross-belts, his head bare. His body shivered in the morning air, the cold and fear setting his muscles trembling, the shaking obvious to the hundreds of eyes that watched his progress. Had Tom lifted his gaze he would have seen little sympathy in the impassive faces of his fellow redcoats, their expressions betraying none of their emotions. Yet more than one soldier wondered what thoughts were going through Tom's mind, what fear he felt, what they would feel if they ever found themselves in his place.

Tom looked small, puny, his escort in their tall shakos seeming to tower over his slight frame. The young soldier's face was puffy, his skin blotchy. The tracks of tears smudged his face and a thin smear of snot crusted around the meagre moustache on his upper lip. When he reached the waiting triangle, he lifted his head, a look of pleading on his face as he searched the watching ranks for some final assistance.

With deft hands the corporal in charge of the escort stripped the young soldier to the waist, his scarlet coat and thin shirt quickly removed. Tom looked around piteously, his beseeching look ignored by the two sergeants who tied him fast to the triangle.

Jack was transfixed. He could see every shaking rib in Tom's thin frame. He could see the tears coursing down the young soldier's cheeks.

The adjutant spurred his horse forward. In a loud, braying voice, he read the charge that had been brought against the redcoat. The words passed Jack by, the adjutant's voice droning on, the convoluted passages he read out barely making sense.

His role completed, the adjutant pulled hard on his reins, moving away from centre stage with indecent haste. The sergeants cleared the area, leaving just the drum major and his two young drummer boys, who shuffled forward, reluctantly taking their places like actors pushed from the wings to face a difficult audience.

"One."

The whip landed on the young soldier's back with a wet slap. Thin trails of blood traced across Tom's back, the first blow starting the sordid process of turning the boy's back into minced meat.

Jack closed his eyes.

"Two. Three."

Jack kept his eyes closed. Like a drowning man reaching for the rope that would pull him to safety,

Jack's mind grasped for memories of better times, searching for an escape.

"Come on now, boys. Lay it on properly. Four. Five."

The redcoats stood in silence and endured the grim spectacle. Forced to watch as a fellow soldier was scarred for life. Flogged bloody for nothing more than falling foul of his sergeant.

"Fifty."

Jack opened his eyes. The long, slow count of the drum major had seemed to last for hours. Finally, it was over.

The corporal of the guard moved forward, cutting down the unconscious soldier from where he hung on the triangle like a carcass of meat. His back had been reduced to a nightmare of flesh and blood, the bones of his spine gleaming as the sun finally dragged itself out from behind the thick, grey clouds to make a tardy appearance on the parade ground.

The punishment was complete.

The example had been set.

Jack crept back from his dreams. Back to the horror of an unjust punishment robustly delivered. His back ached from standing stationary for so long, the dull pain in the pit of his spine throbbing and sending spasms down his legs. The misery of the moment was complete.

Jack turned his head and looked at Slater.

Slater was staring straight at him.

Jack flinched as he met Slater's stare. He would have turned away, his fear instinctive. Yet, instead, he felt his hatred come alive, coursing through his veins.

Slater's mouth twisted into a grin, the smug look of a job well done on his face. He lifted one hand and pointed his thick forefinger directly at Jack. There was no misunderstanding the words Slater mouthed at him.

"You're next."

Jack walked out of the barracks. It was a relief to leave the cloying atmosphere of the battalion behind and not for the first time he was grateful his officer had taken a suite of rooms in town rather than staying in the rooms allocated to the officers in the barracks. The liberty to leave the barracks was something to be savoured and Jack felt the freedom act as a balm to his raging emotions.

The punishment had cleared his mind, the display scouring away the doubts that had dogged him since Sloames had announced his departure.

He would not stay with the battalion, not with Slater looming over his future and with a posting to the Indies in the offing. It was time to leave the life of a garrison soldier behind and become the fighting redcoat he had always dreamed of being. He would go with Captain Sloames and face the challenge of a campaign.

But he would not forsake Molly. He would ask Captain Sloames for permission to marry her. They would be apart but it would not be forever. The war would be short, perhaps even over before Christmas. Then they would be together.

CHAPTER
EIGHT

Jack whistled tunelessly as he carried the bundle of soiled shirts. Even the tart smell of spilt wine and sweat could not dampen his happy mood. He had left Sloames to lie in his stinking pit. His captain had staggered home just after the dawn and Jack had helped to strip him of his clothes before abandoning him to sleep off the wine-induced stupor that the night's excess had brought on.

He walked to the laundry doing his best not to break into a run. He might not have been dressed in the armour of a fairytale knight but he was determined to rescue Molly from the future she so dreaded.

He could already picture her face when he asked her to marry him. He imagined her delight, the sparkle in her eyes when she said yes. He might only be an orderly but he would prove to her that he could succeed and make good the ambition that burned so brightly inside them both.

He turned to the corner and walked towards his new future with a smile on his face.

Then he heard a scream.

The sound was so sudden, so unexpected, that Jack wondered if he had been mistaken. The barracks were quiet, most of the battalion's redcoats out on a day's march. A scream of such horror simply did not belong in an empty army barracks on an English spring morning.

Then it came again.

Jack shook his head to clear the fog of disbelief. He looked around, half expecting to see other redcoats come stumbling out of the barracks, summoned by the dreadful sound.

No one appeared. The peaceful sounds of the spring morning returned as if they had never been interrupted.

His body lurched into motion without conscious thought, his hard boots hammering into the ground as he raced towards the laundry. He never thought to discard the bundle of dirty washing he still carried in his arms. His only thought was to reach Molly, to make certain she was not the source of the nerve-jangling sounds.

The outer door to the laundry was shut. The stifling heat of the huge boiling coppers meant the door was never closed, the fresh breeze offering some respite from the steamy, suffocating rooms. Jack knew then that something terrible was happening behind its ordinary everyday facade.

He hit the door hard with his shoulder, his hands still gripping the bundle of washing. He half expected the door to be locked but it flew open and crashed heavily into the wall inside.

Jack half fell into the laundry's outer room. He lost his footing and would have hit the wooden floorboards hard were it not for the bundle of washing that cushioned his fall, protecting his ribs from the worst of the painful impact.

"No!" Molly's voice screamed out in warning.

Jack was still on the floor but he turned his head in time to see the black shadow of a hobnailed army boot aimed at his head. He rolled to one side and the boot whispered past his face, missing a violent connection by a hair's breadth. His assailant hissed an oath and in a heartbeat Jack scrabbled to his feet, throwing himself at the huge figure that had attacked him. He still didn't know who it was but it did not matter. He had heard Molly scream. It told him all he needed to know.

Jack smashed into his assailant with his full weight and the two of them went crashing down in a twisting frenzy of limbs. They scuffled on the floor, arms and legs thrashing wildly. Fists bounced off arms and elbows, glancing blows, neither man gaining the advantage. Jack could feel the strength in the body that was wrapped round his own, could sense the power in the punches that came down with terrifying speed. One vicious blow connected with his skull and his ears rang and his vision faded. He tried to fight back but his attacker twisted powerfully, pushing him backwards, a huge meaty paw pressing hard against his chest, crushing him where he lay.

Jack aimed a wild blow at the man's head but there was no strength in the punch and his fist bounced off the thick line of his opponent's jaw.

As Jack lay beaten and defeated, the face of Colour Sergeant Slater leered down at him.

A thick line of saliva trembled at one corner of Slater's mouth. Jack saw the red patches on the sergeant's skin where some of his punches had found their mark and a thin stream of blood flowed from one nostril to congeal in the thick, bushy moustache.

Slater spat a globule of bloody phlegm on to Jack's chest.

"Oh dear, Lark. You appear to have got yourself in a spot of bother. I warned you that you would be next but I hadn't dreamt it would come so soon." Slater wiped a hand across his mouth, smearing the blood and saliva across his cheek.

Jack noticed Slater had removed his red coat. His cotton undershirt was unbuttoned nearly to the navel, thick curls of dark hair peeking through the opening, and his breeches were loose, held together by a single button and threatening to fall. Slater would never allow himself to be seen in such disorder, especially in a public room such as the laundry. Jack's heart stopped as he realised what it meant.

His body tensed as the anger surged through him. It was all-consuming, a wave of such loathing that all his fear and pain left him. Nothing mattered except the need to fight. To pound into oblivion the man who had attacked the one person Jack held dear.

"You bastard!" Molly's shriek of rage took both men by surprise.

The dolly paddle in her hands was made from pine. It was thick, shaped like a short-handled oar, and it made a vicious weapon. Molly swung it round like a cudgel, smashing it with all her strength into the side of Slater's skull.

Slater was flung to one side and hit the wall with a thud.

Jack staggered to his feet. If he noticed Molly's torn clothes or the dark red mark that coloured her pale cheek then it did not give pause to his actions. Heedless of the pain in his battered body, he leant down and grabbed hold of Slater's shirt collar, jerking his head off the ground.

"You fucking bastard. How could you? How could you?" Jack was barely coherent, his spittle flecking the stunned sergeant's face.

Slater's head lolled backwards, the effect of Molly's terrible blow leaving him almost senseless. Yet the sergeant was still conscious, his dark eyes full of hatred. Looking in their dark depths was like staring into the very pits of hell.

Exhausted and sick to his soul, Jack let go of Slater's collar and turned to face Molly. He reached out a hand, his fingers tracing the outline of the puffy red mark on her cheek.

Molly didn't make a sound. She swayed on her feet and Jack reached out instinctively to steady her. He saw the panic in her eyes as she felt his touch and she flinched away, pulling backwards, holding her torn blouse together and hiding her bruised flesh from view.

Her eyes were blank. Jack had never seen such a haunted expression, the sparkle of life he found so appealing in her extinguished by the horror of what she had endured.

Jack reached out with his free hand again, moving it slowly until it came to rest on her arm.

"It's alright, Molly. I'm here. You're safe now."

She looked up. Her mouth moved but no sound came out. He could feel her body tremble under his touch.

"My, oh my. What a touching scene." Slater rolled awkwardly on to his shoulder before getting to his feet.

Jack saw Molly's hands tighten their grip on her clothes, her terror bubbling to the surface as she heard the voice of her tormenter.

"Now the fun can begin." Slater walked slowly to the laundry-room door and pushed it shut. His fingers searched the back of the door for the bolt, his eyes never leaving Jack. He found the bolt and shot it across, locking the door. This time there would be no interruptions.

"You want to watch, Lark?" Slater stood facing them. He lifted a finger to his ear, his face creasing in concern at the blood he found coming out of it. "You want to watch me as I take my pleasure? Because I don't reckon you're man enough to stop me. You tried and I beat you easy. It was only thanks to that bitch that I didn't finish you off."

Jack's anger burned but he felt fear clenching his heart.

He turned and looked at Molly. Her face was ghostly white.

"I'm so sorry." Jack gently pushed Molly backwards, holding her elbows to manoeuvre her away.

Slater threw back his head and laughed. "That's it. You just keep out the way, miss, and get ready for me. It won't take long for me to deal with young Lark here."

"You fucking bastard."

Slater greeted the insult in stony silence. His laughter was gone. "Shut your muzzle. It's time to teach you a lesson. And this time I don't expect it will be one you will forget in a hurry."

"No!" Molly's scream did nothing to stop the two men. Jack threw himself forward, moving with a speed that the larger, bulkier sergeant could not hope to match. Like a backstreet prizefighter, Jack came at his opponent, darting his right hand forward, aiming to strike before Slater could react.

Still dazed from Molly's wild blow with the dolly paddle, Slater was slow, his movements ponderous. Jack's fist struck him on the cheek, snapping his head to one side. The left hand struck a heartbeat later, catching him on the point of his chin. Slater reeled, hurt by the twin blows. His counter-punches were slow and Jack easily avoided them, dancing to one side, letting Slater's fists pass by his face before darting back in to land more punches on the sergeant's massive torso.

"Come on!" Jack screamed his challenge as his fists struck twice more. He was aware of nothing save for the huge target that stumbled around in front of him. He had no notion if Molly had fled or if she still cowered in the corner of the room and at that moment he did not care. Nothing mattered except the need to fight, the need to pound Slater into the ground.

Jack hit out, striking Slater from every angle, moving faster than the staggering sergeant could react. Slater's arms waved out, trying to catch Jack, attempting to halt the relentless stream of punches he was raining down. Time after time, he aimed a punch at Jack's face only to hit thin air.

Jack was delivering punch after punch, he could sense Slater faltering. He would beat the invincible sergeant. The whole battalion would hear of the brute's defeat and realise that David had faced Goliath and, just as in the bible story, David had won.

Then Jack's head exploded in agony and the world went black.

Slater's fist had come from low down near the ground where the huge sergeant had bent nearly double as he tried to weather the storm of punches. The massive fist was clenched hard and it connected with Jack's jaw like a sledgehammer. The blow lifted him from his feet and the violent impact threw his body to one side.

Goliath was not following the script.

Jack's body smacked hard into the floor. His vision greyed out, the blow knocking him nearly senseless. He rolled as he hit the ground, desperate to get back on his feet. He never saw the shadow of a heavy boot moving towards him. The kick slammed into his ribs, sliding him across the floor, the breath driven from his lungs. The pain flared white across his vision but he twisted on the ground, his fingers scraping at the floorboards as he battled to get back to his feet.

Slater grunted as he kicked out again, his boot driving hard into Jack's body.

"No!"

It was the sound of a young woman driven to madness. A shriek of rage that echoed around the small room as Molly threw herself at Slater.

She came at him with all her strength. Her torn blouse billowed around her, the bruises on her body dark against her pale flesh. She leapt at Slater with hands like claws.

Jack lifted his head, his blood warm on his face. He saw Molly rake her nails down Slater's face like the talons on a bird of prey, inflicting wounds that were vicious and deep.

Jack levered himself to his feet, ignoring the spasms of pain that tore through his body. It took all of his strength but he staggered upright.

Slater reeled from Molly's sudden assault. He felt her nails rip through his flesh, the pain sudden and bright. He thrust his arm out, using his full strength to push her off. But her desperate strength resisted his efforts.

The touch of her naked flesh stalled him. He brought his hand round, feeling the hard mound of her breast against his grasping fingers and he hesitated, raw desire making his hand linger on the firm young flesh.

Molly screamed and pummelled his face. Slater kept his grip on her body, his hot, rough hands pawing her. In desperation, she thrust her fingers upwards, jamming them brutally into his eyes, her fingers like daggers as she tried to gouge out his sight.

Slater roared. He let go of her breast and punched with all his might. His fist smashed into Molly's face. The blow sent her sprawling backwards, the blood pulsing from the ruin of her nose.

Molly fell hard. Her head crunched with sickening force into a hard metal soap tin.

Jack staggered forward, and his heart stopped when he saw Molly's body lying in a heap on the ground. Her hair had escaped from the pattern of clips and clasps that held her curls in check, fine strands whispered over her bloodstained mouth. But there was no breath to blow them away. Blood was splattered across her pale skin. The bright blue of the staring eyes was dull, the sparkle of life gone.

Jack went to her side, unable to believe what he was seeing. He wanted to fall to his knees, to give in to the horror that gripped his heart, to bury his head in her hair just as he had done so many times before. His throat closed and he felt his breath constrict in his chest as his soul chilled, icing over with grief.

He didn't hear the sound of the bolt scraping back or the door to the laundry being thrown open, or feel the draught of fresh air on his skin. He could do nothing but look at Molly, the waxy pallor of death already stealing the vitality from her skin.

Molly was dead.

CHAPTER
NINE

Jack slowly became aware of the shouting, the cacophony of bellowing voices, the noise and bustle of soldiers, the dusty floor reverberating to the thump of army boots, the air full of braying voices of command.

"Stay where you are, Lark."

Firm hands took hold of his upper arms, holding him hard as if he was expected to make a bolt for the door at any moment.

Jack blinked hard at the tears clouding his vision and tried to make sense of what was happening.

The room was full of redcoats. Half a dozen soldiers crowded into the cramped confines of the laundry's outer reception room.

"Molly?" Jack's voice wavered as he spoke.

"Easy, lad. Behave yourself now." The voice was firm, devoid of compassion.

"Where's Slater?"

"Colour Sergeant Slater is in the guardroom. God alone knows what happened here but it's over now."

The horror surged through Jack's mind. His head sagged with despair and he would have fallen had the two redcoats not been holding him.

"Come on, lad, time to sort yourself out. You have to come with us. You've raised one hell of a shit storm and you're right at the damn centre."

"It was Slater, he —"

"Stow it. Save it for the colonel because I ain't interested. I've been told to take you to the guardroom and keep you there."

"Guardroom?" Jack's head lifted and he stared at the corporal of the guard. He felt the redcoats holding him tighten their grip on his arms. Jack closed his eyes as he realised the small party of redcoats had not come to his rescue, they were here to detain him. To lock him away while the officers made sense of the dreadful events that had led to a young woman losing her life.

"Attention!"

The door to the guardroom was snatched open and the corporal stationed outside the room commanded the room's occupants to rise. The three wooden chairs scraped the floor in unison as the officer strode in. Jack had been sitting in morose silence, guarded by two of his fellow redcoats. Now he stood and stared at the figure of Captain Sloames who looked back at him with a mixture of disappointment and embarrassment.

"At ease. Thank you, Corporal, you and your men may leave us." Sloames dismissed the men charged with guarding the prisoner. He kept up his scrutiny of Jack's face as he did so, as if trying to discern his orderly's guilt in his expression.

"This is a most distressing episode, Lark, most distressing." Sloames held his hands behind his back and paced slowly around the room, looking more like a lawyer than an officer in the Queen's army. "I have sent a message to the colonel and he has charged me to discover what events led to today's terrible accident and to take whatever action I deem necessary. I have listened to Colour Sergeant Slater's account of the events and in the interests of justice I would like to hear your side of the story."

Jack looked at his officer, barely hearing the words spoken to him. He didn't feel the pain in his body, the effects of Slater's beating not registering in his mind. But his soul felt as if it had been cleaved in two.

"Silence won't help you now, Lark." Sloames spoke slowly as if to a difficult child. "You must tell me what happened."

"Slater." Jack whispered the name. "Slater killed her."

Sloames closed his eyes as if in sudden pain. He looked at Jack for what seemed like a long time before he spoke again.

"Slater accuses you."

"Slater's a fucking liar." Jack's voice was raw.

Sloames's mouth twisted in distaste. "Mind your tongue. Need I remind you that you are in a great deal of trouble? One more such outburst and I shall leave this room immediately and abandon you to your fate. Is that clear?"

Jack struggled to contain his grief. He knew how the battalion worked; Tom Black's savage flogging on a false charge was all the evidence Jack needed to understand that nothing he could say would make a jot of difference. Slater had committed the foulest crime but Jack could not touch him.

Sloames took Jack's silence as leave to continue.

"Now. I have listened to Colour Sergeant Slater's account. It is clear there has been a most dreadful accident."

"Accident?" Jack could not fully believe what he was hearing. "Slater was trying to rape her! I stopped him and he killed her." Jack felt his eyes fill. "He killed her!" he shouted, his voice wavering with pain.

The room returned to silence.

"I will carry out a full and proper investigation, Lark, I can assure you of that." Sloames's discomfort was obvious. "However, without any witnesses the situation is very . . ." he paused, an apologetic smile on his face, "difficult. It may not surprise you to know that Slater blames you for the incident. He claims he tried to stop you attacking the girl and you fought him."

"And because Slater is a fucking sergeant he gets away with it."

Sloames scowled. "There is a proper process that will be followed." He lowered his voice, coming to stand next to Jack so he could speak softly and still be heard. "But it really is better for everyone if the details of this most dreadful accident are cleared up without delay."

"Better for who?" Jack sneered the words.

Sloames didn't rise to the bait. "We have to think of the regiment, Lark."

Jack looked into his officer's face. He could see Sloames's distress, he was too used to being with his master to miss it. He let his head fall so that his chin rested on his chest. None of this was Sloames's fault. And nothing would bring Molly back. Jack felt his grief wash over him, obliterating his anger in a wave of misery.

"Slater will not be allowed to get away with this, Jack. He will be punished." Sloames placed his hand on Jack's shoulder.

Jack inhaled deeply. He knew who was to blame. It didn't matter what the army did or didn't do.

Molly was gone.

Sloames patted Jack's shoulder. "I will speak to the colonel. In the circumstances I'm sure he would be content if we were to leave quickly."

"So the whole thing will be hushed up." Jack spoke in a matter-of-fact manner, holding on to his calmness with a huge effort of will.

"We must consider the name of the regiment. Nothing good will come of a scandal."

Jack felt defeat wash over him. He let the tears come, felt them scalding his cheeks as he wept for his loss.

Sloames backed away, sensitive to his orderly's distress. As he reached the door, he turned to speak one last time.

"We are to go to war, Lark. I said we would go together and we shall. We shall leave this place and find us both a new life." Sloames paused. "You will always have a place at my side, Jack. No matter what happens, I shall not abandon you."

Sloames quietly opened the door, leaving Jack alone for the first time since Molly's death.

Jack slumped back into his chair and succumbed to his grief. Through his tears he felt a part of his being harden. Like a rock in a wild, surging river, his desire for revenge stood firm against the torrent of despair.

One day Slater would be made to pay for his crime.

It was dark when the coach pulled through the barrack gatehouse and trundled on to the road that led to London. The lamps on the coach cast out a miserly light, throwing shadows on to the streets. The barracks and the sentries stationed outside for the long dreary hours of guard duty quickly melted into the darkness.

From his perch on top of the carriage, Jack stared back at his former home, his lonely vigil kept long after it had disappeared from sight. As the coach picked its way out of the confines of the narrow streets, he buried his head in his heavy greatcoat, turning up the wide collar so that it smothered his face. Hiding the tears that flowed freely down his cheeks.

Beneath him, from within the warm fug of the coach's interior, the sound of comradely laughter could be heard. Captain Sloames and the other passengers had already enjoyed the first of numerous bottles of claret they had with them to keep out the cold. The sound of their laughter did nothing to warm the chill in Jack's soul, their mirth only adding to his loneliness.

His back ached abominably, the jarring ride sending sharp spasms of pain running up and down his spine. He closed his eyes, concentrating on the pain, savouring the stabs of agony, using them to forget his despair.

He had been taken under guard from his confinement directly to Sloames's rooms where he had quickly packed for their hurried departure. He had remained in the rented rooms until the hired coach had arrived to spirit them away, taking them away from the place where Jack had hoped to find such happiness. Like a felon fleeing the scene of his crime, he was disappearing into the night.

The carriage quickly picked up speed as it bucked and scrabbled its way on to the turnpike. Jack gripped his seat hard, enduring the discomfort and the cold as best he could. Despite everything that had happened, he felt a tremble of excitement deep inside him, a tiny frisson of expectation that he had embarked on a great journey that would take him to the far reaches of the globe. He was a soldier on his way to war.

A new path to the future was opening up before him. No one, least of all him, could see where it would take him.

CHAPTER
TEN

"Lark! For the love of heaven attend to me at once!"

"Sir!" Jack hurried into the room. He had been dozing in a scuffed leather armchair in what passed for a sitting room in the lodging they had taken at a coaching inn in the depths of the Kent countryside. The inn was dank, a rotting, mildew-infested dump of a place that survived by fleecing any traveller foolish enough to spend time in it. Ordinarily, Sloames would never have tolerated even a single night in such a foul establishment but he had been given little choice.

For Sloames was sick.

"I have been ill again." Sloames's voice wavered with emotion.

Jack did his best to hide his distaste. "Very good, sir. I shall fetch some clean water."

He admired the genteel turn of phrase that Sloames had used but there was no hiding the stench of shit that overwhelmed the room's more usual smell of rot, damp and decay. For the third time that day, Sloames had shat himself, the relentless disease that had him in its bitter grip turning the young officer's insides into so much slurry.

Jack bustled from the room, determined to keep his mind on the task at hand. Better that than dwell on the shame or on the fear that was stamped so clearly on Sloames's drawn and whey-coloured face.

The illness had been sudden, violent and unstoppable. What had started as a mild summer cold soon developed into an uncontrollable fever that had rendered Sloames delirious and forced them to seek shelter. The days had passed by in a blur as Jack undertook the distasteful process of cleaning the diarrhoea from his officer's body and trying to slake his constant thirst. Throughout it all, Sloames had drifted in and out of consciousness, enjoying only occasional periods of lucidity as the illness laid waste to his body.

"Here we are, sir. Soon have you sorted." Jack did his best to reassure his officer as he applied himself to the unpleasant task, swallowing the urge to retch as the stench of his officer's voided bowels clogged his throat. He worked as quickly as he dared, trying to avoid the patches of livid broken skin that made Sloames hiss in pain if a careless fingernail scraped it. Yet, even working with haste, it took many long minutes to wipe away the last of the foul fluids.

Throughout it all, Sloames lay quiet. It was only as his orderly pulled the clean cotton drawers to his navel that he spoke again.

"I thank you, Lark. You do me a kind service."

Jack rose from his knees, hiding the cloth with its shaming brown streaks behind his back. It was hard to find the right words to form a reply. He felt he should try to make light of the situation, offer his sick officer the traditional bland reassurances that he would soon be well. But they had already been said too many times before, the blandishments of the healthy to the sick worthless in the face of such a ravaging illness.

So Jack said nothing, merely nodding in acknowledgement of the words of thanks.

"Lark."

"Sir?"

"I need to speak to you." Sloames sucked in huge gulps of air as he struggled to control his distress. "I need to speak of the future."

The future, which had once seemed so full of promise, now hung around their necks like a gravestone. The word mocked them. Jack, who had already lost so much, had clung to a future with Sloames with all the fervour of a religious convert. Now that lay in tatters, destroyed by the illness that was laying waste to Sloames's body.

"We must discuss what is to happen." Sloames delivered the words with stony determination.

"You'll get better, sir."

"Don't be a fool." Sloames delivered the admonishment with some of his former force. "I am dying. There, it is said. I am dying and nothing you or I say will alter that fact."

"We can call back the doctor."

Sloames shook his head. "Do not even suggest it. I've had quite enough of that fat fool blistering and bleeding me to last a lifetime." Sloames shuddered, whether at the memory of the local doctor's enthusiastic treatment or at the ill-chosen phrase, Jack could not tell.

72

"I'll look after you. I'll get you well."

"You are many things, Lark, but I doubt you are a worker of miracles. Now, be quiet and listen. When I am dead, you'll be cast adrift. You'll be without a place. I think we both understand that you cannot go back to the regiment even if they would accept you. That leaves you at the mercy of the damned clerks and I wouldn't wish that on anyone. So, we must apply ourselves to conjuring an alternative. We must find you a future." Sloames's voice had died to a barely audible whisper and Jack was forced to lean close so he could make out the words. With an effort, Sloames took his weight on to his elbows, lifting his head clear of the stained bed.

"You must find your way to our new regiment and go on campaign." Sloames fixed his orderly with a determined stare, a fierce glimmer in his eyes. "You must seize the glory that is rightfully ours. Do you understand? You must do it. You must. Find my glory."

The effort of speaking had taken its toll on Sloames and he slumped back into the stinking sheets and closed his eyes.

Jack sat in the scuffed and battered leather armchair, his fingers absent-mindedly picking at its scarred surface. He was alone with his thoughts and with his fears.

He did not know what would become of him when Sloames finally succumbed to the illness. Sloames wanted him to join the campaign that was about to start. But if he joined the regiment of fusiliers as Sloames had urged, he would have no place there, he would be a stranger, bereft of the ties that bound the men in the ranks together.

The thought of that loneliness made him think of Molly. He had convinced himself that going on campaign as Sloames's orderly would numb the pain of her death. But he now knew he had been foolish to think that. He had lost the woman he loved, just as he was about to lose the man who held the reins to his future. When Sloames died, he would have lost everything.

Molly had once told him to get a grip and make his own future if he wanted to get anywhere in life. The words haunted him. He got up from his chair and pulled Sloames's uniform coat from its peg. The fabric was soft, the weave so much finer than the drab, clumsy cloth of the ordinary red coat he wore. Jack ran his hands over the heavy bullion epaulets that defined the captain's rank, searching for the courage to dare to do something which would, if he were discovered, lead only to the scaffold and a long, drawn-out death.

It was time to prove he could do it. He owed Molly that at least. He would gamble his life to better himself and he would do it for his Molly.

He would do as Sloames had suggested. But he would do it in a way that his officer would never have imagined.

For he had nothing left to lose.

The room was as cold and clammy as a corpse. The fire had died down as Jack slept, a muted glow in its smoky depths the only reminder of its former warmth. A solitary gas lamp that Jack had balanced carelessly on the edge of a battered travelling chest hissed and spluttered, before its light went out, fuel exhausted, its flame untended and ignored.

It was quieter without the harsh hiss of the gas lamp, almost silent except for the slow, methodical tick of the silver fob watch which Jack had placed on the mahogany dressing table, its chain neatly coiled round its case. The watch lay at the head of a formation of tortoiseshell-handled brushes, combs and razors, next to their brown leather carry case, precisely as Sloames liked them to be laid out.

Sloames listened to his fob watch, cursing the sound of each second ticking by, hating the audible acknowledgment that his life was nearly over, the passing of time as inexorable as the approach of his death. He lay on his back in the darkness, his head bent to one side so that he was facing the room's single garret window. The window was streaked with filth, congealed bird muck covering much of the uneven glass. He longed to enjoy one last view of the stars. Yet even that simple pleasure was denied him.

He yearned to rise from the filthy sheets. To peel back the stained and stinking counterpane and cross the scuffed, soiled, floorboards. To throw the window open so he could drink in one last mouthful of the crisp night air. Instead, he was a prisoner in his putrid bed. His ruined body his jailer. The illness that had reduced him to a living cadaver his immutable sentence.

The seconds ticked by, bringing Sloames ever closer to his end, this last period of consciousness a final misery his illness chose to inflict upon him. He cursed the irony of fate that should condemn him to die of disease in the benign surroundings of the Kent countryside when he had spent a small fortune to avoid a posting to the fever-ravaged Indies where sickness and death were commonplace.

In the quiet of the room, Sloames could detect the faint sounds of his orderly snoring as he slumbered in the winged-back chair in the adjoining room. It would have been easy to hate his servant for his ripe health and vitality. Instead Sloames felt tied to the man he had saved, whose life he had changed, whose future he had set and which now looked almost as bleak as his own.

Sloames would have wept if his body had still had the faculty. He would have railed against the merciless disease that had reduced his body to a desiccated husk, at the injustice, the unfairness, the casual callousness of his fate. Yet his imminent demise brought on such lethargy that it was an effort to focus his mind even on the appalling spectre of his own death. His thoughts, meandering and vague as they were, turned to what might have been.

These should have been the best days of his life, the great adventure of going to war certain to bring the glory he had always craved. The campaign against the might of Russia should have been his finest hour, the much longed for opportunity to lead a company of soldiers into battle.

As Sloames sank ever closer to oblivion, he dreamt of the battles that were to come, imagining the future that had been stolen from him, the laurels of glory that would have been his. The room was silent, yet Sloames's sick mind echoed to the sounds of battle, to the calls of the bugles and the beat of the drums, the crash of cannon, the rattle of musketry, the screams of pain and the cheers of victory. His thoughts filled with the grandeur of battle in all its splendour.

The first rays of daylight pierced the gloom of the attic room, illuminating thousands of specks of floating dust. It reached Sloames's face, the thin beam lingering on the sallow cheeks and wasted features.

A cloud passed over the sun, shutting off the warming light, and the gloom quickly refilled the spaces that had enjoyed the momentary glow.

The shadow of the cloud passed over Sloames's face and he died.

CHAPTER
ELEVEN

14 September 1854. Kalamata Bay, Crimean Peninsula

For countless leagues, the rolling grasslands of the Crimean peninsula stretched as far as the eye could see. In places, a scattering of ancient barrows, mounds of earth that had been used as burial places in centuries long past, interrupted the undulating steppe. Elsewhere, the grass gave way to cultivation, the dark, fertile soil a rich foundation for the acres of vineyards and orchards that produced an abundant supply of grapes, pears, nectarines, apples and peaches. Pockets of snug dwellings nestled in the folds and creases of the plateau, scattered through the landscape as if the squat buildings had formed naturally, grown out of the fertile soil of the steppe.

It was a place of calm and tranquillity, a land that stoically endured the wild weather and slept through the good. It had remained unchanged and undisturbed for centuries, far from the trials and tribulations at the heart of the Russian empire, distant, forgotten, and ignored.

Then the invading armies arrived.

They had landed the previous day at Kalamata Bay, twenty-five miles north of the Russian naval base at Sevastopol on the Crimean Peninsula. Even now, on the second day of the landing, the inauspiciously named Kalamata Bay was a frenzy of activity. The grey waters were crammed with ships and yet more sails filled the horizon. Large, powerful men-of-war, the leviathans of the fleet, sat immobile on the cramped margins of the bay, while smaller gigs and cutters swarmed around them. The new war steamers, with their shallower draught, came closer to shore before they, too, disgorged their own flotillas of small craft, their smokestacks belching out columns of dirty grey smoke towards the dreary sky.

A thin spit of sand and shingle ran along the landward rim of the bay, separating the sea from a large, stagnant and foul-smelling salt lake. The newly landed men would have to march along its entire length before they could turn inland for the higher ground. The remote beach was normally deserted, even the local Tartar population finding little reason to visit. Now, two hundred and fifty ships were disgorging nearly sixty thousand British, French and Turkish soldiers on to it, a coalition of forces brought together to fight the might of the vast Russian army.

The landing site had only been picked the previous day, an ill-omened indication of how indecisive the combined allied command structure was. Nonetheless, the generals' staff had done their best to plan the landing in minute detail, producing eight pages of printed regulations that listed everything from the landing timetable to which flag each troop-carrying vessel should display. Now, the sheer scale of the operation was overwhelming all that planning and the beach was descending into chaos.

Dozens upon dozens of sailors stood knee-deep in the surf, hauling in boats full of men and turning freshly emptied craft around to return to the transports for yet more troops. Newly landed soldiers gathered on the shingle in their thousands, among mountains of equipment. The officers watched in dismay as the military might of three countries was dumped in one bewildering heap on the sand.

"Company! Form line!"

The command would ordinarily have brought the company of redcoats sharply to attention. It should have sent the sixty-three men and three sergeants moving through well-practised drill.

Should have, but did not.

Two weeks on board ship had stiffened their limbs but that alone could not explain the sloppiness with which the men responded to the order. The soldiers moved lethargically, shuffling into the semblance of an ordered line with little grace and even less military precision. Despite such a glaring lack of discipline, none of the company's three sergeants found the energy to chastise their men. They too ambled their way to their allotted positions behind the line, every sluggish movement displaying their displeasure at being forced through the unnecessary drill.

"I am not impressed, gentlemen. Not impressed at all. Would either of you care to offer any defence for this shameful performance?"

This was addressed to a pair of young lieutenants who stood dejectedly to the front of the Light Company of the King's Royal Fusiliers. Behind them, the company stopped shuffling, having finally formed the two-man-deep line the British army still favoured. Modern manufacturing might have advanced the army's weaponry but its generals still clung to the principles and tactics of their former commander, Lord Wellington, who dominated the thinking of this most modern of armies even though he had been dead and buried for nigh on two years.

Neither of the two young subalterns was willing to meet the uncompromising stare of their new commander. He stood in front of them, hands placed petulantly on his hips, his disgust at the wretched performance of his new command obvious.

The sun disappeared behind the bank of threatening, dark-grey clouds that had rolled over the hills to the south and west, leaving the Light Company standing sullenly in the sudden gloom as they waited for the next order.

Even standing still was uncomfortable for the exhausted fusiliers. The men had to keep repositioning the awkward, improvised containers they had fashioned to carry their necessities. Their generals had commanded the army to leave their familiar "Trotter" backpacks on ship, issuing the men with only a few days' worth of food and ammunition which they believed would be more than adequate for the lightning-quick raid on Sevastopol they envisaged.

To the front of the Light Company the captain waited for his subalterns to try to explain the men's lethargic drill, something neither was keen to do. He let the silence stretch, unconcerned at his junior officers' discomfort.

Unable to bear it any longer, Lieutenant Simon Digby-Brown, the senior of the two officers, stopped his intense survey of the ground around his boots and risked a reply.

"Well, sir." He cleared his throat nervously before pressing on. "I know you only arrived shortly before we embarked at Varna, but even in that short time you must have been seen what a festering hole we were forced to live in. It is no wonder that the men are so out of condition."

The captain snorted his derision. "You are quite correct. I understand why the men have reason to be in a sorry condition. However, what I do not understand is why you appear to have done so little to correct it."

"Sir, I must protest. That is grossly unfair." Digby-Brown's voice rose in protest. "We sat in that filthy place watching our men fall sick and die. We could do nothing but nurse the sick and do our utmost to prevent more of the men succumbing. You saw the appalling condition of the camp, sir. Filth everywhere, barely any clean water and every type of loathsome insect constantly swarming over us. It was simply awful, sir, and I do not believe we could have done anything further to make such an awful situation better."

The captain smiled at his subaltern's impassioned reply. "In just a matter of days, we will be fighting the

Russian army. I very much doubt they will stand and listen to your excuses as to why the men are not fit. They will happily slaughter us to the last man and if we are too ignorant, or too indolent, to prepare properly, then we will deserve little else. Do I make myself clear?"

Digby-Brown repressed the urge to continue his defence. Unable to look his captain in the eye, his replied was forced. "Yes, sir. Abundantly clear."

"Lieutenant Thomas. Do I make myself clear?"

The Light Company's junior lieutenant nodded firmly in reply, unable to summon the courage to match his fellow subaltern's passionate defence of their actions. At nineteen, Lieutenant James Thomas was one of the youngest lieutenants in the battalion, having only recently moved up from the rank of ensign.

"What was that, Thomas? Did you mumble something?"

"No, sir. I understand you perfectly, sir."

"Good, I hate mumbling. You are an officer. Your every word must be audible and enunciated clearly." The company's new commander seemed to be enjoying himself. Indeed, he gave every impression of savouring his subaltern's discomfort. "How long have you been in the army, Thomas?"

"Nearly two years, sir."

"How much did your lieutenancy cost?"

"Sir?"

"I think I made my question perfectly clear, Thomas. Please do me the courtesy of answering."

"Two hundred and fifty pounds, sir." Lieutenant Thomas swallowed hard.

"Plus the value of your ensign's commission, correct?"

"Yes of course, sir." Thomas's face betrayed his anxiety. "With an extra consideration of twenty pounds to facilitate the transaction."

"Goodness me. That is a fortune, Thomas. Do you know how much your soldiers earn?"

"Sir?" Thomas was unsure how to answer the sharp question. As a rule, officers never discussed money. It was not a topic of conversation for gentlemen.

"Really, Thomas. If you and I are going to get along you will have to stop behaving in such a contrary manner. It is a simple enough question. How much are the soldiers under your command paid for their service to the Queen?"

"A shilling a day, I believe, sir."

"You believe or you know?"

"Sir. A shilling a day, sir."

"You are nearly correct. The men are supposed to be paid a shilling a day, but that is before deductions. Deductions take away most of that pitiful amount and leave them lucky to see a few pence. Yet you, Mr Thomas, are prepared to spend two hundred and fifty pounds on a new commission. Is your family rich?"

"No, sir," Lieutenant Thomas was sweating under the fierce barrage of questions. "Well, my parents are financially comfortable, I would say, sir."

"How very nice for them. Mr Digby-Brown, how much would it cost you to buy a captaincy?"

"One thousand one hundred pounds is the current army list rate, sir."

"One thousand one hundred pounds. Do your family's comfortable finances have such an enormous sum ready for you, Thomas?"

"I do not know, sir. I would like to think they would be willing to invest such a sum in my advancement. It is, after all, the way things are done, is it not?"

"So do you believe you are ready for a captaincy? Do you feel that your two years' service, and not forgetting your family's two hundred and fifty pounds, has properly prepared you to lead the men?"

"Yes, sir. I would say I am confident in my own abilities."

"I admire your certainty." The captain let out a tired sigh before continuing. "As officers, the men expect you to lead them, not to pander to them. That is an art you must learn. You are not born to lead, whatever you may believe, and a privileged upbringing does not endow you with the qualities you'll need if you are to succeed as an officer. In my company, I expect you to lead by example. To prove to the men that you are willing to share their discomfort and to fight as we expect them to fight. You do not learn to lead from a book. You do not learn it in the officers' mess and you most certainly cannot purchase it. You learn it here. Here with your men."

Lieutenant Digby-Brown studied his new commander as the lecture ended. Now that the captain had finished speaking, he had turned away, suddenly awkward in front of his subalterns. Digby-Brown would have judged the new commander of the Light Company to be of an age close to his own twenty-four years. They were similar in build, both standing just short of six feet tall, but where Digby-Brown was fair-haired, pale-skinned and showed the benefits of a privileged upbringing in his portly build, the captain was dark and gaunt, his face hard, his eyes uncompromising and intense. The captain sported several days' growth of beard. Digby-Brown would never dare to do the same. He struggled to grow even a pair of sideburns, his attempts at which, to his shame, were often thin and patchy. The Captain's face was more often than not creased in a scowl, as if he were constantly irritated by what was going on around him. Digby-Brown knew he would have to try harder to understand his new officer.

The Light Company had learnt little about the man behind the stern expression. It would take time to find out what he was like as a leader, to discover if he would prove a dynamic commander or a hopeless tyrant. The Russian army would be the harshest test of his talents and no amount of rhetoric would help when the men were called into action.

The whole army was under intense scrutiny; advances in communication would keep the home audience fully informed of events in the campaign. The British public would soon find out how good their modern army really was.

A fine rain started to fall as the men sullenly re-formed into company column and marched to join the main battalion. It soaked into the men's red jackets and dark blue woollen trousers, adding to their discomfort and wearing away their last reserves of energy.

Wearily the fusiliers trudged into the battalion's assigned bivouac area on the wide, grassy plain a mile inland from the beach at Kalamata Bay. The rest of the battalion had got there before them and now lay sprawled on the ground, the men already exhausted, their physical condition pitiful after months languishing on transport ships or in the fever-inducing swamps at Varna.

The captain of the Light Company buried his neck as far into his sodden greatcoat as he could while trying his best to ignore the rivulets of rainwater that dripped from the peak of his Albert shako. The stubby, six-inch plume on top of the shako drooped under the weight of the water it had absorbed, its green hue darkened to a grey-black.

The dress uniform he had been ordered to wear showed the damage a day's slog through sand and mud had inflicted. His greatcoat was splattered with filth and soaked by the incessant rain, and underneath, the gold of his shoulder epaulets was already tarnishing.

The Light Company's new leader stood alone in the rain on a small island of grass in the sea of mud, enduring the discomfort as he watched his company fall out and prepare themselves for the night ahead. It would be spent in the open, with only the salted pork and hard biscuits in their improvised backpacks for nourishment, and brackish water in their canteen to drink. There was little prospect of a fire for warmth.

A thin smile flittered across the captain's face as he heard the first grumblings emerge from the grubby forms of his men, surprised that it had taken so long for the complaining to begin. As sure as dogs greet each other by sniffing arses, soldiers always follow a day's work with a bout of whingeing; the soldiers' right to grouse and grumble was inalienable.

"There you are! By God, what a damned awful day. How are your boys getting on?"

The commander of the Light Company chose to turn his whole body to face the newcomer rather than turn at the neck and thus risk a waterfall of icy cold rainwater running down the back of his shirt. The diminutive figure of Captain Michael McCulloch strode towards him. McCulloch commanded the battalion's 2nd Company and he had appointed himself the new captain's friendly guardian.

It was an honour the Light Company's captain would have happily forgone. McCulloch was well known for his prissiness, especially with regard to standards of dress. Such pickiness irked the newly arrived captain, although it was the martinet's orderly who bore the brunt of his obsessive demands for perfection. Even now, after hours of slogging through rain and sand, McCulloch seemed to gleam, as if he had been buffed from head to toe.

If McCulloch noticed the lack of an enthusiastic greeting from his fellow captain, he did not remark on it.

"I have got someone I would like you to meet. I know you have some absurd notion that you can manage without an orderly but by the look of that greatcoat, it is obvious to us all that you are deluding yourself. More importantly, the colonel agrees and so, as of this minute, he insists that you utilise the services of one of the men." McCulloch raised a hand immaculately clad in a tan kidskin glove to wave away the protest that he knew was about to emerge from the small gap between greatcoat and shako in front of him. "None of that. The colonel insists and that is that. So allow me introduce the man we, your fellow officers, have selected for you. He has been nagging us for this opportunity for ages now, more fool him." McCulloch turned to a figure wearily trudging towards them. "Keep up, Smith, for goodness sake. Now then, Fusilier Thomas Smith, meet your new lord and master," McCulloch gestured theatrically at his fellow captain, "Captain Arthur Sloames."

CHAPTER
TWELVE

The rain stopped shortly before dawn. It was small relief to the thousands of British soldiers who had spent the night trying to rest in the stinking quagmire that had formed around them. They were bereft of any comfort other than a single blanket each. Even the generals had to endure the pitiless storm without cover. The general commanding the Light Division, Sir George Brown, was forced to sleep with only an overturned cart for protection from the elements.

Jack had given up trying to sleep long before the rain stopped, preferring instead to endure the misery of the night awake, waiting for the day to break, shivering through the cold and lonely hours. He looked in envy at the tumbled heaps of bodies spread around the muddy bog that had been assigned as the Light Company's bivouac area. The fusiliers huddled together in small groups to keep warm, any desire for privacy overwhelmed by the bitter cold and the pervading damp.

Jack well remembered what it was to sleep jumbled up with his messmates. He had never thought he would miss it but, as he sat, cold, wet, and alone, he was jealous of the small comfort the men obtained from their closeness.

It had taken all of his courage to take Sloames's uniform jacket from its peg and place it on his own shoulders. It felt as if it had doubled in weight, the responsibility and power it gave its wearer physically manifest in the bullion epaulets and gold buttons. The innkeeper had been all too willing to help dispose of Sloames's body. He had quietly palmed the guineas and summoned a local undertaker content to take away the corpse of a dead orderly, the name of Jack Lark now buried along with the body of the officer he had served.

Once he had taken those first, terrifying steps, everything had fallen into place. He had been accepted and brought into the fold of the regiment without so much as a murmur or raised eyebrow. There had been plenty of time to practise his deception, first at the fusiliers' depot in Woolwich, then later on board the steamship during the long, tedious voyage to the East. By the time he had finally joined his new battalion he had become so accustomed to his new role that he occasionally forgot he was not truly the person he claimed to be.

Yet the long journey to meet up with the battalion at its camp at Varna had done little to dull the pain of his loss. The circumstances of his departure festered in his soul, a canker he could not resist picking over, keeping the scab fresh and the wound painful. But he refused to give in to grief and bitterness. He vowed he would succeed in his deception to prove that Molly had not been wrong to choose him. He would show her just what he could achieve.

The King's Royal Fusiliers had never been a fashionable regiment. Very few members of the aristocracy would willingly choose to spend even a short part of their military career in such parsimonious company. Instead, the regiment was officered by the epaulet gentry, the sons of tradesmen, of clergymen or of small-town gentlemen, for whom their commission was their only evidence of respectability. In such company, Jack thrived, revelling in the deceit, the motley collection of fusilier officers never once suspecting that there was a charlatan among them. Jack grew in confidence with every week that passed. Now, months later, much to his surprise, his deception was still intact and he found himself facing the prospect of leading Sloames's company to war. The trial of battle awaited him. Jack feared it would be a damn sight harder to fool the gods of war than it had been to pull the wool over the eyes of his brother officers.

"Coffee, sir?"

Jack looked up to see his newly acquired orderly standing in front of him, holding out a chipped tin mug brimming with steaming coffee. Gratefully Jack took hold of the mug, luxuriating in its warmth.

"Thank you." Jack was sensitive to the nervousness of his new orderly and he was determined to make the man's life as pleasant as possible. He sipped the scalding liquid, grimacing as the bitter coffee scoured the night sourness from his mouth. "Good coffee."

"Have you got something you'd like me to knock up for your breakfast, sir?" Smith kept his voice low lest he disturb any of the other men in the company who were still desperately trying to cling to the last moments of rest they would have that day.

Jack smiled at the suggestion. "Only the same rancid salt pork and hard biscuit as you have, Tommy. You don't have to worry about preparing anything for me. I plan to eat the same as you men, and, as you well know, even the finest chef at the Savoy could not make that foul offal taste any better. Unless you happen to have some juicy kidneys or some chops tucked away."

"No, sir, I'm afraid I don't have anything like that, more's the pity."

The silence stretched uncomfortably between the two men, both feeling ill at ease with the stilted conversation. Smith swallowed and broke the uneasy silence.

"Is there anything else I can do for you instead, sir?"

"No, this coffee will have to suffice. Where did you get the beans from?"

"Captain McCulloch's orderly ground some up this morning, sir. He's the only one who has a roundshot and shell case with him. I hear the officers usually club together to buy enough beans to go around so I expect they'll tap you up for some rhino soon enough, sir."

"I am sure they will, most of them don't have a silver sixpence between them." Jack smiled, hoping to break the awkwardness between the two of them. One very tangible benefit of impersonating Captain Arthur Sloames was the acquisition of his pocket book.

The annual pay for an infantry captain was one hundred and six pounds a year. It sounded like a fortune to Jack but it was far short of the amount even an unmarried officer was required to pay for a year's worth of mess bills, uniforms, weapons and the many other expenses an officer accrued. The bill for the privilege of serving the Queen was high. Some officers did manage to survive on their salary. These parsimonious men kept a very different style to those with private incomes, creating a two-tiered world in the officers' mess. The army had class barriers just as strong and as impenetrable as in wider society.

Jack forced his frozen joints into action, trying not to spill any of the precious coffee in the process. As he stood up the ground squelched obscenely under his feet and a puddle of water immediately formed around his mud-encrusted boots. His hand instinctively reached to the small of his back where painfully cramped muscles sent spasms of pain shooting down his legs. Backache was the bane of his life, inescapable and wearing, the legacy of a childhood spent heaving barrels of ale or shifting drunken bodies and made worse by the current damp and rain.

Around him, the rest of the company was starting to stir even though reveille was still some time off. The first hardy souls began to emerge from their blankets, their breath condensing in front of their mouths as they yawned and stretched their aching limbs.

"Where are you from, Tommy?" Jack was determined to find out about the man the battalion had foisted on to him. It was unheard of for an officer not to have an orderly but Jack had hitherto resisted all offers, hoping to be spared the intimate attentions of a servant. The idea of having an orderly poked at his usually untroubled conscience.

"Kent, sir, a small place called Womenswold, not far from Dover."

"I cannot say I have ever heard of it."

"I doubt you would've, sir. There's not much there, it's a farming village, you see. Everyone works on the land."

Jack took in his orderly's narrow shoulders and bony hands. He looked the archetypal British redcoat, if a little taller than average, with a height and build not much different to his own. Smith had an open, honest yet pinched face and a smattering of scars that revealed a childhood brush with smallpox. Jack's new orderly looked more like the undernourished product of one of modern Britain's overcrowed and polluted cities than a man raised in the fresh fields of the country, but Jack was not about to question another man's past.

"So what made you take the Queen's shilling?" Jack asked as he stamped his feet in an attempt force his frozen circulation into action. "Was it some scandalous affair with a farmer's wife? Or did you steal the local squire's daughter and tumble her in a haystack?"

Smith looked at his new officer, his face reddening, before he answered. "It was boredom, sir, plain and simple. There's nothing so dull as farming. I wanted to do something, anything, to get out of that place. The life of a soldier just seemed so grand, sir. When I saw the colour party at the hopping fair, that was it. I just had to go."

"Well, it seems to me like we both had the same idea. Let's hope we both live long enough to enjoy the glory." Jack flung the last gritty liquid from his mug and handed it back to Smith. "Thank you for the coffee. If you can make a brew like that, in as Godforsaken a place as this, then I am sure we will get on fine."

"I'm glad to hear it, sir. Do you think we'll be in action soon?"

"I am certain of it. We certainly did not come all this way for a holiday. Although, judging by the number of travelling gentlemen on board ship, that is exactly what some people have in mind. There were even a number of women on board, although General Raglan forbade it. I heard a story that one lady married to an officer in the cavalry was smuggled aboard right under Lord Lucan's nose."

"Well, that doesn't surprise me, sir. Old Lord Look-on couldn't spot a doxy in a whorehouse."

The conversation was brought to an abrupt conclusion by the call of the first bugles sounding reveille.

The call sounded muffled, the damp and chill in the air strangling the notes. This was the first time the bugle call had sounded on Russian soil, the raucous notes a challenge to the sleeping Russian bear.

CHAPTER
THIRTEEN

The Light Company drilled alone. Since early that morning, they, along with the rest of the battalion, had been toiling in fatigue parties. The army was desperately trying to bring order out of the chaos of the landings that were still proceeding through a second day. When the battalion's services were finally dispensed with, Jack had asked his colonel to give him leave to march his company a short distance from the battalion lines in an attempt to try to inject some much-needed vigour into the lacklustre fusiliers.

Colonel James Morris cherished his battalion. He fussed over it like an over-proud parent and he had been delighted that his new Light Company commander showed such enthusiasm. With the colonel's blessing, and despite the sullen protests of the exhausted company, Jack had marched his fusiliers half a mile inland, seeking space away from the prying and critical eyes of the battalion. They were by no means the most forward British troops and neither Jack nor the colonel had been concerned that the Light Company would be marching into any danger — complacency that Jack would soon bitterly regret.

"Captain Sloames, sir. Cossacks!" Lieutenant Thomas could barely contain his excitement as he spotted the enemy troops on the crest of a ridge a thousand yards from where the Light Company was being drilled.

The men of the company stopped in mid-evolution, looking up to stare with fascination as the Russian irregular cavalry fanned out, forming line along the ridge. Stories of Cossack ferocity had been the talk of the army for months, their reputation as hard, vicious fighters growing with each retelling. Now the Light Company was privileged to be some of the first British troops to see their foe in the flesh.

"Thank you, Mr Thomas. A little less excitement, if you please," Jack said with as much sangfroid as his racing heart would allow. "I'm sure they are just here to watch how well we can perform our drill and I'm equally sure they are as unimpressed as I am." Jack turned to face his company. "No one told you to stop. You look like frightened serving girls caught with their hands down the master's trousers. Now, stand to attention and shoulder arms! Let us at least try to look like fusiliers. Sergeants, dress the ranks!"

The Light Company brought their rifles to their shoulders at the command while the three sergeants hurried down the line, pushing at a man here, pulling at another there, to make sure the line was dressed and ordered. Jack strode ahead of the line and as he walked he opened the leather case that held his field glasses at his hip. Captain Sloames had never scrimped on his equipment and the field glasses were new; they still smelt of their protective oil. They were manufactured

98

by Dollond of London, the best that Sloames could afford, and the heavy brass they were made of felt lumpy and cold in Jack's hands as he extended the lenses.

Jack took a deep breath as he focused on the Russian cavalry, both to settle his nerves and to steady his hands. He panned slowly down their line. The Light Company was being observed by half a Cossack *sotnya*, around fifty irregular cavalry armed with fearsome ten and a half foot long lances that rested on a leather strap attached to the right foot. The light glistened off the iron tips of the alarming weapons, and Jack's shoulder blades twitched involuntarily as his imagination dwelt on the deadly purpose of the wickedly sharp blades.

The Cossacks sat high in their saddles, feet above the belly of their horses which snorted and pawed at the tussocks of grass beneath their hooves. The men's dress was loose and baggy, with a wide variety of different jackets. On their heads most wore a fur shako, often with a double pom-pom hanging to one side. The rest wore a motley array of differing headgear that served to enhance their foreign appearance.

In addition to the terrible lances, Jack could see a sabre hanging at the side of every man and a mixture of muskets, carbines and pistols strapped to their horses' saddles. The Cossacks were well armed and looking for trouble. It was dawning on Jack that his small command might just be the sort of target the Cossacks had been waiting for.

Lieutenant Digby-Brown walked forward to join his captain. "They look a shabby crew. Are they truly Cossacks?"

"I believe so." Jack kept his field glasses trained on the enemy cavalry.

Digby-Brown was trying his best to adjust to his commander's curt and dismissive manner, even though it never failed to nettle him. It was obvious that in their short acquaintance his new captain had taken a dislike to him. Digby-Brown could not think with what justification Sloames had formed his poor opinion but he was certain the best way to proceed was to ignore the barbed remarks and prove his worth to his company commander.

"There's about fifty of them, I would say, sir."

Jack ignored him, continuing to pan his field glasses slowly along the line of enemy cavalry.

"Yes, definitely fifty."

Jack's mouth twitched in annoyance as his subaltern confirmed the obvious. "Are you of the opinion that I need assistance observing the enemy?"

"No, sir, of course not."

"And do you think that I managed to make it all the way to the rank of captain without possessing the ability to count?"

"No, sir! I was trying —"

"Be quiet," Jack cut across him. "I can assure you, Lieutenant, that I am quite capable of counting the number of enemy troops without your damn interference."

Jack went back to studying the Cossacks, his thoughts in turmoil. By keeping the glasses pressed to his face, he could avoid giving any orders. Right now, that was a good thing, as he had no idea what he should do next. He felt the gaze of his men burning into the back of his scarlet coat as they watched and waited for his command. It was as if their expectation was a physical presence leaning down on him, its weight pressing on his shoulders.

As he watched, the Cossacks started to move. Unlike the fusiliers, they moved fluidly and with confidence. Jack could not make out who was commanding the enemy troops. If there were any officers present then they were dressed in the same drab garb as their men, unlike their British counterparts who stood out against their troops like peacocks in a chicken coop. The left half of the Russian cavalry moved forward and down the slope, crossing obliquely in front of the right-hand troops and forming a new rank to its front. It was a calm demonstration of proficiency that was utterly chilling.

Jack finally pulled his field glasses away from his face, the purposeful deployment of the enemy forcing him to act. His last glimpse of the Cossacks showed them to be lifting the foot of their lances from the leather stirrup that held it in place as they rode, positioning it under their right armpits and readying it for use.

Jack turned to face his men, forcing himself to turn his back on the threat of fifty deadly lances. His throat felt constricted and dry so that he was forced to clear it noisily, despite knowing that it would make him appear nervous in front of the men.

"Company! Prepare to load!"

The men stiffened, their bodies tensing as they readied themselves to load their newly issued Miniè rifles.

Like any rifle, the inside of the barrel was grooved. When fired, the conically shaped miniè bullet deformed at the base, allowing it to engage the rifling whilst sealing in the power of the exploding charge. The spinning ball was said to be accurate to six hundred yards, but the soldiers maintained it would penetrate a soldier at double that distance, pass through his knapsack and still have enough force to strike down men in the ranks behind.

The process of loading the rifle took around thirty seconds. Slower than the veterans of Waterloo could load their Brown Bess muskets, but the reduced rate of fire was more than made up for by the rifle's vastly increased range, better accuracy, and the hitting power of the Miniè balls themselves. A volley from a battalion armed with Miniè rifles would devastate any opponent in a battle of musketry.

"Company! Load!" Jack bellowed the command and the men reacted immediately. In a sequence of movements they had practised until it had become second nature, the men of the Light Company loaded their rifles. Their rifle butts hit the wet soil as one, each the regulation six inches in front of the soldier's body. The weapon was held in the left hand while the right hand deftly extracted a cartridge from the ammunition bag. The top of the cartridge was bitten off and the powder poured down the rifle's barrel, swiftly followed by the Miniè ball.

Their hands and arms moving in unison, the fusiliers whipped the ramrod out of the loops that held it suspended underneath the barrel and used it to ram the bullet down on to the powder. As soon as they had rammed it home, giving it two final taps to make sure it was resting on the powder, the ramrod was withdrawn and returned to its loops. The rifle's butt was brought up from the ground to rest against the soldier's right hip while a fresh percussion cap from the cap box on the front of his belt was fitted to the firelock.

The two ranks of Cossack horsemen stood ominously still. The Light Company finished loading, the fusiliers now as primed for a fight as their weapons. The company was formed into two ranks with the three sergeants and two lieutenants making a third line three paces behind the second rank.

Jack ordered the men to fix bayonets and then, with as calm a demeanour as he could muster, walked to his station on the right of the line. His men were in a precarious position. Sixty-three fusiliers, three sergeants and three officers were not much of a force but it had to be at least the equal of fifty mounted Cossacks. But Jack was not confident.

Twice he cleared his throat to order the men to withdraw and twice the order died on his lips. Trying to withdraw in an orderly fashion whilst being harried by the best light cavalry in the Russian army would be a desperate affair. Jack could sense the men's growing unease. They were starting to fidget. He knew they needed firm leadership to steady them. He tried to imagine what any of his former captains would have done. What the real Captain Sloames might have said to calm the men's anxiety. The responsibility of command was more daunting than he could ever have imagined. His right hand gripped and re-gripped the hilt of his sword, his indecision infuriating and frightening in equal measure. He sensed the first man in the rear rank make a shuffling movement backwards. The tiny movement rippled through the ranks as if the men were gently stirring in the light breeze that blew inshore from the coast.

The movement shamed him into action. If the men took it into their heads to run, they were all doomed. The Cossacks would pounce on them as soon as the tight formation broke up. On their own, the men would be slaughtered. He could not let that happen.

He strode forward to stand in front of the company, the heels of his boots hitting the ground with such force that each step sent an explosion of water out of the ground.

"Stand fast!" Jack demanded of his command, his eyes roving over the two ranks. "You are British fusiliers. Where is your goddamn pride?" He raised his voice, challenging his men, hiding his lack of experience under a covering of anger.

The few fusiliers who had been stalwart enough to meet his gaze dropped their eyes.

"We stand together and we face the enemy. We don't show fear. We don't show panic. We stand in silence and let them know they are facing the finest soldiers on this whole damn earth!"

Jack turned to observe the enemy. His show of anger might have disguised his indecision but it did nothing to stop the Cossacks. They began to advance before his eyes, the line of horsemen moving forward as one.

CHAPTER
FOURTEEN

The pit of Jack's stomach lurched as he stared at the Cossack advance, transfixed by their control and discipline. The horses pulled at the bits in their mouths, sensing their riders' quickening excitement, but the Cossacks kept them in check and the pace was steady. This would change soon enough, Jack knew, and if the Cossacks caught the company in line then the redcoats were dead men. The two-man deep formation was perfectly suited to blasting volleys of musketry at opposing infantry but against a cavalry charge it would be torn apart in a brief frenzy of bloody hacking.

"Sir!" Digby-Brown arrived breathless at Jack's side, the young officer's face devoid of all colour. "Sir, we must retire. Sir!"

Jack ignored him, his concentration focused on the Cossacks.

"Sir! I must insist that we retire!" Digby-Brown was speaking in an icy whisper lest the nearest men hear his desperate plea. The need to maintain a facade of proper behaviour was deeply ingrained, despite the threat of fifty charging Russian Cossacks.

"There's no time." Jack felt himself come to life. "We'll form square."

"Sir?"

"A square, damn you!" Jack was desperately trying to remember all the conversations he had overheard in the officers' mess, discussions on tactics that kept the battalion officers entertained for hours on end. He knew the evolutions of the drill itself inside out, the manoeuvres needed to move the company from one formation to another. But that was as a redcoat, a single cog in the complex machinery that was a British army battalion. It was not as an officer. No one told the men why they changed formation or why the drill had to be learnt so perfectly. The redcoats were only so many cattle blindly obedient to the commands they were given. Commands Jack would now have to give.

"Sir, I disagree. We must retire!" Digby-Brown argued, his face ashen.

"No. There's no time," Jack snapped. "We'll form square and if they are foolish enough to attack then we'll fight the bastards off."

The oath had come to Jack's mouth unbidden, the stress of the moment revealing the cracks in the veneer of his imposture. An imposture that would end in the destruction of the company if the fusiliers did not form the protective square in very short order.

The Cossack force split in two, each wing banking away from the Light Company with the grace of swallows turning on the breeze. Jack twisted his head from side to side, desperately trying to watch the movements of both groups of Cossacks at the same time. The Russian riders were curving back towards the fusiliers' thin red line. Deftly and without audible words of command they had changed the direction of their attack and were now closing in fast against the Light Company's exposed flanks.

"Form the rallying square!" Jack bellowed at his men. The fusiliers looked at each other in silent terror but countless hours of incessant training had buried their instincts deep and, despite their panic, the men reacted to the command.

The square was the only defence that could provide protection against the charging cavalry. The fusiliers needed to form a wall of bayonets round the company and force the Russian horses to veer away.

The three sergeants screamed themselves hoarse, pulling the ranks together. The square started to emerge.

The Cossacks were horribly close.

"Prepare to resist cavalry!" Jack yelled, readying the men to fire even as they still jostled with each other to form the walls. The soldiers on the outermost wall of the square squatted on the ground, the butts of their rifles jammed into the soil. Their position was the most terrifying, forced to sit and wait for the enemy to close, without being able to fire back. Yet their bayonets were what would hold the enemy at bay, for no horse would be willing to charge the ring of steel no matter how hard their riders urged them on.

Those men still standing raised their rifles. The formation was ragged but it would have to suffice.

The Cossacks thundered towards the huddle of redcoats. To Jack they resembled a locomotive moving at full speed, the noise and the power of the charge seemingly irresistible. Yet his men stood their ground, defiant in the face of their terror, standing firm when lesser men would have run screaming for their lives.

"Independent firing, at one hundred yards." Jack's voice cracked with tension. It was not meant to be like this. He was about to fight for the first time yet there was none of the glory that his former master had dreamt of. This was nothing save a squalid, meaningless skirmish which would quickly be forgotten, lost in the annals of the huge campaign that would surely see bigger, more important battles.

"Ready! Commence firing!"

This was the command to begin firing at the enemy. The rough square erupted in a drawn-out ripple of gunfire. The disordered formation forced the men to fire independently, denying them the effectiveness of devastating volleys.

The ragged square was immediately smothered in a foul-smelling cloud of smoke that flickered with the flash of rifles firing as more men opened up on the Cossacks.

Jack's fear had been banished with the blast of the first rifle. Nothing mattered now that the fight had started. He caught glimpses of the Cossacks through the smoke. His eyes were watering and the noxious smell of rotten eggs filled his nostrils but he could see that the rifle fire had emptied at least half a dozen saddles and left three horses heaped on the ground, their hooves drumming in pitiful frustration as the valiant animals still tried to respond to the urge to gallop. More riders fell as they swerved round the square and fusiliers snapped off a shot at them.

Jack got the briefest impression of the Cossacks thundering by, a fleeting glimpse of bearded faces set in a vicious snarl of impotent anger as the redcoats stood firm.

"Cease firing! Reload!" he commanded. The Cossacks were turning, bringing their dreadful lances back towards the huddle of redcoats.

Rifle butts thumped in the ground as the fusiliers began the ritual of reloading their weapons. Jack looked around at his men, his heart hammering in his chest as he willed them to load faster. His own weapon, a revolver, hung at his hip, its chambers empty. It was another mistake, another oversight that he would never allow to happen again. Never again would he be so ill prepared for a fight.

CHAPTER
FIFTEEN

"Prepare to resist cavalry."

The second rank of riders were discarding their lances, tossing them carelessly to the ground and drawing their firearms. The Cossacks had clearly expected the redcoats to break and run as the line of powerful horses bore down on them. The Cossacks had turned fast, their even ranks as precise as when they first charged. The gaps in their formation had been closed and their files were ordered, as if not a single rider had been knocked from the saddle. The cloud of rifle smoke had dispersed enough to give Jack a good sight of the enemy.

Without command the front rank of cavalry surged forward.

Jack stood in the centre of the square, his attention focused on the enemy. He was aware of his men moving around him, the sergeants pulling at the ranks to force the men into a better formation, closing the gaps in the wall of bayonets, their industrious bustle steadying the men as they watched the Cossacks charge for a second time. He could sense his men's resolve, their determination hardening as they realised they had survived the first desperate moments of the fight. Jack was beginning to understand the confusion that swirled around him, making sense out of the chaos. His heartbeat slowed as he felt his confidence build. If the fusiliers stood firm then the Cossacks were powerless to touch them.

"Commence firing!" Jack ordered, his body flinching as the fusiliers discharged another storm of shot towards the Cossacks.

This time Jack was prepared for the thick, pungent smoke and he turned on the spot, looking for a gap in the smog so he could watch the Cossacks thundering past in a repeat of their opening charge.

He saw nothing but open plain. He twisted back round, pushing himself to the front of the side of the square that had faced the charging Cossacks, using of his elbows to force a passage in the tightly packed ranks.

The redcoats' fire had been dreadfully effective, killing men and animals with cruel abandon as the heavy bullets punched through flesh and bone. The front rank of Cossacks had borne the brunt of the punishment, screening the second rank of horsemen who now rode forward with calculated steadiness, each rider clutching a firearm.

"Jesus Christ!" Jack swore aloud as he realised what was about to happen. Instead of being safe in their tight ranks, the redcoats were suddenly staring at death. When the second line of Cossacks closed the range, their firearms would not be able to miss the packed ranks, every enemy bullet would find flesh.

"Stand firm and reload," Jack ordered, his heart contracting in horror as he waited for the inevitable. He caught Digby-Brown's eye and saw the same terror reflected in his expression.

The first line of Cossacks swung round, splitting into two groups that would attack the corners of the square, the weakest points in its formation. This time they would close slowly and use the long reach of their lances to stab down on the fusiliers.

"Reload!" Jack screamed. "Faster, damn you!" The redcoats worked furiously, careless of skinning their knuckles on their bayonets, desperate to reload and drive the enemy away before they unleashed a storm of bullets of their own.

As every second crawled by, the fusiliers got closer to being able to fire once more. Jack could not fathom the Cossacks' lack of fire. At any second he expected to feel his flesh being ripped apart yet still the Cossacks did not fire.

As the cloud of smoke from the fusiliers' volleys was dispersed by the freshening wind, Jack stopped screaming at his men and gaped.

The Cossacks had gone.

The Light Company stood in silence, the tension still swirling through the men. It took several long moments for the fusiliers' fingers to relax their grip on the trigger, a few seconds longer for the men to remember to breathe.

Jack moved first, pushing through the shaken redcoats to stare at the Cossacks disappearing over the crest of the slope.

"The bastards." He was barely capable of coherent thought, such was the feeling of relief coursing through him.

His two lieutenants came staggering out of the company to join him, the same mix of disbelief, astonishment, and relief etched on their ashen faces.

Lieutenant Thomas spoke first. "What in the name of God was all that about?"

"God is the right person to ask." Jack took a deep breath to steady his nerves. "I don't have a bloody clue."

"Were they testing us?"

"Who knows?" replied Jack.

Lieutenant Thomas struggled to cope with the wave of emotion coursing through him. "Thank God."

"Thank God indeed," Digby-Brown echoed with a withering glare at his captain.

"But why do it?" Thomas asked, his face now flushed with a rush of blood. "Why did they not press home the attack?"

"I rather think those fellows over there might have had something to do with it." Digby-Brown waved his hand to the south.

Jack looked up and immediately saw what Digby-Brown meant.

To the south, a full squadron of greenjacketed horsemen and a column of blue-jacketed troops flowed across the plain.

The French army had arrived.

The old enemy, Britain's most constant foe, the Crapauds, had rescued the Light Company.

★ ★ ★

114

The French cavalry galloped past, clods of earth thrown into the air, the ground drumming with the staccato rhythm of the fast-moving horses. The Cossacks rode away, driven from the field by the superior numbers of French cavalry whose bright yellow facings and gleaming sabres added a touch of gaudiness to the miserable scene. Two companies of French infantry manoeuvred to take station on the Light Company's right flank.

Jack's men began to deal with the aftermath of the fight, scraping shallow graves for the bodies of the Cossacks that had fallen. They paid little attention to their allies. The fusiliers worked in bitter silence, the grotesque evidence of the power of their Miniè rifles shocking the inexperienced soldiers.

Their rescuers were no ordinary French soldiers but the French elite, the Zouaves. Originally formed of Algerian troops, the battalions of the Zouaves had become something of a legend. The French authorities might have replaced the original colonial soldiers with true-blooded Frenchmen, but the regiment's reputation remained, as did their colourful uniforms. From their deep red, baggy trousers to the elaborate gold embroidery on their dark blue jackets, they looked as foreign as their name implied. A red fez perched elegantly on their heads, and bright white gaiters round their ankles completed their spectacular attire.

A French officer strode forward jauntily, a smile spread wide under his thick black moustache. He wore a longer and more traditionally cut dark blue jacket with gold-braided cuffs and epalets, his red trousers were less baggy, with a thick blue stripe running down

115

the seam, and a kepi replaced the more exotic fez; he looked a great deal less outlandish than the soldiers he commanded.

"A very good afternoon to you, gentlemen," the French officer called out to Jack and his two lieutenants. "I must apologise for our rude interruption. I rather think we spoiled your fun, no?" The French officer's English was impeccable and bore only a hint of an accent.

Jack was in no mood to be sociable. His indecision when the Cossacks first charged stung his pride. He should have had the men form a square earlier, his tardy orders had placed the company in danger when a more resolute and disciplined response would most likely have deterred the Cossacks from charging. His mistakes had nearly cost his men dear.

"You must excuse me, my manners are terrible." The French officer pronounced the last word in the French way and Jack's mouth tightened with dislike. The French officer's own expression hardened, his eyes never once wavering from Jack's belligerent glare.

"I should introduce myself. My name is Octave Marsaud." The Frenchman smiled, an expression that sat well on his battered face but which did not reach his hard, pale-blue eyes. His face was lean, a large Romanesque nose dominating his features. A thin scar ran down one side of his jaw and another smaller one flecked the cheek on the opposite side of his face. He looked as hard and as tough as his men. "I have the honour of being a captain in His Majesty's First Battalion of Zouaves."

Both British lieutenants inclined their heads at the French man's introduction, acknowledging his words as if they were meeting in more dignified surroundings than a muddy Crimean field.

"Sloames. Light Company, King's Royal Fusiliers." Jack kept his introduction short. "Lieutenants Digby-Brown and Thomas." He gave the briefest of nods towards his two subalterns as he introduced them.

Marsaud smiled politely. "Those Cossack bastards. They think they can do whatever they like. I am sorry my appearance drove them away. I should have liked a fight. We have had enough of all this bloody waiting." The Frenchman smiled wolfishly.

"Indeed." Jack kept his reply non-committal, wanting the conversation over as fast as possible.

"You do not sound convinced, monsieur." Marsaud's hard eyes bored into Jack's.

"Is there ever a good time to fight?" The battle was too fresh to be casually dismissed.

"Of course! But you only fight when you know you can win." Jack heard the censure in the Frenchman's words; the experienced officer was admonishing the British captain's performance in the face of the charging Cossacks.

"We are British soldiers. We always win."

Marsaud smiled wryly at the bold claim. "You British. If God had given you brains then you would be truly dangerous."

Jack let the comment pass. Another Zouave officer was standing, hands on hips, glaring in their direction, his hostility obvious even from a hundred yards away.

Jack nodded towards him. "I do not think your chum over there is pleased to see you fraternising with the enemy."

Marsaud looked across and snorted as he spotted his fellow captain's posture.

"Do not concern yourself with Saint-Andre. He hates the British. One grandfather died at Waterloo, the other at Talavera. He was taught to hate you *rosbifs* since the day he was born." With a final bow, the French captain took his leave of the British officers and walked back to his men. Jack let him go, his thoughts returning once more to the disaster the Zouaves had prevented.

In a matter of days, the company was certain to face the Russian army. They could not always rely on the timely intervention of an ally to save them from destruction. They would have to depend on their officers to do that. Jack was painfully aware that his fusiliers would have little confidence left in their officer's ability.

The knowledge humbled him. He had stolen a life and a rank that was not rightly his and his lack of experience had nearly cost his men their lives.

CHAPTER
SIXTEEN

Jack left the dismissal of the Light Company to Digby-Brown. He had borne the men's despondency like a shackle round his neck during the weary trudge back to the battalion lines. The fusiliers had marched in a sullen silence, the confrontation with the Cossacks leaving them in no doubt about their captain's ability to command them in battle. Indecision cost lives, their lives. It was unforgivable.

The Cossacks had outmanoeuvred the Light Company with the ease of a vicious child plucking the legs from a captured spider. Jack's arrogant self-belief that he could lead a company into battle had brought him to this place. At the very first opportunity, he had shown himself to be completely lacking in any of the skills needed for such a task. He truly was a fraud.

"Ah, Captain Sloames!" Captain McCulloch spied his fellow company commander and called cheerily out in greeting.

Jack was too despondent and too weary to reply, so he simply pulled his greatcoat tighter round his body and waited to see what McCulloch wanted. He did not have to wait long to find out, as McCulloch's short legs propelled their owner across the muddy ground.

"Captain Sloames? Ah good, it is you. Bad news, I'm afraid. Still no tents! I cannot think what the commissariat is playing at. But still, no croaking, what? No one likes to hear a fellow griping on. We shall just have to make the best of it."

Jack took in the news. No tents meant another night spent in the open, enduring whatever foul weather came their way. It was not news to lift his spirits.

"However," McCulloch continued when it became clear that Jack was not going to respond, "we are told to expect a draft from the second battalion. Apparently they were meant to meet up with us back at Varna but, like most things, the army managed to lose them for a while."

"How many men?" Jack's interest awoke at the news of reinforcements.

"I have not heard the exact details. Are you short?"

"Of course. But who isn't? I don't think there is a single company that is up to strength."

"Well, let us hope the draft is not just made up of raw recruits." McCulloch rapped Jack's arm with the kidskin gloves he carried in one hand to emphasise the point. "So I hear your company was in action." He tried to steer the conversation towards the real reason he had sought out the Light Company's commander.

Jack's brow furrowed. He was not surprised the news was already racing around the battalion. It was the first skirmish of the campaign and would be the talk of the brigade if not of the whole army.

"The battalion will be quite famous. We are the first to fight."

120

"It wasn't much of a fight. We formed square and drove them off." Jack was uncomfortable discussing the day's events.

"The company fought well from what I hear."

Jack grunted in reply, refusing to be drawn.

McCulloch took the lack of reply as a rebuke. "Apologies. One mustn't harp on about such things. So let us hope the draft brings us fresh blood." He hid his disappointment well.

"Indeed." Jack struggled to shake off his apathy. "I could use a new colour-sergeant. Mine went down with the cholera before I even had a chance to meet him."

"Lieutenant Flowers did not say if there would be any such specimens in the draft, but you may be fortunate." McCulloch looked up as a few fat raindrops started to fall from the gloomy sky. "We could all use some luck."

Jack could not have agreed more. As he took his leave of McCulloch, the heavens opened. Jack sloshed his way through the muddy quagmire underfoot, lost in a gloom that soaked his soul in misery more thoroughly than the deluge could soak his bedraggled greatcoat. He prayed the new draft contained an experienced sergeant, a veteran soldier he could rely on to prop up his faltering authority. Jack knew he needed assistance if he was to bring his company through the battles that surely lay ahead.

Jack shivered in the damp mist that heralded the arrival of dawn. A watery sun was rising slowly, ending another night of ceaseless discomfort and misery. The long and wretched hours of darkness had left them all weary, draining their already feeble reserves of strength. Jack, like his men, faced the dawn chilled to the bone, mud-splattered and clammy, his body fatigued and aching.

As soon as the battalion stood down, Jack ordered Digby-Brown to organise the men into the necessary working parties ready for the quartermaster's instructions. Then, leaving his senior subaltern to manage things by himself, Jack squelched his way through the mud in search of Lieutenant Flowers, the battalion's harassed adjutant.

Jack found Flowers perched on an ammunition crate, wrestling with three thick, black leather ledgers which Jack recognised as the company returns. It was a risk approaching the adjutant. Jack was well behind in the mountain of paperwork that the army expected him to keep up to date; his basic numeracy skills and dubious handwriting forced him to rely on his lieutenants to maintain the company accounts. He was not alone in his unwillingness to tackle the ledgers, many of his fellow captains put a great amount of effort into avoiding coming into contact with the thick black books.

This state of affairs drove Flowers to distraction. The staff officers at brigade headquarters perpetually harassed him for correctly completed returns, which he could only provide with properly kept company ledgers. It was a never-ending battle between himself and the captains that Flowers knew he would never win. Nevertheless, the resourceful lieutenant did his best, and he would try any means to ensure some of the record-keeping was at least partially completed. The result was that any request made of the adjutant came at a price, a quid pro quo arrangement that had to be carefully negotiated.

Jack arrived just in time to catch one of the ledgers as it slid from the adjutant's lap, grabbing it by the corner before it fell to a muddy grave on the filthy ground.

"Steady there, Flowers."

Jack gave the cover of the ledger an exaggerated polish with his sodden sleeve. He generally enjoyed a battle of wits with the adjutant. Flowers was quite the dashing young officer and he sported a fine pair of whiskers that any cavalry officer would have worn with pride. By rights, Jack should have loathed him. Like Digby-Brown, Flowers came from a wealthy family, by the meagre standards of the King's Royal Fusiliers at least. His passage through the junior ranks had been effortless, as would the climb on to the next rung. But whereas Digby-Brown carried himself with a precocious superiority, Flowers was charming, his easy company and propensity to share a joke smoothing any ruffled feathers among his fellow officers. He was impossible to dislike.

Jack grinned at him. "I cannot imagine Captain Devine would be happy to see his precious accounts ruined through your carelessness."

Flowers greeted Jack with a warm smile. "I believe Captain Devine would give a loud sigh of relief if I somehow contrived to destroy his company's books. It's good to see you, Sloames. Somehow, we have managed to miss one another since we came ashore. Hard to believe, I know. It's as if you are avoiding me."

"Never!" Jack tried to look suitably shocked at the preposterous idea as if he hadn't in fact ducked out of sight whenever he spotted the adjutant. "I've been rather preoccupied preparing my company to fight. You are aware that we're about to fight the Russians, aren't you?"

"Very amusing, Sloames. Unfortunately, the staff officers at brigade do not think this should interrupt my returns so I really would be very grateful if you could get your company's books in order. Then I will only have to make up around half the information brigade is requesting."

"Well, you do such a good job of it. What does it matter if you make it up or if I tell Digby-Brown to do it?"

"The reason is very simple, as you well know. If you don't provide me with your completed ledger and I am forced to guess, we may be left dangerously short of something we would rather like to have."

"Such as?"

"Such as, oh, I don't know, new blankets or new boots or some other necessity we cannot manage without."

"Like tents."

"Exactly. Imagine how awful having insufficient tents would be in this Godforsaken place!"

"We don't have any tents, Flowers."

"You see! It's happening already. Perhaps if we had completed our records properly we might have enough tents by now."

"No one has any tents. No one. Not even General Brown."

"Then the whole damn army is probably guilty of incomplete accounting. I can't think of any other reason why we would not be provided with the most essential equipment. Why, we might even run the risk of not having enough medical supplies or ammunition."

"Do we have enough medical supplies? Or ammunition?"

"Now you come to mention it, that must be another item we have not properly accounted for as we seem to have barely any."

"Good grief." Jack grimaced, his jocularity faltering. "Very well. I'll get Digby-Brown on the case. I even promise to help him spell the long words."

"You will?" Flowers seemed surprised at such rapid capitulation. "Capital. Is there anything you wanted to see me about?"

"No, nothing at all. It was just a social call. I thought we'd not spent enough time together recently."

"Bosh!"

"Well, since you insist, there is one thing you can do for me. I was wondering if you knew the constituents of the draft that is due to arrive today."

"I do. What do you need?"

"A sergeant. Preferably one with years of experience and a vast amount of patience."

"I see." Flowers placed the ledgers on another crate that had been pressed into service as part of his makeshift office. He carefully picked up a sheaf of papers that had been kept in place underneath his revolver. He flicked through the pile with an ink-stained thumb before plucking one short scrap of paper from the middle. He ran his finger down the list. "Forty-three other ranks, two corporals and, yes, you are in luck, one sergeant. I have no more information than that. Why are you so interested?"

"Well, I only have three sergeants and I've a feeling I'm going to need more than that. I was hoping you could see your way to allocating any new arrival to the Light Company."

"It may not be so easy." Flowers looked pensive. "You're not the only one short, after all. McCulloch has only got two, as has Captain Taylor and that's only because we gave Corporal Jones his third stripe back. I'd planned to allocate him the new sergeant as Jones is almost certain to get into another fist fight before the week is out."

"I'd be very grateful, Flowers."

Flowers looked up from his papers. Something in Captain Sloames's tone caught his attention. As a rule, captains did not usually ask so nicely. "I'll do all I can. Colonel Morris will have the final say but I'm sure I can make it happen."

Jack passed Captain Devine's ledger back to Flowers. "My thanks, Captain Sloames."

Jack turned and left the adjutant to his bookkeeping.

Flowers watched him stride purposefully away. For the first time he noticed that Sloames marched rather than walked, his gait more regimented than the languid stroll of most officers. The commander of the Light Company was proving to be something of an enigma.

He maintained a reserve quite unlike any of the other officers, as if he were hiding something of his real personality. Flowers pushed the thoughts from his mind; he had too much to do to waste time on idle reflection. He was satisfied to have succeeded in persuading at least one of the company's captains to sort out his paperwork. It usually took days of threats and cajoling, and more often than not the colonel's intervention, to make any sort of headway.

Flowers stood and placed the ledger Sloames had handed to him neatly on top of the other two. As he did so, he noticed the name on it.

It belonged to the Light Company. Sloames had humbugged him.

CHAPTER
SEVENTEEN

The new arrivals trudged in late that afternoon. The battalion had spent another laborious day organising the mountain of supplies that continued to be brought ashore. Hour after back-breaking hour was spent moving the tons of supplies the army would need if it were to untie itself from the apron strings of the navy and strike inland.

The arrival of new men would usually have brought the battalion to its feet to scrutinise the newcomers and subject them to a barrage of catcalls and insults. Today was different, the fusiliers were simply too exhausted after their day of labour to show much interest in their reinforcements.

The newcomers, too, were in a wretched condition after weeks of being incarcerated on the transport ships. Many were raw recruits, naïve impressionable young men who had fallen for the blarney of the recruiting parties or were desperate to escape poverty, using the army as a refuge and a better alternative to the grinding misery of the workhouse. Most would have joined up in London, the fusiliers' traditional recruiting ground where all manner of Englishmen, Scotsmen, Welshmen and the Irish could be found. A rare few would already be soldiers, volunteers from the regiment's depot companies, who were drawn to the campaign to escape the mind-numbing boredom of garrison life.

The new recruits would also include a substantial number of felons who had been given the option to serve the Queen. The authorities were always willing to empty the dregs from London's gaols into the ranks rather than go through the lengthy process and costs of a formal trial. The army took them willingly, its insatiable appetite for manpower overriding any qualms about arming the country's criminal classes.

The battalion would have to absorb these newcomers, embrace and train them, turning them from ordinary redcoats into fusiliers.

This motley collection of soldiers stood about waiting to be welcomed. The sky had cleared and the late-afternoon sun did nothing to improve their appearance. A few fusiliers looked them over, a swift appraisal that invariably finished with a snort of derision. They were outsiders, foot soldiers not fusiliers, therefore not worthy of consideration or attention.

Lieutenant Flowers bustled over to greet the bedraggled replacements he had left waiting for close to half an hour. The adjutant was carrying several pieces of paper that he was trying to read as he walked. He paused to finish the last sheet of paper before tucking the pile under his arm and grinning warmly at the men who had the good fortune to be joining the King's Royal Fusiliers.

"Good afternoon. What glorious weather! My apologies for the lack of ceremony but as I'm sure you can imagine things are a little busy around here at the moment. Now then, I'll not detain you for long. We'll soon have you away to join your companies." Flowers noticed the enormous sergeant who stood alone at the head of the column. "Goodness me. Welcome, Sergeant. You'll be pleased to hear you are assigned to the Light Company. The best of the best for you."

The sergeant snapped to attention. "Sir!" He was a bear of a man who would surely command the immediate respect of his new company. Flowers was certain Captain Sloames would count himself very fortunate indeed.

The lieutenant's attention was diverted for a moment by the sight of a most welcome surprise hidden at the rear of the column. Standing forlornly behind the formed ranks was a single horse and cart. Battered and broken, both had almost certainly seen better days and looked thoroughly clapped out. Nevertheless, Flowers was too delighted by the cart's contents to worry about its condition.

"God bless you! Tents! It's about time they turned up."

He immediately summoned the closest company to unload the cart's precious contents and haul the stone-coloured canvas sacks to where the rest of the battalion's stores were piled up. It was immediately obvious that there would not be enough of the large and cumbersome bell tents to go round but on first inspection there appeared to be enough to get most of the battalion's officers under canvas even if it meant some very cosy sleeping arrangements. The subalterns and the fusiliers would not be so lucky and would be forced to continue enduring whatever weather the Crimean peninsula chose to inflict upon them.

With the unloading of the cart well under way Flowers was pleased to spy the regimental sergeant major leading a gaggle of sergeants and corporals towards the sullen ranks of newcomers.

Flowers supervised the distribution of the reinforcements, handling the process briskly and efficiently, allocating the new arrivals to their allotted companies and into the care of the sergeants and corporals. Soon, only the new sergeant was left, along with the six men who would join him in the ranks. Sergeants Adams and Shepherd from the Light Company eyed the imposing figure of their new sergeant warily.

"Right," announced Flowers cheerfully. "I'll escort you chaps to your new company personally. Follow me."

Flowers found Captain Sloames perched on the edge of a crate of ammunition, his feet stretched out lazily in from of him while he cleaned his fingernails with the end of a tortoiseshell comb. His shako lay discarded on the ground beside him and for the first time the weather was clement enough for him to have removed his mud-encrusted greatcoat, which was draped over a stand of rifles in a vain attempt to dry it out.

The captain's dress uniform showed the ravages of days spent in the field. The dress jacket was splattered with grime, the vibrant scarlet already dulled, and the bullion epaulettes and fine brass buttons were tarnished, and flecked with dirt. The uniform was slowly degrading in the harsh climate, much like the man who hid beneath its folds.

Jack looked up as Flowers led his little procession towards him, casually tossing his tortoiseshell comb into his upturned shako as he stood to greet them. He had used the afternoon's decent weather to shave off his beard, something he never enjoyed doing. His skin was red and sore from the razor's abrasive attention and a few spots of blood welled up under his jaw line. At least the razor's blunt service had distracted him from fretting over whether or not he would obtain the service of a new sergeant. Now that concern came back and Jack anxiously scanned the approaching men.

With relief he caught a glimpse of white sergeant's chevrons on the arm of the man following behind Lieutenant Flowers. Jack smiled warmly and was about to offer his most profuse thanks to Lieutenant Flowers when his smile died and his body went rigid. Fear and loathing coursed through him, his fingers twitched towards the revolver at his hip. Flowers was bringing to the Light Company a man who could recognise their captain for the charlatan he was.

Flowers saw the colour drain from Jack's cheeks. "Captain Sloames, are you quite well?" He moved forward and reached out to steady the visibly shaken officer in front of him, blocking the new sergeant's view of Jack.

"I'm fine." Jack spoke barely above a whisper, desperately trying to gather his fleeing wits.

"Are you sure? You have me quite concerned but let me try to improve your spirits. The colonel has granted

132

your request and let you take the new sergeant. I'm sure you will find him of considerable value to your company, not least because the man is a damned Goliath."

Flowers turned to one side and held his arm out to bring the replacement sergeant into the conversation. The towering soldier took a purposeful step forward and stood rigidly to attention in front of his new commanding officer.

Jack stood face to face with the man he hated more than any other. His mind was racing, his memory replaying that brutal fight in the laundry. He could remember every bitter moment of it and now the cause of all his misery stood in front of him, about to reveal his true identity.

Slater was staring straight ahead, his gaze focused on a spot six inches above Jack's forehead. It took several agonising moments before the sergeant sensed that his new officer was waiting for his attention.

Slater finally lowered his gaze. Jack saw the flare of recognition deep in the dark brown eyes. But the moment passed and Slater's gaze returned to its original position. He stood rigidly at attention, his pose the very embodiment of a British sergeant waiting for a command.

"Right, I'll leave you to it." Lieutenant Flowers playfully punched Captain Sloames on the shoulder. "Are you sure you are quite well? The last thing we need is you falling sick. There has been quite enough of that sort of thing already."

"Thank you, Flowers, you may go."

There were a thousand questions running through Jack's mind as he struggled to understand how the brutal sergeant had arrived in the Crimea.

There were many questions but just a single conclusion. His charade was over.

CHAPTER
EIGHTEEN

The hastily erected tent already smelt musty, the gloomy interior thick with the stink of sun-warmed canvas. Jack stood back, politely holding the tent flap open so that his fellow captains could enter first.

The darkness of the Russian steppe enveloped the British camp; the few flickering watch fires the men had managed to get started created menacing shadows in the surrounding darkness. The army's piquets stared anxiously outwards, seeing danger in every shifting shadow, their nerves fraying, their fragile confidence eroding as the minutes of their duty ticked slowly by.

The single tent would normally have been the temporary residence of one officer. Tonight it would hold four. Jack would be sharing the small space with McCulloch and Captain Brewer, the commander of the battalion's Grenadier Company. The three captains would also have to find room for Major Peacock, the battalion's second-in-command, a proposition made all the more onerous due to Brewer's sizeable girth.

It was traditional that the Grenadier Company was formed of the tallest men in the battalion and many of them measured over six foot. Brewer was half a dozen inches shorter but made up for his lack of height by being very, very fat. It would be a tight squeeze in the confines of the tent but Jack appreciated how lucky they were to be spending a night with some shelter from the elements. The junior officers and their men would not be so lucky, forced to spend a third night exposed in the freezing night air. It was not lost on Jack that, as ever, the senior officers claimed the best of the scarce resources, their privileged lifestyle extending even to the furthest reaches of the campaign trail.

Brewer carelessly tossed his shako, knapsack and scabbard to one side. He lowered himself awkwardly to the floor, the muddy ground covered by a creased and mildewed groundsheet, letting out an enormous explosion of wind as he did so. Unrepentant and ignoring the looks of disgust on the faces of his fellow captains, Brewer lay flat on his back and groaned in satisfaction.

"Do you know, this is the first time I've actually lain down since we came ashore. I'm exhausted already and we have yet to move more than a damn mile."

"Now, now. No croaking." McCulloch was carefully arranging his knapsack to one side of the tent. When it was lined up to his satisfaction, he unbuckled his sword and scabbard, which he placed meticulously alongside it, followed by his holstered revolver. He produced a handkerchief from his trouser pocket and laid this on the floor of the tent, then delicately sat down, using the crumpled linen to act as a barrier between the seat of his trousers and the soiled groundsheet.

Jack watched McCulloch's fussy preparations with wry amusement before he slung his own knapsack on to

136

the ground on the opposite side of the tent, following it with his weapons. He tossed his shako to one side and sat on his knapsack. A spasm seared up his aching spine and his hand automatically went to the small of his back in a vain attempt to massage away the worst of the pain.

"Curry," announced Brewer suddenly as he lay supine on the floor, his arms crossed behind his head. "Nothing would hit the spot, right now, better than a curry."

"Curry?" snorted McCulloch who was rooting through his knapsack. "Vile foreign muck! I've only had the misfortune to endure it once when I visited a cousin in London. Why anyone would want to eat such a loathsome concoction is beyond my powers of comprehension."

"Nonsense, man." Brewer scratched hard at his full beard. "It may be a heathen food, I'll grant you that, but there are few things better." Brewer lifted one hefty buttock as he broke wind for a second time. "Excuse the old boiler. Now, a good steak and kidney pudding might just win the day. Or perhaps a well-crafted game pie." Brewer was warming to his favourite subject. "Sloames, care to venture an opinion?"

Jack started at hearing the name. His mind had been elsewhere, his thoughts dwelling on the return of Sergeant Slater into his life. He tasted the emotions that had stirred at the sight of the brutal sergeant. Hatred. Fear. Grief. Slater's appearance had brought back all the memories he had wished to hide away in the darkest recesses of his mind. Now they rose to the

137

fore like the scum on an old keg of ale, bitter and sour for having been kept in the dark for so long.

"Jellied eels." Jack offered the suggestion curtly, attempting to convey his intention to stay out of the discussion.

"You have the taste of a costermonger! Jellied eels, indeed. Now, pie and liquor, that I would understand if you must indulge a fancy for the food of London's less salubrious parts. Or perhaps —"

The tent flap was violently snatched open and Major Peacock stormed inside. He surveyed the interior of the tent with obvious distaste. His prominent Adam's apple bobbed up and down as he swallowed a mouthful of the ripe air.

Peacock smoothed his razor-thin moustache with a thumb and forefinger. "Goodness me, could you not have at least allowed us a moment's rest before you fill the air with your noxious flatulence, Brewer?" The major immediately turned round to shout to his orderly who was hovering just behind him. "Coffee, Spalding," he snapped. "Bring it as soon as you have it ready." Peacock cautiously sniffed the air. "I shall dine outside tonight."

Jack hid the look of distaste that crossed his face. Peacock represented much that he disliked in the officer class. Over-bearing, bombastic, small-minded, ignoble and arrogant, Peacock was universally disliked throughout the battalion. To the men he was a bullying tyrant, an officer who gained immense satisfaction from his rank and his right to command. To his fellow officers he was unprofessional and discourteous. He enjoyed his position due to his constant toadying to Colonel Morris, the only man in the regiment who had not found cause to dislike the supercilious major.

In peacetime Peacock had thrived on the army's many rules and regulations which he viciously enforced, ensuring that the lives of both officers and men were made as unpleasant as possible. Any misdemeanours were ruthlessly pursued, no matter how trivial. For the men that meant punishment, for the officers it led to public censure and ridicule.

The major removed his shako and ran the palm of his hand over the bald dome of his head. "Has no one given a thought to arranging some furniture? We cannot all be expected to sprawl on the floor, can we, Brewer?" Peacock nudged him with the toe of his boot, which the grenadier captain chose to ignore.

"I can arrange for something if you insist," volunteered McCulloch, a barely discernible hint of disdain in his voice.

"Good fellow, McCulloch. Then we can make ourselves as comfortable as the circumstances will allow."

McCulloch rose to his feet and Peacock made a point of clapping him on the shoulder as he left the tent.

"You see, Brewer. Not everyone is as slothful as you. You really should follow McCulloch's example or even take a leaf out of Sloames's book. He has already engaged the enemy, while you, lazy good-for-nothing that you are, lumbered around the battalion cadging food."

"I resent that, Peacock," Brewer said mildly, refusing to be drawn by the major's hectoring. Traditionally officers addressed each other by name rather than by rank when they were not in front of the men. Colonel Morris was the only exception; he was only ever addressed as "Sir" or "Colonel". "My grenadiers are in tip-top condition, as we shall prove when we finally get off our collective firmament and take on the damn Russkis."

"Bravo, Brewer. Bravo. *Aut vincere aut mori.* That's the spirit. What do you say, Sloames?"

Jack did his best to look composed in the face of Peacock's schoolboy Latin. He had no idea what it meant. The knowledge of ancient, long dead languages had been lacking in the rudimentary education that he had received from his mother, yet for an officer it would be unthinkable to have no knowledge of it whatsoever. His usual tactic of hiding his lack of education behind a curt reply would not deflect someone like Peacock.

"What do you say, man? To conquer or to die?"

"I'd sooner do the conquering than the dying," Jack replied with more honesty than he intended, something he was immediately made to regret.

"Come now, Sloames. *Deficit omne quod nasciture.* Surely it is better to die gloriously than to live your life in the shadows and die wondering what you could have achieved if only you had dared to live a little. *Qui audit adipiscitur!*"

Jack had a fair idea that dying gloriously meant having your body shredded, your insides spilling on to the ground while you writhed in unimaginable agony, an opinion he felt sure the major would not take kindly to hearing. Fortunately, he was saved from having to reply by the timely return of Captain McCulloch who came into the tent followed by half a dozen fusiliers carrying an assortment of ammunition crates and ration boxes.

"It is the best I could find," McCulloch announced. "At least we shall have something to sit on."

The private soldiers deposited their burdens and scurried out of the tent, each man keen to avoid being given any more unwanted errands.

Peacock perched on the edge of one of the crates and looked round at his companions for the night. All were avoiding his eye, busying themselves with routine tasks or, in Brewer's case, simply lying in an exhausted stupor.

Peacock sniffed in disapproval. None of the captains was offering him any sort of entertainment so he determined to make his own.

"Well, then. I trust you and your companies are ready for the off." Peacock spoke far louder than was necessary. He was pleased to see Sloames look up from cleaning his revolver while McCulloch sat down on a crate and appeared to be giving him his full attention. Brewer gave no sign of having heard him, but Peacock was reasonably certain that the captain of grenadiers would be listening if he were not already asleep.

"The colonel and I have been told we should be ready to move in a day or so." Peacock continued. "The French are eager to move inland as early as tomorrow but Raglan will not let us go until he is satisfied that we are ready. Quite rightly, the general does not intend to allow us to be ordered around by that decrepit old crone, Saint-Arnaud. Raglan will not order an advance until he is certain that we have adequate supplies. I expect that is something he learnt from the old duke."

Peacock spoke confidingly, as if Raglan had offered the opinions to him personally. It was typical of Peacock's conceit to speak in such a self-important manner. Jack went back to cleaning his revolver.

McCulloch, however, was intrigued. "I wonder why the French seem so much better prepared for the campaign than we do. Their soldiers have their own tents, the army is well served by a commissariat brought with them from France and they have more than enough transport, having brought that with them too. They even have a number of these new-fangled 'ambulances' to move the sick."

"I'm sure the general has everything in hand." Peacock disapproved of McCulloch's negative comments. It would never dawn on the major to think ill of his betters, even if their incompetence was staring him in the face.

"I'm not croaking, merely observing that our allies seem a great deal better prepared for the campaign than we appear to be."

"*Per aspera ad astra*, McCulloch. I admit we may not appear to be as prepared as our allies are. However, remember this. A Frenchman cannot survive for two minutes without his comforts. They are a nation of dancing masters. We British, on the other hand, function far better when confronted with adversity."

Jack gave up the unequal struggle to remain silent in the face of Peacock's crass comments. "What utter claptrap! I have yet to find a soldier who fights better when he is wet and exhausted. Are you seriously saying that driving the men to breaking point is part of some grand strategy?"

"Sloames! *Cave quid dicis, quando et cui.* I cannot, and will not, tolerate such talk."

Jack may not have understood Peacock's Latin but the message was clear. He rebuked himself for getting involved in such pointless pontificating. Slater's arrival had shaken him to the core and he was letting his carefully constructed character slip.

"My apologies. I did not mean to sound disrespectful. I'm sure our commanders are fully in control of the situation."

Peacock was not about to let him off the hook so easily. This was just the kind of entertainment he had hoped the officers would provide. "I would remind you, Sloames, that you are a captain in one the finest regiments in this army. You hold a position that comes with onerous responsibility. A responsibility that requires you to set an example to the officers and men under your command." Peacock was enjoying himself. This was the first time he had been given an opportunity to give the captain of the Light Company a dressing-down. He gave every impression of being a capable and competent officer but the man kept himself to himself far too much for Peacock's liking. He needed to be reminded of his place in the battalion's pecking order.

"As officers we must maintain a character that is without blemish," Peacock continued. "A character *nulli secondus*. Without it, you will be unable to command the respect of the men. Respect, Sloames. You must earn respect. It is not given freely. The men are the scum of the earth, as the late duke so eloquently put it. Without gentlemen to lead them they are no more than a rabble."

Jack bridled at Peacock's words. "The men are not scum. If you only took the time to get to know your bloody command you would know that. Of course that would mean taking your head out of your own damn arse first."

"Sloames!" McCulloch cried out at Jack's outburst. Even Brewer was shocked enough to push himself to his elbows to stare at the source of such a scandalous eruption of anger.

The reaction of the two captains was as nothing compared to Peacock's outrage. Sloames had barely spoken in the weeks since joining the battalion. This sudden transformation was startling.

"How dare you!" Peacock shouted. "The colonel shall hear of this!" He rose to his feet and so did Jack. It looked as if the two officers would charge at each other. McCulloch leapt up, physically interposing himself between the two officers who continued to shout at each other.

"Jesus Christ! What are you going to tell the colonel? That I dared to speak the truth?" Jack no longer tried to hold back the flood of emotion that surged through him. He felt the charade that shackled him fall away and was glad of it.

"Why, you devil! I am your senior officer and you will speak to me with respect."

"Respect?" Jack spat the word out with venom. "Respect has to be earned, remember. I have no more respect for you than I do for the fleas in a whore's drawers."

Peacock was dumbstruck, his mouth hung open as he tried to speak through his fury. He was not silent for long. "You swine! Never have I been spoken to like that. Never! You viper! There is no place for scum like you in the King's Royal Fusiliers. I shall see to that. *Aut viam inveniam aut faciam!* When the colonel finds out about this, you will be damn lucky to keep your commission! If you were a private soldier, I'd have you flogged until I could see your spine and —"

"Alarm! To arms! To arms!"

The call to arms resounded through the army. Something had stirred in the darkness of the Russian steppe, scaring the already nervous sentries and triggering mayhem. "To arms! To arms!"

Men scrambled from their bivouacs, redcoats rushed to find their weapons, officers came stumbling from their tents undressed and unprepared. Sergeants rapidly formed their men into some kind of rough order before their officers dragged them off to where the line of piquets had begun firing into the night.

CHAPTER
NINETEEN

Peacock stormed out of the tent as the alarm sounded. Jack would have charged after him, nothing now left to lose, his charade about to end in a blaze of scandal that would see his name go down in the folklore of the battalion. But the threat of an attack was very real and, despite everything, his duty to his men and to his regiment came first.

Jack bent to reassemble his revolver, ignoring the tension that filled the tent and refusing to acknowledge either of the astonished captains who had been struck dumb by his outburst.

Brewer was the first to recover his wits. He levered himself to his feet, exhaling loudly with the effort, and hurried out of the tent with a sharp look of reproach at Jack. Brewer might have treated Major Peacock with less reverence than his rank was due but that did not mean that he would ever condone the loutish behaviour and foul-mouthed abuse he had just witnessed.

McCulloch let out a long sigh, shaking his head at the distressing scene he had just witnessed.

"What came over you, Sloames? What possessed you to speak to Peacock in such a ..." McCulloch struggled to find the right words, "such an appalling manner?"

Jack looked up as he snapped the last parts of the gun back together, his expression grim. "It is no more than he deserved and I damn well enjoyed it."

"Enjoyed it? You perverse lunatic! You cannot speak to your superior officer like that."

"You heard the pompous fool."

"If anyone is playing the fool then it's you, not Peacock. He'll drag you over the coals for this, you dolt. You'll have to apologise."

"Apologise? I'd rather rub my arse with a brick!"

"Please refrain from using your foul language with me. You'll have to apologise or you'll face ruin."

Jack chuckled at the threat. "We're about to fight the biggest bloody battle since Waterloo. What punishment can Peacock possibly inflict that is worse than what the Russians have in mind?"

"Worse? Why, he could ruin you! Don't you understand? He could blacken your reputation so that no other regiment would ever accept you. You would never live it down. Never! Your career would be finished."

"Reputation! Is that all you lot really care about? What a load of pompous claptrap!" Jack felt his anger returning.

"What on earth do you mean? You lot? As officers we are nothing without our reputation and without us, the men would never fight."

"Is that right? Oh, I forgot. The men are just scum and it takes a true gentleman to be an officer and lead them," Jack fired back, his face taut with anger.

"Of course it does and well you know it."

"I know no such thing. You're being as much of an arse as Peacock if you believe it."

McCulloch stepped back as if Jack had physically hit him. Jack thought McCulloch might actually strike him but although he was shaking with anger, he managed to bring his rage under control.

"You are a fool, Captain Sloames, a fool and a viper. Peacock was quite right. I only wonder how you kept your true character hidden for so long."

McCulloch snatched up his weapons and strode out into the night.

Left alone, Jack stood still, savouring the momentary peace. It seemed to him that his imposture lay in tatters around him in the tent. Yet he felt no fear, only relief. Giving up the deception was perversely liberating.

He thrust his revolver into his waistband and snatched his sword and scabbard from the ground. He would face the Russians and do his duty. Peacock, McCulloch, Slater and the rest of the bloody officers could go to hell.

He whipped back the tent flap and strode out into the chaos of an army on the verge of panic.

Soldiers ran in every direction in complete disorder, some armed, some seeking weapons, everywhere a frenzy of movement and sound. The bellow of orders and counter-orders, shouts of confusion, the jangle of equipment and thud of booted feet resonated in the night. Through it all came the sound of gunfire. Sometimes it rippled out like a child running a stick along an iron fence. Then it would die down to single shots, before the noise built to another crescendo as more soldiers fired at shadowy targets in the darkness.

A vicious blow smashed into the side of Jack's head and sent him reeling back into the tent, knocked half witless. The attack had come out of nowhere. He desperately tried to locate the source but his vision was blurred and his senses dazed.

The second blow came in low, punching into his stomach, driving his breath from his body. He doubled over, unable to recover, incapable of doing anything but absorb the blows that came out of the darkness. As his head went down, his attacker threw his knee forward, connecting with Jack's unprotected face, snapping his neck backwards and throwing him on to his back.

Jack hit the ground, agony searing through his body. He could feel the blood running freely down his face from his battered nose, with more filling his mouth where his lips had been driven into his teeth. Before he could even begin to struggle, a huge body thumped down on top of him, pinning him to the tent floor. Barely able to breathe, Jack tried to raise his arms but his opponent merely punched down, sending another searing lance of agony into his already battered face. His arms were thrown backwards and pinned underneath his attacker's knees. Pain seared through his arms and shoulders as his assailant leant his weight forward, bearing down on him.

He was helpless and barely conscious.

"Wake up, damn you," Jack's assailant hissed through gritted teeth, leaning over his face.

Though the pain was terrible, Jack forced his eyes open and looked up into the terrifying gaze of Sergeant Slater.

"Good evening, Lark. Even dressed as a Rupert, I knew it was you." Spittle flew from Slater's mouth, mixing with the blood that covered Jack's face. "I thought I must've been dreaming. But there you were, bold as brass, and looking quite the part, I have to admit." Slater leant so close that Jack could smell his foetid breath. "You almost had me. You seemed so at ease, like you truly were an officer. So I didn't say anything. I needed some time to think. But when this little shindig kicked off I thought it was too good an opportunity to pass up. So here I am, come to say hello to my old chum, Jack Lark."

Jack could see every pore on Slater's sweating, florid face.

"Fuck you, Slater."

Slater cackled, showing the blackened stumps that were all that was left of his teeth.

"I'm going to kill you, Slater. You hear me? You are going to pay —"

Slater swatted one meaty hand across Jack's face, cutting off his words. The blow sent droplets of blood splattering across the floor of the tent.

"Enough." Slater looked down at Jack. He was as calm as could be. "I must hand it to you. I never knew you had it in you to be so daring. Oh, I admired you for standing up to me. That took real guts, that did. But when you and that fool, Sloames, scuttled away, I can't

150

say I was surprised." His face creased into a smile. "What did you do with Sloames? Did you kill him?"

"He died."

Slater nodded solemnly. "So, Sloames died. That was convenient, wasn't it? Then you pinched his uniform. But coming out here was plain stupid. It's going to be bloody dangerous in these parts soon enough."

"I had nothing left. You saw to that."

"You sad little fool." Slater seemed genuinely amused. Then his expression hardened. "I lost my colours and got shipped out to this rat hole because of you." His face twisted. "That fat fool Stimpson said I had brought the regiment's name into disrepute and had me sent away. Just because that stupid doxy banged her bloody head." The huge man shook his head. "But now I reckon things will turn out all right. This is quite a nice little swindle you've got going here, I'm almost proud of you." Slater cackled at the notion. "From now on, you do what I tell you, or I'll gab on you and let the army hang you for the fake you are. So you make life nice and easy and do what you're told." He paused as he let the threat sink in. "Now then, I'm going to stand up and there's no need for any fuss and nonsense. Just take it easy and think on what I said."

Slater eased his weight cautiously backwards, releasing Jack's arms, ready for any sign of resistance. He need not have bothered. Jack lay immobile, his pain-wracked body unable to move after the beating.

Slater eased himself on to his haunches, giving Jack a cruel smile as he did so. "I knew you'd see sense. Now, you lie there like a good chap while I walk my chalk.

151

We'll have another chat on the morrow. And remember, I'll be watching you."

Slater pushed himself to his feet, watching Jack warily the whole time.

Jack could do nothing. He could not even force his bruised arms to move. He closed his eyes against the pain, holding them closed for several long seconds.

When he finally opened them, Slater was gone.

Gingerly Jack tried to sit up, his body protesting loudly. His arms felt crushed, as if the muscles had been pulped, while his face was a single orb of pain. The months had not diminished Slater's ability to deliver a slating.

Jack slowly forced his body upright, meeting every fresh lance of pain with a stream of expletives. He staggered across the tent to his kit, the act of bending down to open the knapsack releasing another flurry of oaths as sharp needles of pain surged through his back. Clutching the scrap of linen he had used to clean his revolver in one hand and his canteen of water in the other, he lurched painfully out of the tent, grateful for the darkness that would hide his battered features from casual scrutiny.

The first thing he noticed was that the rifle fire had died down. Then he realised that the fusiliers were streaming back into the battalion lines, their eyes bright with the excitement of blasting the night air with their Minié rifles. The British soldiers had been shooting at shadows. The Russian army was safely tucked up in their tents and in the cosy houses of Sevastopol. There was no attack. The alarm had been false. Like revellers returning home late from the local fair, the fusiliers were laughing and joking with each other, their exhilaration obvious even through Jack's blurred and pain-filled vision.

Keeping his head down, Jack slowly made his way through the men, his only thought to seek out a refuge where he could tend to his wounds away from the prying eyes of his fellow officers. He skirted round the bigger groups of redcoats, walking as briskly as his injuries would allow, hoping that the men's excitement would allow him to pass through them unremarked.

Jack spotted a gap between the last of the officer's tents and a column of empty wagons. The small space offered a sanctuary away from inquisitive eyes.

He was so intent on reaching his goal that he did not notice a burly redcoat come hurrying out of the officers' tent closest to the carts. The soldier barged into Jack and for the second time that night he was knocked to the ground.

"Jesus Christ! Sorry, I didn't see you there, mate." Tommy Smith reached out a hand to help him to his feet. As he did so, he realised that he had knocked over an officer. "Blow me! Sorry, sir. I didn't see you, I swear. Oh, sweet Jesus." A fusilier could find himself flogged for knocking an officer off their feet, even accidentally, something that Smith was well aware of.

"Oh, my God!" he exclaimed when he saw the officer's injuries. The man looked terrible, as if he had fought the Russian army on his own. Blood was encrusted around his nostrils and caked around his bruised and swollen lips, and the imprint of a hand was clearly visible on his right cheek. Smith kept a firm grip on the officer's arms, as it was obvious that he could not support his own weight.

It was only as the officer wearily lifted his bloodshot gaze that Smith recognised the battered features. His eyes widened in shock.

"I've got you, sir. I've got you. Let's sit you down, sir. Before you fall down." Grimacing with the effort of supporting Jack's sizeable frame, Smith gently lowered his officer back to the ground, sitting him down so that his back was leaning up against one of the wagons' wheels. "There you go, sir. Now, let's have a look at you."

Jack hovered on the brink of unconsciousness. Through the fog of pain, Jack recognised the square-jawed face of his orderly.

"Sorry, Tommy. I'm a bit of a mess." Jack's swollen and bloody mouth made his words barely intelligible.

"That you are, sir, that you are. Now, then." Smith's thick fingers gently prised the cleaning cloth and canteen of water from Jack's grip. "Let's clean you up so we can see the damage. You just sit tight."

Jack let his head fall back so that it was resting on a spoke of the cart's wheel and submitted to his orderly's administrations. For a farmhand Smith was surprisingly gentle, his deft movements efficiently removing the worst of the blood.

As Smith worked, Jack nurtured his hatred for Slater, using it as a balm for the wounds to his body. He had stolen Captain Sloames's identity and gambled that he could make a new future for himself. Now his past had caught up with him and that bastard of a sergeant held all the cards.

154

CHAPTER
TWENTY

"There you are, sir. Best I can do." Smith stood at last, his knees cracking as he did so. He looked at his captain where he lay slumped against the cart's wheels. Smith thought he had lapsed into unconsciousness but eventually one eye partially opened.

"Thank you." Jack could not raise the energy to speak above a whisper but Smith heard the softly spoken words.

"What happened, sir? It looks like you went ten rounds with a backstreet prizefighter."

"I fell." Jack's voice was still thick with phlegm mixed with blood, and he spat a fat globule on to the ground. "Tripped over one of the damn guide ropes."

Smith snorted at the obvious lie. "Nonsense, sir, if you'll forgive me for saying so. I know a slating when I see one and I can see some bugger has used you for a punchbag."

Jack looked at his orderly. Pain and tiredness threatened to overwhelm him and he craved respite from the fear of his impending doom. Peacock hated him and would surely make it his business to bring about his disgrace, McCulloch and Brewer likely felt the same. Then there was Slater, revelling in his discovery and certain to make the very most of his knowledge before leaving Jack to face the consequences of his imposture.

Jack felt very alone.

"Slater." The name was out before he had finished thinking, the first drop of water through the crack in the dam that was on the brink of collapse inside him

"What?" Smith barely heard the name. He sensed his officer was wound tight with tension. He did not try to speak again; instead he lowered himself to the damp ground so that he sat alongside Jack.

"Slater. Slater beat me. He knows who I am."

Smith opened his mouth to speak but he was too confused to form a coherent question. He remained silent and waited for his battered captain to explain himself.

Jack gingerly turned his head so he could look at the effect his words were having on his orderly. Smith's close presence was reassuring, reminding him of the times when he would sit among his mates after a hard day's drill.

"Slater knows who I really am. He knows I'm Mudlark. God, of all the damn men, why did he have to come here?" Jack was rambling, his aching brain making heavy weather of stringing sentences together.

"Excuse me for asking the bleeding obvious, sir, but who the hell is this Mudlark?"

"I am."

"You are not making any sense at all, Captain Sloames, sir."

156

"No, for the first time in a long time I am making perfect sense." Jack painfully lifted his arm and offered his hand to the bewildered fusilier. "Jack Lark. Pleased to make your acquaintance."

"Sir?" Smith frowned. "What are you talking about?"

"I'm an imposter. We are of the same kidney, you and I. Look behind the gold and the scarlet and I'm just the same as you."

Smith started to push himself to his feet, clearly uncomfortable to be having such a conversation with his captain.

"Stay where you are, Smith." Jack gave the order with the snap of an officer and it immediately stopped his orderly in his tracks. "You see? I'm bloody brilliant at playing the officer. Now, sit tight and listen so you'll be able to retell the story in full. You'll be quite famous, the orderly of the scandalous Jack Lark. You could well drink off the tale for the rest of your life."

Jack took a deep breath, causing his ribs to protest. "I was an orderly, just the same as you. In truth, you could say we have both been served the same officer. My officer was called Captain Arthur Sloames. He died, God rest his soul, leaving me alone in the arse end of nowhere. What I should have done was carry the damn corpse back to the army and let them pack me off to some place new. It would've been simpler but I couldn't bear the thought of joining a new regiment on my own, without my old mates."

Jack paused, tentatively inspecting the tattered ribbons of flesh on the inside of his lips with his tongue before continuing. "I could've deserted, I suppose.

Used the opportunity to take myself off and forget the whole damn army. But more fool me, I liked being a soldier. So there I was, presented with the chance to stop serving an officer and to actually *become* one. To be a captain, something someone like us could never even dream of becoming. I even thought I'd be better at it than half the fools God endowed with enough damn money to be able to buy their rank." Jack had to stop himself, the pain in his head was increasing as he became more agitated.

'So I stole a life," Jack eventually continued when the worst of the pounding in his skull faded away. "Jack Lark died and Arthur Sloames lived again. I became Captain Sloames and not one of the bloody useless clots we call officers ever questioned me. The fools never suspected a thing. It's no wonder this army is a shambles; the bloody idiots couldn't even spot a fraud as damn queer as me. Then Slater turned up." Jack paused to see how Smith was reacting, but the fusilier was just staring into the darkness. "Now he truly is a bastard. He knows me from my old battalion."

Jack's speech trailed off. The talk of his past had reawakened the pain of Molly's death. He wanted to thrust it away, to deny its presence and with it Molly's place in the story of his imposture. He let his head fall forward so his chin rested on his chest, his bitter grief threatening to overwhelm him.

The silence stretched out. Around them, the battalion was quietening down. Jack could make out the shadowy forms of the officers in the tent next to where he sat, their silhouettes picked out by a single candle. It was like watching a puppet show at the fair. Their braying laughter sounded loud in the dark and Jack was heartily relieved to be away from the bombastic company of the battalion's officers, even if it meant sitting on the damp soil, beaten, bruised and exposed to the elements.

Finally Smith spoke. "We're a pair of rummy coves, all right." He chuckled softly to himself.

Jack looked at him. "What's so funny?"

"You."

"Me?"

"You think you're some great villain, some scandalous cove who has committed a daring crime that will shock the whole army."

"Haven't I?"

"Come off it. Half this damned army is pretending to be someone they're not. Most of us would be in the clink or been packed off to the colonies if we'd not taken the Queen's shilling. You think you being an imposter makes you special. But like the rest of us you're just trying to stay one step ahead of the rich who piss on us without a second thought."

Smith's casual dismissal of his crime needled Jack. "So what's your story, Smith? What makes you such an authority on the lowlife in this army? You seem to know a lot about it for an honest country bumpkin."

"I'm a thief," Smith said quietly. The word hung between them, silencing them both for a while.

Jack swallowed. "What did you do?"

"Anything really. A bit of this, a bit of that. Hoisting stuff, bit of the pannie, passing queer screens, anything to earn some bloody money. Until I was nabbed, that is. Serve the Queen or go to bloody Botany Bay. That's the choice they gave me. So here I am. You're a charlatan and I'm a thief. Proud redcoats all."

Jack suddenly recalled where Tommy Smith had been when they had collided. "You're still at it! You're still a bloody thief! A regular Jack Shephard!"

"Of course I am, you fool! Why else do you think I wanted to be an orderly? Do you think I wanted to feed some toff his victuals or clean his shitty drawers?" Smith saw the growing look of horror on Jack's face. "Oh, don't worry. I didn't pinch anything of yours. Just don't you go raising a shine when Lieutenant Price croaks about losing his precious bloody pocket watch."

"You scoundrel!"

"Well, you were right. We're both of the same kidney."

"No we're not. You're a bloody thief!"

"Jesus Christ! What are you then? I just pinch stuff. You stole some poor sod's whole life!"

The sharp comment hit home. Jack had never considered himself a thief. In his own mind, his charade had been a way of doing his duty. Of serving his Queen and country by making the most of the abilities he knew he had. Smith saw it in more simple terms.

"So where are you from, Jack, if it ain't Hampshire or some other place where all the posh folk live?"

"London. Whitechapel."

"No wonder your loaf's all messed up. What about the poor bastard who died?"

"What about him?"

160

"What about his family?"

Jack's brow furrowed at the unexpected question. He had never given Sloames's family much thought. "He has a younger sister. I don't think they were close. He didn't mention her much."

"So she thinks he is still alive then? Maybe one day you can find her and tell her what happened."

Jack chuckled at the thought. Something he immediately regretted as the laughter magnified the pain in his skull. "I doubt she would be happy to see me."

"You'd be surprised. Women love returning heroes. Maybe you can even go and visit your ma one day."

"If she hasn't drunk herself to death yet."

"Like a tipple, does she?"

"You could say that. She runs a gin palace."

"You left a ginny to join the redcoats?"

"It's not as good as you think, believe me. I near broke my damn back in the bloody place. It was full of drunks and whores and piss."

"Sounds like my idea of heaven."

"Then you're a fool."

Smith snorted at the notion. "So where was your guv'nor while you were having such a horrible time of it getting pie-eyed with your dear old ma."

"He ran off with a whore when I was a nipper."

"So at least someone in the family had some sense then."

"Not really. He was found in a gutter a week later. The bitch had slit his gizzard and disappeared."

"Sounds like a nice place, your Whitechapel. Remind me to steer clear."

"It was not so bad. The one good thing I remember was the recruiting party that came by once a month. I used to watch them as they gulled the local lads into taking the shilling. I thought those soldiers were the finest men I had ever seen. They were so clean and smart and you should have heard the stories they told. I couldn't get enough of them. I wanted to take the shilling myself but my mother wouldn't hear of it. She needed me to help run the damn place. It took me years to pluck up enough courage to leave her."

"Well, more fool you, leaving a gin palace just so you could take a turn at being a bleeding Rupert." Tommy Smith shook his head.

"I think it's all over now anyway, or nearly. I advised Major Peacock to take his head out of his arse." Jack winced at the memory.

"You did? Blimey." Smith sounded impressed. "Well, you'll have to sort that one yourself. But dealing with Slater, that's easy."

"Easy? Have you seen the size of the bastard? He beat me tonight without breaking a sweat."

"I'm not suggesting you fight him. Not if you can help it, anyway. But fixing Slater couldn't be simpler. I'm astonished you haven't thought of it for yourself."

"Well, why don't you enlighten me seeing as I'm too stupid to see it for myself?"

"You let the army fix him."

"And why would I do that?" Jack shook his head at the notion, grimacing with the pain the sudden

162

movement caused. "He knows who I am. He'll peach on me and then it's all over. I'll be drumming my heels on the scaffold within a week."

"Who are they going to believe, Jack? A sergeant who has just arrived or one of their captains?"

Jack was silent. It was so obvious. Hadn't Slater been the one who had once mocked him for being powerless against the will of a sergeant? No one would disbelieve the word of an officer.

"You would have to get in there first. Have him up on a charge for being drunk, or for pissing on your boots, or something. Take away his stripes for starters and if that doesn't quieten him down then get him flogged. You're the officer. He can't stand against you."

"He'd go insane. He'd kill me." Jack did his best to imagine Slater without his stripes. He couldn't do it.

"Well, it sounds like he might do that anyway. Once you have him up on a charge, the army will do the rest. And no one will believe him if he starts ranting on about your past. If anything, that would just give more credence to your punishing him in the first place. And anyway, what have you got to lose? It can't exactly make things any worse, now can it?"

Jack stayed silent as he considered the idea. The pain of Slater's beating was fading as he contemplated a new future.

The power of an officer over a redcoat, even a sergeant, was absolute. It would take one word, one accusation, and Slater would be at his mercy.

CHAPTER
TWENTY-ONE

"I would like to apologise for my behaviour, sir."

The colonel's tent was stuffy, despite the fact that the canvas flaps of the entrance were tied back as far as they would go. The smell of the colonel's lunch still lingered, and a half-empty glass of claret added its heady aroma. Jack did his best to hide his distaste, the sour air in the tent made all the worse by the bitter taste of the thick wedge of humble pie he had had to swallow. He was standing at attention in front of the colonel, his shako under his left arm.

The colonel turned to the side to look at his second-in-command.

"Mr Peacock, do you accept Captain Sloames's apology?"

Peacock sniffed in disapproval. If he had had his way Captain Sloames would already be on board a steamer heading back to England in disgrace. He had argued for that very punishment as vociferously as he dared but Colonel Morris would have none of it.

Peacock nodded his assent with ill grace. "I do, sir. *Absit invidia.*"

Morris looked hard at both officers. Seated behind a makeshift desk that his orderly had fashioned from empty ammunition crates, he looked more like a stern schoolmaster than a colonel in Her Majesty's army.

"Capital. I expect to hear no more of this episode. From either of you."

Peacock did not take the caution well and opened his mouth to protest. Morris raised a hand to quell his words. "I will hear no more. The battalion will soon face the Russians and I will not allow my officers to be distracted from their responsibilities by petty squabbles. Captain Sloames has apologised and his apology has been accepted. That concludes this matter. Am I clear on that, gentlemen?"

"Yes, sir." Jack was quick to reply.

"Good. Major Peacock, I am sure you are anxious to be about your duties. Captain Sloames, if I could detain you for a moment longer I would be obliged."

"Of course, sir," Peacock replied punctiliously and swept out of the tent.

Despite the politely worded request, Peacock felt sure Morris had asked Sloames to remain on his own so that he could administer the dressing-down the odious captain so obviously required. Peacock had enjoyed seeing Sloames standing in front of the desk like an errant schoolboy and with a face that looked as if he had received the type of beating reserved for newly arrived fags at Peacock's former school. The man was obviously a bounder and a severe reprimand was exactly what was needed to bring him down a peg or three. Peacock hoped the colonel spared no punches. It was just a pity he could not stay to witness the spectacle in person.

Inside the tent, Colonel Morris addressed the captain of his Light Company.

"Captain Sloames. I should not have to remind you that the successful operation of my battalion requires all of its officers to work together and to treat each other with the utmost respect." Morris steepled his fingers and tapped the tips against his bearded chin.

"No, sir."

"Nor should I have to remind you that altercations between my officers are unacceptable under any circumstances."

"No, sir."

"Any act that is prejudicial to the smooth operation of this battalion is an offence I take personally. I will not tolerate another foul outburst such as the one Major Peacock reported to me. Do I make myself perfectly clear?"

Jack stared into the space six inches above the colonel's tightly cropped, iron-grey head of hair, grateful that his years in the army had taught him how to deal with discontented officers.

"Yes, sir."

"Yes, sir. No, sir. Three bloody bags full, sir. You are barely listening to a word I say, are you, you damn scoundrel?"

The outburst took Jack by surprise. He dropped his scrutiny of the tent wall and looked at the colonel.

"That's better." Morris smiled at Jack with surprising warmth. "Oh, I recognise the tactic. I wasn't born yesterday. I appreciate it is the best way to deal with a superior officer. I still use it myself on occasion."

166

Jack watched the colonel warily, keeping his guard up and his face neutral.

"It is a shame that we did not get to know one another before this campaign began." The colonel paused to see if Jack would speak but it was obvious that he was still wary of his commanding officer. As well he should be. "Peacock is a stuffed shirt. I do appreciate that."

The sudden admission startled Jack into a response. "Sir?"

"I know how Peacock is regarded in the battalion. I appreciate how difficult he can be. However, that does not excuse one of my captains insulting him."

Jack bowed his head. "I know, sir. I was wrong."

"Goodness me. You disappoint me. You are a damn sight meeker than I had been led to believe."

The barbed comment stung. "I'm not sure what you mean, sir."

"I mean, Captain Sloames, that I have heard many things about you, but none of them included tales of your meekness."

Jack did not respond.

"I have heard," Morris continued, "that you are a capable and efficient officer who is turning the Light Company into an excellent unit. Yet I also hear that you are taciturn, some would say withdrawn, and a loner. From Major Peacock I hear you are a vile, foul-mouthed brute who deserves to be shipped home in disgrace. In short, the Light Company appears to be led by a man I know very little about and who now presents himself in front of me looking like a backstreet brawler."

Again, Jack chose not to comment. A gentle sigh of disapproval was the only evidence that his silence was not to the colonel's liking.

"I shall speak plainly. My battalion is shortly to be involved in a battle that will test us all but I am confident of my men. We will not let the regiment down, I am certain of that. Yet I find myself faced with a dilemma." Morris paused and fixed Jack with a firm gaze from under his furrowed brow. "You, sir, are the cause of this dilemma. There is something about you, Sloames. I am a good judge of character and my instinct tells me that you are not quite what you seem."

Jack was feeling uncomfortable under the colonel's intense scrutiny and it was an effort to stand still and let no sign of his anxiety show.

"So I have to ask myself if I trust you and to be honest I have no clear answer to that question. I do not expect my captains to be milksops. I need men of strong character and iron self-discipline to lead my companies. You, Mr Sloames, showed singular lack of self-control in your dealings with Major Peacock. That concerns me a great deal."

Morris paused and looked down at his fingers. "However, on this occasion, I shall give you the benefit of the doubt. I will be expecting great things of you and your men. Do not let me down."

Relief coursed through Jack. "I won't, sir. I give you my word." His voice cracked with emotion as he spoke.

Morris nodded and rose to his feet, extending his hand. "I will be watching you," he said as he took Jack's hand in his firm grip. "God help you if you fail. Because I shall not, I promise you that."

Jack walked out of the stuffy confines of the colonel's tent and into the bright morning sunshine. The lecture had shamed him but the colonel's firm support had left him determined not to let the battalion down.

"Captain Sloames!"

The portly figure of Lieutenant Digby-Brown lurched upright from where he had been perching on a water butt a short distance from the tent.

"Digby-Brown. What a delightful surprise."

"Sorry to you bother you, sir," Digby-Brown replied, and then stopped as he saw the state of his captain's face. "You look like you've been in the wars, sir." Digby-Brown tried not to smile.

"What do you want, Digby-Brown?" Jack's positive mood faded in the face of his subaltern's grating presence.

"We have a problem, Sir. Fusilier Hayward has reported sick."

"Why is that a problem? Half this bloody army is sick."

"Yes, sir. However, half this army has not been beaten to a pulp. Hayward has and the fool is refusing to tell us who did it."

Jack felt a sinking feeling deep in his gut. Slater was more than capable of beating one of his own men. It was typical of his brutal tactics. Beat one man in the company as a warning to the rest. The sergeant was moving fast; soon he would have the whole company eating out of his hand. He had to be stopped and stopped quickly.

"You'd better take me to him."

Fusilier Hayward was a mess. Digby-Brown had at least had the sense to leave the battered young fusilier with the company, away from the gaze of rest of the battalion. Jack could not help wincing as he took in Hayward's injuries. He looked even worse than he himself had done after his own bruising encounter with Slater's fists. Both of Hayward's eyes were closed behind thick purple swellings. Welts and gouges covered his face, and his mouth had been reduced to a pulp. He was barely recognisable. The rest of the fusilier was surprisingly intact, Slater presumably concentrating on the face to give the most vivid demonstration of his viciousness to the rest of the Light Company. It would take a brave man to risk receiving such a battering.

"Have him taken back to the beach, by two of our own men," Jack ordered Digby-Brown. "I don't want some callous bandsmen making the trip a torment for him. He's suffered enough."

"Yes, sir. I'll take him myself." Digby-Brown noticed the concern on his captain's face at seeing Hayward's injuries. It was obvious Sloames cared rather more about his men than Digby-Brown had given him credit for. "How do you think this happened?"

"How do you think? Some vicious bastard gave him one hell of a beating."

"One of our men?"

170

"Most likely."

"But why? I mean, we are all in the same company. I cannot believe one of our men is guilty of such brutality."

"Don't be so damn naïve," Jack snapped. "Half of the men come from the poorest backstreets of London. Violence is the common currency of their sorry lives." Jack did not try to hide his contempt for Digby-Brown. The lieutenant had no concept of the lives formerly led by the men he commanded. Digby-Brown was not to blame for the station into which he had been born. But Jack did blame him for having neither the wit nor the intelligence to learn about the men he was responsible for. To Jack that was unforgivable and all too typical of the supercilious officer class.

"Get Hayward to the medical staff on the beach." Jack finished curtly, dismissing his troubled lieutenant.

His thoughts turned to the perpetrator of the cruel beating. It was time to make Slater pay for his crimes.

CHAPTER
TWENTY-TWO

"Drunk!"

"Not only drunk, Flowers, but drunk on duty. I also have grounds to believe he was responsible for an assault on another of my men."

"I can scarcely credit it." The adjutant was appalled. "Why, he has only just joined the regiment."

Jack shook his head, as if he too could not believe what he was reporting. "I fear we now know why he was thrown out of his former battalion. He was a colour sergeant there, I hear, but he lost his colours for victimising the men under his command. It would also appear he has a habit of making up fanciful tales to suit his spite. It's a bad show all round."

"He'll have to lose his stripes, of course."

"Of course." Jack tried to look suitably sombre.

"I'll arrange for him to transfer to another company. The timing is not ideal but it would be for the best." Lieutenant Flowers shook his head. "What possessed him? Drink really is the devil. Perhaps the temperance movement has it right."

Jack thought of the toothless drunks who begged or stole all day simply to be able to buy the watered-down gin his mother sold. There could not be a better example of the evil of drink but it had never made him hesitate when the ale was being poured. "Can you really imagine living without a drink, Flowers? No claret? No porter? No whisky to dull the pain of an evening listening to Major Peacock?"

"You do have a point." Flowers sighed. "Captain Devine can take him. His company is at the lowest strength. Let him make a fresh start in another company."

"I'd rather keep him. Give him another chance to prove himself." Jack wanted Slater close. There was no telling how he would react to losing his stripes and Jack was determined not to give the brutal man any opportunity to spread his poison around another officer's company.

"That's very generous of you, but do you think it's wise? The man is obviously a malcontent."

"I'd rather not. He's my problem. I don't like to hoist him on someone else."

"Well, it's your decision, and one that does you great credit. I'll arrange for the colonel to deal with it this afternoon. He won't be best pleased. He has other things on his mind."

"Such as?" Jack sensed news.

The adjutant looked around to check that no one could overhear them and dropped his voice. "Look, I shouldn't be telling you this. The colonel wants to make a big announcement after church parade this afternoon and he'll have a fit if he finds out I have stolen his thunder. Orders have come through from brigade. Raglan has agreed to march. I've no idea why he thinks we are ready to move but there you have it. I'm told the French have been making one hell of a fuss as we sit here dilly-dallying. So, ready or not, we're to be off."

It was the news the army had long waited to hear. The campaign was about to begin in earnest.

There was barely a cloud to trouble the grey-blue expanse of sky that, to Jack, seemed to have taken on a vastness he had never seen. It stretched from one distant horizon to the other, one great canopy of such immensity that it left him feeling very small. The sun did nothing to lift the spirits of the men who knew they must shortly suffer a long, exhausting march under its unseasonal heat. It brought back memories of the dire period they had endured in the feverish heat at the camp in Varna prior to their departure for the Crimea.

Jack found Tommy Smith working with McCulloch's orderly, Johnson, using a shot case and a roundshot to grind up more of the green coffee beans that the battalion's officers consumed at a terrific rate.

"Good morning. Nice to see you both working on such an important task." Jack forced himself to sound jovial in front of McCulloch's orderly.

"Mornin', sir. Lovely day."

Johnson's familiar London accent made Jack smile. "It is indeed, Johnson," he agreed, "but I'm afraid I need to borrow Smith."

"Course, sir. No bother. He's no bleeding use anyhow. You're welcome to him."

"Thank you, Johnson. Smith, come with me please."

174

Jack led Smith away from the keen ears of his fellow orderly. The officers' servants thrived on gossip, as he himself knew only too well.

As soon as they were far enough away, Jack confided the adjutant's information to his orderly who took in the news calmly and immediately understood the need for caution. Any advantage to the Light Company would disappear if the news spread and they had to compete with nearly six hundred men all trying to grab a share of the meagre supplies available.

"What would you like me to do first, sir?" Smith asked, keeping his voice low and slowly scanning the surrounding area for anyone who could overhear them.

"Well, for starters you can stop looking so damn furtive."

"Sorry. Bit out of practice."

Jack chuckled. "I'm glad to hear that. I can't keep checking to see if you've filched my pocket book every time I stand near you."

"Now, sir, as if I would turn your pockets. Besides, I was never a pickpocket. I had more class."

"Truly? You never cease to amaze me." Jack shook his head. "I have some good news about Slater. I spoke to the adjutant and it's done. He'll face a battalion court martial this afternoon. I'll be there and it's just a formality. He'll be reduced to the ranks."

Smith smiled at the news "It's no less than he deserves after what he did to young Hayward, not to mention yourself. So what do we do about Slater now? He'll be after you."

"For now there is nothing more we can do. But watch my back." Jack looked at Smith keenly, seeking reassurance.

"Just let me get a clear shot of the bastard, sir. I'll sort him out."

"After me, Tommy. After me." Jack put the happy notion to one side. "Now, as soon as the colonel announces that we are finally to march inland, all hell will break loose. The most important thing is water. I know it's already hard to get enough but we need to make certain the men's canteens are full and that we get as much extra as we can carry."

"Right you are." Smith nodded.

"Next, ammunition."

"No, that's done," Smith said. "Digby-Brown carried out an ammunition check after roll call this morning. We all have our full tally. Not even Welsh Davies can have flogged any to the tinkers yet."

"Very good." Jack was surprised. Perhaps Digby-Brown was finally starting to contribute to the effective running of the company. "So that leaves the rations. We'll have to wait for whatever the rest of the battalion gets issued but looking around the place," Jack gestured towards the many heaps of supplies that lay dumped around the battalion lines, "there is no way in hell we can take everything with us. Forage around a bit and see what you can square away. And see if you can sniff me out some tea. I'm getting heartily sick of all that bloody green coffee."

"I'm sure I can manage that. I'll say you're planning to take us off for another drill first thing in the morning so we need to get ready today. No one will question that. Moan like buggery and call you every name under the sun, but question it, no."

"I think I'll ignore that last remark, Fusilier."

"As you choose." Smith hesitated. "The men think you're doing well, sir. They seem to like you."

"What?" Now Jack was truly surprised. He had not forgotten the near disaster of facing the Cossacks and he did not think the men had either.

"Oh, they think you're a rum cove, all right, and they'd as soon see you piss off and leave them alone. But they're coming round to you. Especially since they heard about you taking a pop at Peacock."

Jack looked his orderly in the eye, suspecting some flummery or banter in the words. But Smith met his gaze, his expression serious.

"Well, I'm damn pleased to hear it. It's about time I got some bloody recognition."

"But of course they don't know you're a fraud, so don't let your head swell too much, will you, or it's likely to get shot right off."

Jack grinned. "Not much chance of that with you to remind me, Smith."

CHAPTER
TWENTY-THREE

Reveille sounded in the darkness. The bugle call was picked up and repeated throughout the three armies, strident and remorseless, demanding immediate action.

The British army scrambled to its feet, resembling an anthill that had been poked violently with a stick. They were still woefully unprepared for the long-awaited march. Despairing officers tried to organise their commands and bring order from the confusion, a hopeless endeavour made worse by the ill-informed staff officers to whom they turned for orders.

To the bewilderment and consternation of their French allies, the British were not ready to march at four o'clock as had been agreed the previous evening, nor were they ready at five o'clock. As the early-morning light pushed away the darkness the chaos in their lines was all too apparent.

The failure of the British commissariat was complete. Seven hundred wagons had been expected but barely one-third of that number had arrived. Mountains of supplies would have to be abandoned where they lay. The more enterprising soldiers were taking advantage of the disorder by pilfering the stores, filling their pockets and their greatcoats with extra rations, adding more confusion and delay.

Dealing with the mountains of stores was not the only task left outstanding. There were dozens of sick to be stretchered back to the beach and handed into the dubious care of the army's medical staff. Water still had to be found for the soldiers' canteens, no easy task given that the few wells that had been dug now produced only a little brackish water. Rations waited to be distributed, the meat to be carried raw, no time left for the soldiers to cook the salted pork that was all the army provided. The British army was in total disarray.

The French looked on appalled. Their bandsmen bugled and drummed impatiently, as if the martial music could inspire, cajole or shame their maddeningly disorganised allies to order. The French troops had been ready to march since before dawn. They sat despondently on the ground, wondering at the sanity of their masters who had tied their fate to the bungling British.

The coolness of the early morning gradually melted way, the heat building steadily as the sun rose. Miraculously, at nine o'clock in the morning, the British army was finally ready to march. The redcoats had muddled their way to readiness, the enterprise and industry of the battalion officers succeeding where the professionals in the commissariat had failed so completely.

In all their martial splendour, the armies of three countries would march directly for the Russian port of Sevastopol, the key objective of the campaign. Sunlight glinted off metal, battalion colours were unfurled, uniforms of every colour were massed in ranks of infantrymen, guardsmen, fusiliers, grenadiers, gunners, hussars, dragoons and lancers. It was a sight to stir the heart of even the most reluctant soldier.

The French would march on the right flank, with the sea and the might of the two navies on their right. With the French marched Suleiman Pasha and his six thousand Turkish soldiers. The British would march on the left. To smooth the ruffled feathers of the French generals, Raglan, ever the politician, had acceded to their demands to dictate the order of the march. Perhaps the politics of the joint command had distracted the British commander. Or perhaps Raglan saw no danger in the station the British had agreed to occupy in the combined column. Whatever the reason, the British marched with their left flank dangerously exposed. In the days of Wellington, cavalry outriders would have been despatched to patrol and protect the exposed flank. Intrepid young officers on fast, corn-fed horses would ride into the wide plains, probing for danger, so that no enemy formation could approach the open flank undetected. But Wellington was dead and the British army marched in one compact mass, its flank exposed save for a thin screen of light cavalry.

But this was not the morning for doubts. Led by their colours the British soldiers left their fears, their misgivings and their complaints behind them, the brave and stirring tunes from their regimental bands propelling them forward.

The cavalry led the way, the dandies and the aristocrats at the fore, their horses prancing in the excitement. Lord Cardigan, with the 13th Light Dragoons and the 11th Hussars, formed the vanguard of the army. His bitterest enemy, Lord Lucan, who also happened to be his brother-in-law and his commanding officer, led the 8th Hussars and the 17th Lancers on the left flank.

Behind them marched the Rifle Brigade, the feared Greenjackets who had once so tormented Napoleon's veterans on the battlefields of Portugal, Spain and France. Then, the Greenjackets had been the acclaimed masters of the skirmish line. Now, their descendants were desperate to prove their superiority once again, even in the modern world where every soldier bore the once coveted power of the rifle.

Behind them came the infantry, the men Wellington so harshly titled the scum of the earth. They were the least regarded yet the most important of all the troops that marched that day, for it was the humble redcoat who would decide the fate of the battle to come. Victories were not won by the glamorous cavalry, or by the hard-bitten professionalism of the rifles. Even the deadly killing machines of the artillery would not decide who was victorious. Battles were won by the tenacity, the bravery and the sheer bloody-mindedness of the massed ranks of the infantry. Whether they were guardsman, fusiliers, grenadiers, or just plain redcoated infantrymen, all battles came down to their ability to deliver the power of their massed volleys, their willingness to endure the carnage inflicted upon them and the raw courage that would see them close to butcher the enemy with their bayonets.

The King's Royal Fusiliers marched at the head of the Light Division. The fusiliers had suffered their fair share of disorder that morning. Many of the men marched with half-full canteens of water or with barely enough rations to last them the day. Yet they marched with pride. It was a day to savour being a fusilier in the service of the Queen.

Jack marched proudly at the head of his company. It was hard for him not to look smug so he did not even try, instead merely nodding his head in acknowledgement of the scowls of his brother officers whose men marched inadequately prepared. The Light Company marched with full canteens of water, and the sergeants and corporals carried numerous spares. Their ration bags were full and Tommy Smith even marched with one of his spare stockings crammed full of tea liberated from one of the many abandoned supply chests. One company, at least, would not be going short.

The fusiliers' band struck up the opening bars of "Cheer, Boys, Cheer!" It was a firm favourite in the battalion and Jack grinned as he heard the men begin to sing in their deep and surprisingly melodic voices.

The company had come a long way in the few days since they had landed. The men now marched with a cocky air about them, a sureness that had been missing earlier. Watching them, Jack could almost believe they took a certain pride in being one of the first troops to have engaged the enemy. Only the looming presence of Slater cast a shadow over his own confidence.

He turned and saw the enormous redcoat marching easily in his allotted station, his long, loping stride and confident demeanour a reminder of the man's power. If the whole company had, at first, been wary of the new arrival, now they were openly fearful of him. The loss of his sergeant's stripes had added a chilling bitterness to the man and not even the boldest redcoat wanted to spend a moment in his company.

The first Light Company fusilier collapsed shortly before the march was one hour old. Fusilier Macclesbridge had been convinced he had been dying for days. His messmates, long used to his complaints, ignored his whines and daily litany of distress. If Macclesbridge was not complaining of dying of thirst then he was starving to death. He did not get a fever without being certain he had got the plague. That morning he had woken convinced that he had the cholera and his comrades had laughed at his malingering ways. Yet this time he was right. One moment he was cursing as the men marching around him belted out the chorus to "The Girl I left Behind", the next his face darkened and he stumbled forward, crashing into the back of the man in front and falling to the ground choking on a torrent of vomit that erupted from his throat.

Macclesbridge was the first to fall but he was not the last.

The heat of the sun cooked the fusiliers in their thick woollen coats, stewing them in a soup of sweat that chafed their skin. Another two men from the company collapsed before midday, unable to find the strength to march under the maddening heat. After the first few hard miles, barely one fusilier had more than a few mouthfuls of warm brackish water left in his canteen. The march had barely begun but already the men trudged in misery.

They soon marched in silence, the joy of the early morning forgotten. The bandsmen had been forced to stow their musical instruments and carry out their secondary role as stretcher-bearers, hauling the sick out of the line of march lest they be trampled into the dust by the never-ending procession that ground its way forward. All too soon, the bandsmen were overwhelmed by the sheer number of men falling to the ground and by the dozens of redcoats who were too weak to rise to their feet after the halts that were now being called every half hour.

The pace of the march slowed to barely a crawl. The ground behind and to either side of the army became littered with abandoned equipment and with the crumpled forms of those unable to carry on. Men sank to their knees in delirium, their anguished cries for water breaking the hearts of their mates who could do nothing but march on and leave them to the less than tender mercies of the overworked bandsmen.

After another hour picking their way through the detritus that littered the path ahead of them, the fusiliers could march no more. The men fell out, before the order was given, many sinking to the ground where they stood.

The army was disintegrating. The heat and the cholera threatened to end the campaign after barely ten miles.

Jack observed the pale faces of his men as they sank to the ground. He saw their drawn, haggard expressions, their mouths tinged blue from dehydration. Worst of all was the listlessness and the exhaustion in their eyes. It would be a relief to sink to the ground with them, to give in to the pain that wracked his body. A terrible thirst tormented his every thought. Anything was preferable to the torture of carrying on in this living hell. But Jack refused to give in. Everything he had gone through since the army had landed a few short days ago would be for naught if he gave in to the demands of his battered body.

A mocking laugh caught his attention. Jack turned his head to see which of his men had the energy to find something in this terrible situation to laugh about. Sitting to one side of the company, Slater took a long drink from a full canteen, carelessly letting drops of the precious water spill from his mouth. Against his will, Jack licked his cracked and swollen lips, helpless in the face of his desire to drink. He could smell the water, the mere thought of drinking made his body tremble with desire.

Slater watched the company's reaction as he drank. He lowered the canteen slowly, his lips wet from the long draught. He leisurely wiped the back of his hand across his mouth and belched. The men turned away.

Jack watched the performance, his hands clenching into fists at his impotence to deal with the bastard's mockery. Slater would pay for this particular pantomime, as he would pay for all his violent thuggery.

But revenge would have to wait. With the column of infantry stalled, staff officers galloped backwards and forwards to rouse the men, the flanks of their tired mounts lathered in sweat.

"To your feet!" Colonel Morris shouted. On horseback, the colonel looked imposing. His charger was huge, jet-black save for a white blaze on its forehead and of such an evil temper that only the colonel could ride him. Now the fine horse was streaked with sweat, its eyes rolling in their sockets as Morris paraded him past the slumped ranks of his battalion.

"On your feet, my boys! On your feet my brave, brave boys!"

Jack expected the colonel's call to go unheeded but, to his surprise, the men dug deep into their reserves of strength and struggled to their feet once more, responding to their beloved colonel. Like an army of the dead, the fusiliers rose from the ground and stumbled back into formation.

"That's it, my boys!" Morris applauded the effort, encouraging his men as best he could. "I am proud of you. Proud of all of you," he shouted, moving up and down the flank of the column that was slowly taking shape. "That's the way. It will be time to rest soon enough. But not now. One more effort. One more march."

A handful of staff officers came galloping back down the length of the infantry column, their urgency attracting the attention of those fusiliers with enough strength to still be interested in their surroundings.

One, a cornet from the 7th Hussars, reined in hard alongside Colonel Morris. The hussar officer's bay horse skittered nervously, moving in a tight half-circle, as the cornet leant forward in his saddle to hand a piece of paper to Morris.

The colonel scanned the paper quickly, his brow furrowing. His eyes darted across the few short lines before he looked up, his leathery face creasing into a smile.

"This is it, boys!" he shouted, standing in his stirrups to call down the length of the battalion. "The Russians are ahead!"

The Russian bear had stirred. The road to Sevastopol was blocked.

CHAPTER
TWENTY-FOUR

"Water!"

No other single word could have created more disruption to the order and discipline of a British army battalion. The fusilier had spied the small stream twisting its way along the shallow valley ahead and joyfully announced its presence to the rest of the regiment. The fusiliers had trudged over the low rise footsore, dehydrated and close to collapse. Yet the single word transformed them. Without a word of command the column stopped, the men quivering with eagerness, like hounds smelling the fox for the first time.

Colonel Morris beamed with pride as the men held their ranks despite their desperate desire to drink. Every head turned to stare at the colonel, the same look of longing on all their faces.

Morris could not deny them. "Go, my boys! You have earned it."

Released, the redcoats streamed forward, the men pulling and elbowing each other in their desperate haste to reach the small stream. Men who minutes earlier had felt ready to lie down and die found the strength to race forward down the shallow slope towards the Bulganak

River. They threw themselves into the shallow stream, thrusting their heads into the ice-cold water or cupping their hands and gulping it down their parched throats as fast as they could. And the officers joined them. Colonel Morris alone held back, walking his horse behind the rearmost and slowest moving fusiliers. Only when the drenched fusiliers returned to the north bank of the river, their heavy uniforms soaking but their thirst satiated and their canteens full, did he allow his horse to bow its head so it, too, could drink.

"Would you be so kind, Sloames?"

Jack stood in the centre of the stream, the slow-moving water rippling around his boots. His stomach ached with the cold water he had gulped down. He looked up to see Morris holding out his canteen.

Without a word, Jack reached out, took the canteen and squatted down, removing the stopper as he did so. It was only when he handed the full container back did he see the strain on Morris's face.

"Obliged to you." Morris tipped back his head and took a long draught from the canteen, closing his eyes at the exquisite pleasure of the fresh water cascading down his throat. It took several seconds before he lowered the canteen, leaving a few errant drops of water captured in the wiry grey hairs of his beard.

Morris replaced the stopper. "Mr Sloames, form your company, if you please. We have work to do."

A troop of the 13th Light Dragoons splashed noisily through the river. The horses' hooves flung the water high into the air so that the bright sunlight flashed off thousands of droplets. More dragoons were riding down the shallow slope towards the river. The cavalrymen looked down in disdain at the soaked fusiliers as they rode past, their sneers and shouted insults leaving the redcoats wondering who the true enemy was. Jack looked to the south, the direction the cavalry was taking. There, half a mile distant, Russian cossacks lined the brow of the hill.

A chill ran down Jack's spine. Muttering imprecations, he went to form up his company.

"Jesus Christ! If they could bleeding shoot straight they'd be fucking dangerous."

"Silence in the ranks!" Sergeant Baker snarled from his place behind the company, his eyes scanning the men as he tried to identify the culprit. The redcoats stood stoically in their ranks, as the sun beat down. The sweat poured freely down their bodies and faces but at least they had a grandstand view of the afternoon's entertainment.

The battalion was deployed in a line two ranks deep, spread like a long red chain on the brow of the shallow slope to the south of the Bulganak River. It had not taken the 13th Light Dragoons long to drive off the few cossacks who had been observing the movements of the army and the fusiliers had been ordered forward to take up position on the crest of the slope the cossacks had vacated. To their front, Lord Cardigan had led the light cavalry forward in skirmish order and for the last twenty minutes they had been engaged in a vigorous but so far ineffectual exchange of gunfire with a large body of Russian cavalry. Neither side appeared capable of hitting their targets. From their vantage point on the low crest, the fusiliers watched in disappointment as the brisk exchange of fire failed to inflict a single casualty on either side.

"It reminds me very much of a review day at Chobham." Captain McCulloch had wandered over to join the Light Company, making his observation as he approached where Jack stood observing the afternoon's display. McCulloch's 2nd Company was formed on the Light Company's right flank. The Light Company itself was the furthest left of the whole battalion, with Captain Brewer and his grenadiers at the opposite end on the battalion's right flank.

This was the first time the two officers had spoken since the night of Jack's abuse of Major Peacock.

"I wouldn't know as I never had the pleasure, although I hear review days are about as interesting as listening to Brewer fart. At least our damn cavalry are not spoiling the spectacle by actually hitting something."

McCulloch winced at the colourful language. "So you have not yet learnt to moderate your language, Sloames."

"No, I'm afraid I haven't, nor do I think I ever shall." He turned to face McCulloch. "But I have learnt to appreciate when I'm being a complete fool. I can only apologise for my appalling behaviour. It was unacceptable and I truly regret that it ever happened."

McCulloch met Jack's intense gaze. A moment's scrutiny was all it took for him to believe Jack was telling the truth. "Let us hear no more about it then.

191

Let bygones be bygones and all that." McCulloch lifted his shako by its peak and wiped his hand across his sweat-streaked forehead. He slicked his damp hair down with a grimace of distaste.

"Thank you." Jack offered McCulloch his hand.

"There's no need for that, old fellow," said McCulloch, shaking Jack's hand anyhow. "We all have our off days."

Jack and McCulloch stood in companionable silence watching the British cavalry engage their Russian counterparts in a wasteful and ineffective duel of musketry. The sight of a single Russian trooper silently crumpling over and falling to the ground raised such a cheer from the watching British troops that the cavalrymen of both sides turned to look at the source of the huge hurrah.

The sporadic gunfire soon resumed and proved as wasteful as before. The mute participation of the British infantryman became languid and sleepy.

General Raglan steadfastly refused to allow the infantry to join the attack. He was anxious to avoid a general action until his army was consolidated and so he held his men back, refusing to be drawn into a precipitate advance. There was nothing for the infantry to do other than to roast in the sun and endure the heat, the flies, the boredom and the thirst. The foolishness of the inactivity was not lost on the battalion's officers as a steady trickle of men collapsed from heatstroke, victims to their general's feckless caution.

"Aha! This looks more like it. Action at last," McCulloch said happily, announcing a change in the tiresome skirmish.

Jack had been engaged in a battle of his own as he fought to keep his heavy eyelids from closing. The effects of the long march and the cavalry's ineptitude had combined to leave him struggling to stay awake. It was with some difficulty that he lifted his gritty and sore eyes to see what had caught McCulloch's attention.

A squadron of Russian cavalry spurred towards the British dragoons' left flank, the first purposeful movement either side had managed for the last half hour.

With a precision that put the languid movements of the British cavalrymen to shame, the Russian cavalry opened in the centre, the separate halves of the squadron peeling back left and right, revealing the battery of guns they had so skilfully been screening.

"Oh, well done. Well done indeed!" McCulloch could not resist praising the beautifully executed manoeuvre.

The Russian artillery opened fire as the last of their cavalry spurred their way clear, the puffs of smoke from the mouths of their cannon clearly visible moments before the noise of the cannonade could be heard.

"There! We are privileged indeed, Sloames. We have witnessed the first cannon of the campaign being fired." McCulloch pulled hard on the hem of his jacket and picked a small bit of lint from his lapel as he spoke, as if to be present at such a historic moment made him uncomfortable.

"Let us hope our cavalry is pleased. I'm not sure I'd be so keen to see the first cannon shot of the campaign if I was on the receiving end of it as they are."

McCulloch chose to ignore Jack's somewhat caustic observation. "I had better get back to my company. I'm glad we had the opportunity to talk."

"Enjoy the day, Mr McCulloch, and don't forget, *aut vincere aut mori*." Jack mangled the Latin phrase he had heard for the first time on the night of his confrontation with Major Peacock.

His sarcasm brought a wry smile of acknowledgement from McCulloch. "Mr Sloames, you are incorrigible. God willing I shall see you later and we can work on your pronunciation. You sounded like a constipated clergyman." McCulloch nodded his farewell and left Jack to enjoy the display the cavalrymen were putting on.

A battery of British horse artillery careered to a noisy halt a short distance to the left of Jack's company, stung into action by the skill of the Russian horse artillery.

The suddenness of their arrival stirred many of the Light Company from their sun-induced stupor. The gunners prepared their weapons to fire to the clipped orders of their sergeants. The sight was of much greater interest than the shambolic performance of the skirmishing cavalry.

The Russian artillery fired a second volley before the British gunners were ready to reply. From their elevated viewpoint, the Light Company could trace the pencil-thin track the roundshot left as they flew through the air towards the dispersed ranks of the cavalry. In the widely spaced skirmish order, the dragoons and hussars offered a poor target for the Russian gunners and the heavy barrage struck down only a single dragoon.

An ear-ringing explosion of noise and smoke to the Light Company's left announced that the British battery was returning fire. Far to the battalion's right a second British battery opened up, the deep cough of these guns identifying them as bigger bored nine-pounders.

Despite the cloud of foul-smelling powder smoke that partially blocked the fusiliers' view, it was clear the British were directing their fire with greater effect than their Russian counterparts. Several Russian cavalrymen and horses were struck by the first British volley. The Russian gunners bravely fired again, resolutely sticking to their task despite the storm of roundshot that crashed about their ears. It was a courageous display but one that only served to goad the British gunners to greater energy. With another explosion of noise and smoke, the British guns fired again.

When the smoke cleared, the fusiliers could see that the Russian gunners had seen sense. With a haste born of fear, they hurried to limber their guns before the British fired on them once more.

The British gunners would not let the Russian gunners skulk away unmolested. The artillerymen were serving their guns with intensity and rivers of sweat streamed down their powder-stained faces as they raced to reload. Within moments, another British volley crashed out, and then another, maiming and killing indiscriminately.

The fusiliers watched in subdued silence as the British artillery exacted a dreadful toll on the retreating enemy gunners. Soon they witnessed the devastating power of artillery close up as the few British casualties were brought back towards the rear. One young hussar trooper had been draped unconscious across his saddle. His body jerked like a rag doll, a bleeding, tattered stump all that remained of one of his legs. The gory sight of the man's ripped limb, the bone and flesh mangled into something unrecognisable as being human, turned many a stomach among the watching men.

This time the fusiliers had been able to stand on the sidelines and watch as other young soldiers experienced the raw horror of war. A few miles to the south the main body of the Russian army waited. Tomorrow the King's Royal Fusiliers would have to take their place in the battle line and face the stark reality of battle for themselves.

CHAPTER
TWENTY-FIVE

The battalion spent the night on the same ground they had occupied through the long, dull afternoon. The fusiliers were grateful to be bivouacked close to the River Bulganak. This gave them easy access to fresh water, even if the thin stream had been churned to a muddy soup by the incessant passage of men and horses, and the thick ferns and lavender bushes that grew on its banks provided fuel for their fires. By some miracle, the army had delivered fresh rations, including the blessed casks that would supply them with their treasured ration of rum. Only the columns of smoke on the horizon gave a reminder of what they would face the following day. The Russian army had torched the closest villages, denying any sanctuary to the invading armies.

Four rivers blocked the allies' route to Sevastopol. The first, the Bulganak, was now behind them. That left the Alma, the Kacha and the Belbek. Already rumours were spreading through the army. It was said that fifty thousand Russian infantrymen waited on the formidable heights that bordered the River Alma, supported by a huge number of cavalry and cannon. Their position was strengthened by fearsome fortifications constructed in the time gifted to the Russian defenders by the British army's lethargic preparations and delayed advance. The Russian general, His Serenity Prince Alexander Sergeevich Menshikov, was reputed to have boasted that he could hold the position for weeks, even in the face of the most determined assault. The Alma would run red with the blood of the hated invaders.

Jack closed his eyes in pleasure as he relished the flavour of the scalding hot tea, a welcome contrast to the tartness of the green coffee he was usually forced to drink.

His body ached and he craved the oblivion of sleep but first he would check on his men. He threw the dregs of his tea on to the dusty ground and forced himself to his feet.

The men of the Light Company lay sprawled around their hastily constructed fires. They were now adept at making the best of wherever they found themselves. Jack had released his two subalterns, giving them leave to visit their friends in the other companies. It left him alone and for once he did not feel his usual jealousy of the companionship they shared with their mates. He was content to spend the time with his company. Tonight, it was where he belonged.

Jack felt a fierce affection for the men. The redcoats enjoyed little in the way of comfort, earned a pittance and endured terrible hardships and ferocious discipline. Yet they faced it all with a stoicism that was scarcely credible. With their mates at their side they would go into battle with the same resolute spirit that they dealt with everything else the army threw at them. Jack knew now that to lead a company of soldiers was a privilege that few deserved, him least of all. It had been a terrible presumption to think that he was worthy of the commission he had stolen. He had believed the life of an officer was easy, full of undeserved privilege and comfort. He had not seen the responsibility that the officers carried constantly. Now he understood what it meant to lead men. Yet as heavy as that burden was, he would not surrender it for anything.

"Evening, sir." The greeting came from Fusilier Dodds, one of the company comedians. He was too fly for his own good which got him into far too much trouble with Sergeant Baker and meant he was still an ordinary fusilier even after fifteen years' service. He was also one of the most popular soldiers in the company. He looked a typical rogue, his scrawny frame and gaunt face so typical of the soldiers who hailed from the rookeries of London. Like many of the fusiliers, Dodds had joined the army to get away from the dreadful conditions of the workhouse and a lifetime of grinding poverty.

"Good evening, Dodds. Was it warm enough for you today?"

"Warm, sir? It was fair roasting. Still, it weren't as bad for us as it was for them Turkish fellows."

"And how's that, Dodds?" Jack asked cautiously, sensing this was exactly the question Dodds wanted him to ask.

"Well, they's Hottoman's, ain't they?" Dodds's face creased into a grin. His messmates groaned at the desperate pun.

"I expect you spent all day thinking that up," Jack said wryly.

"He must've, sir," Fusilier Troughton, one of Dodds's messmates, called. "He was pulling such a face all day we thought he was sickening for the bleeding chokey. It must've been him thinking!"

The rest of the small group doubled up. The laughter was much too loud for such low jesting. The men were clinging to their humour to contain the terror that bubbled below the surface. It was the night before battle and no sane man could face the future without fear. The dread picked at their courage and gnawed at their spirits. Yet not one of the fusiliers would admit to their fears.

Jack left the men laughing, his exhausted body and throbbing back finding walking easier than standing in one place. The men at the next fire looked up as he came close, their grimy faces turning to stare at him apprehensively as he approached.

"Good evening." This time Jack spoke first. The group was made up of the new recruits who had joined the company with Slater. In these early days, they found it easier to stick together. It would take time for them to fit in, to be accepted as belonging to the company. It was not something that could be forced or hurried.

Fear and anxiety was etched on the pale faces of the newcomers. Without the easy camaraderie of Dodds and his messmates, the newest additions to the company would have to face their fear quietly, hiding the terror behind the silent domestic rituals of cooking their rations and settling to rest.

The men seemed nervous at the sudden appearance of their company commander and just bobbed their heads in acknowledgement of his greeting. One of their fellow recruits had collapsed on the march, claimed by the searing heat of the sun. The company had lost three men that day, losses it could do without so close to battle. None of the victims had died but all were lost to the confusion of the army's system of caring for the sick and wounded. No one expected to see them again. Even if they returned to health, it was more than likely they would be sent to another battalion and their entries in the company books crossed through.

Jack left the new recruits to eat their rations in peace, remembering how daunting the presence of an officer could be. Nothing he could say would allay their fear or banish the thoughts of what awaited them tomorrow. They would simply have to cope, as every man had to. Alone.

"Hello there, sir. Have you not had your fill of walking? I know I bloody well have." The singsong accent of Welsh Davies welcomed Jack into the group of men gathered round the next campfire.

He walked into the circle of light, its warmth reeling him in like a trout on a lure. "Do you call that walking? I thought it was more like a pleasant stroll in the countryside."

"T'were that, Captain," the broad West Country baritone of English Davies rumbled from the far side of the fire. The two Davies were never far from each other, as if their common name created a natural bond between them.

"Thank you, English." Jack looked round the small circle. "Make sure your rifles are ready for tomorrow. I have a feeling you're going to need them." Jack offered the unnecessary advice more for something to say than for any more practical reason. These were his best men. They seemed to be drawn to each other, their experience and skill forming them into a special cadre at the core of the company.

"I plan to sleep with my Minié, Captain, and I'll caress her sweet curves all night long, so I will." This from Dawson, the smallest man in the company. Hoots and whistles greeted his comment.

"Why you said the same about your old Bessie," Taylor, who was old enough to be Dawson's grandfather, said in mock disapproval. He was referring to the Brown Bess musket that had only recently been replaced with the new, more powerful, Minié rifle.

"Now don't you go getting all excited, old man. At your age it could be the death of you." Dawson chuckled. "I do miss my old Bessie, I'll give you that. But you can't beat getting your hands on a younger model, now can you?" Dawson slapped the stock of his Minié rifle.

Jack grinned at their tomfoolery, glad his fusiliers had the good spirits to chide and tease one another.

Taylor threw a lump of rock-hard biscuit in Dawson's direction. The young fusilier caught it and took a teeth-shattering bite out of it. His grimace of pain set the men off laughing again and Jack used the moment to move on.

A slow and laconic round of applause came from the darkness on the very edge of the Light Company's lines.

"Bravo!" Slater's voice mocked Jack from the shadows. "Trust you to play the toff."

Slater had taken to making his own private bivouac, away from the hatred and fear of the company. Now, like a spider crawling from its web, he slunk out of the darkness, his shadowy form huge in the flickering light of the campfires. Instinctively Jack's hand moved to the handle of his revolver.

Slater noticed. "Oh, you'd like to shoot me, would you, Lark?" Slater stepped forward, suddenly very close and very threatening. "Well, here I am, all on my lonesome. Go ahead, shoot me."

Jack was sorely tempted. He looked into Slater's moist brown eyes and felt a surge of hatred so intense it threatened to overwhelm all reason.

With an effort, Jack brought his emotions under control. "Why don't you just bugger off and desert? We certainly don't bloody want you," Jack hissed.

Slater's thick moustache twitched. "Damn you, I'm no coward. I'm not frightened of the Russians and I'm most certainly not frightened of you. But you, now you should be frightened. You should be shitting in your fucking breeches, boy."

Jack gritted his teeth and said nothing.

"You took away my stripes." Slater's voice quivered with emotion, something Jack had never expected the brute of a man to reveal. It was like hearing armour crack. "I thought about peaching on you, telling the whole world what a fraud you are, you by-blow of a doxy," Slater went on quietly and evenly, his emotion back under control. "But then I figured why give the army the bother of dealing with you when I could get so much pleasure out of doing it myself." He licked his lips. "You'd better take care. There's no knowing what could happen in the heat of battle. Why, I hear some officers have been hit in the back, shot by their own men, can you believe?"

Slater stepped back and without a word Jack turned away towards the nearest fire, as if the heat of its flames could melt the chill that gripped him.

CHAPTER
TWENTY-SIX

Few men were woken by the harsh notes of the reveille. Many were already up and about, abhorring the idea of wasting what could be their last living hours in sleep. The quiet murmur of voices could be heard throughout the army, some in conversation with their fellows, others in prayer, even those most vehement atheists returning to the comforting words of religion.

The sun rose lethargically as if it, too, was unwilling to start the day. The morning was chilly, the men and their uniforms damp from the heavy dew. Fires were coaxed into life and the men breakfasted on salt pork and biscuit. Then it was time to form up.

By six thirty, the men stood ready in their ranks, waiting for the command to march. Their coats steamed gently under the climbing sun. Horses pawed at the ground and flicked their tails, the men fidgeted. And waited.

By seven thirty, there was still no order to advance. Exasperated officers decided enough was enough and ordered their men to sit. The men sank gratefully to the ground and the officers gathered to vent their frustration at the maddening delay and the incompetence of their seniors.

"Digby-Brown!"

The lieutenant heard his captain's loud summons and reluctantly left the circle of subalterns. Already he was sweating profusely, his thin whiskers slick from the steady stream that ran down from underneath his shako.

"Yes, sir?"

"Nothing is going to be happening here for a while so I'm of a mind to see what lies ahead. I'm leaving you in charge of the company. I'll return should the generals condescend to present us with orders to advance."

"Very good, sir." Digby-Brown licked his lips nervously as he risked a request. "Would you mind if I came with you?"

"Yes, I would." Jack wanted to get away from the cloying attention of his fellow officers. Taking Digby-Brown with him would be as bad as joining in one of their pointless discussions.

Digby-Brown's shoulders slumped at the unkind reply. "Very good, sir. Any other commands?"

"No. Stay with the men and send someone to me if I'm needed." Jack made to leave.

"I think I might just about be able to manage that, sir." Digby-Brown's words stopped Jack in his tracks. "It's just the task for a hopeless lieutenant."

"What on earth do you mean by that?" Jack snapped.

"Well, it's clear you don't like me. You treat me like something you've just trod in."

"I have no idea what you mean." Jack could see the emotion in his junior officer's face and it brought him up short.

"Truly?" Digby-Brown's eyes glistened. "You never have a good word to say to me. You treat me like a fool."

"I don't think you are a fool — except when you come up with daft notions like this."

"With respect, sir, I disagree. I've tried my best to help you. Yet whatever I do, you show me nothing but scorn and derision. It is grossly unfair."

"Listen, Digby-Brown. This is the neither the time nor the place for this."

"I think it is exactly the time, sir. There may not be another chance to speak plainly." The young lieutenant paled at the thought of his own mortality.

"Well, consider your views aired and noted. Your function in my company is to assist me as I see fit. If that is unsatisfactory to you then I can arrange for you to be assigned elsewhere. For God's sake, man, we are about to go into battle. This is not the time for a fit of the vapours."

Digby-Brown's shoulders slumped and he lowered his head, his spark of righteous anger extinguished by Jack's damning words.

The sight of the crestfallen officer pricked Jack's conscience. "Look here, Digby-Brown. I need you to help me. Do you understand?"

"You need me, sir? I thought you couldn't stand the sight of me."

"Grow up, man. Of course I need you. I can't do everything myself. The men will look to both of us to show them what is expected of them. For better or worse we are their officers and it's up to us to live up to their expectations."

"Yes, sir." Digby-Brown's head lifted. "I would like to apologise for my outburst."

"Now you're being a damn fool." Jack clapped Digby-Brown on the shoulder. He knew he had treated his lieutenant harshly. He had used the young officer as an undeserving scapegoat for all his loathing towards the officer class. He saw now how his treatment had affected Digby-Brown and for that he did feel a pang of remorse. He had not set out to be such a bastard.

"You have all the makings of a fine officer," Jack told him. "Never let anyone tell you different. Now," he summoned a wry smile, "get to your bloody duties before I change my mind."

"Yes, sir." Digby-Brown glowed with delight, the unexpected praise helping to settle the fear that sat heavily in his stomach. "And thank you, sir."

Jack turned and made his way up the small hillock a few hundred yards in front of the fusiliers' position. At the top he pulled up handfuls of heather and weeds to make a cushion that would spare his backside direct contact with the damp ground. Then he turned his attention on the panorama that stretched towards the southern horizon.

Directly to the south was a ridge and it was carpeted with thousands upon thousands of Russian infantry. Unlike the allied army, the enemy had yet to form up. Sunlight glinted on the infantry's neatly piled arms and reflected off the hundreds of pieces of artillery whose iron barrels were aimed down the slope towards the Alma River.

Jack slowly panned along the enemy's position, Sloames's precious field glasses bringing the Russian men sharply into focus. He watched intrigued as individual soldiers wandered down to a thick band of vegetation that lined the banks of the river. He picked out one scrawny Russian conscript who meandered down to where a thick clump of bushes would screen him from his fellows. The Russian had not reckoned on being observed from far away to the north and Jack had a clear view as he dropped his thick grey trousers and squatted down on to his haunches.

Jack held the man in view. He counted the seconds, deciding that if the Russian was still emptying his bowels after the count of thirty then Slater would die that day. Jack knew it was superstitious nonsense but he could not help feeling hopeful as he reached twenty.

At the count of twenty-seven, the Russian soldier abruptly stood up and hoisted his trousers over his skinny shanks. Jack swore loudly.

Annoyed at his own stupidity, he turned away from observing the Russian line. He shuffled round on his scratchy seat so he could observe the preparations of his own side. The sight of the massed ranks of the allied army astounded him, it stretched for miles; the allied force was far greater than even the huge number he had observed in the Russian lines.

Officers galloped between the formations, full of activity despite the fact that the army was sprawled immobile on the ground. To the rear, the last of the ammunition wagons made their way forward, harried by mounted officers who bellowed at the cart drivers to make swifter progress. Around the Bulganak, the army's pioneers wielded shovels to level the riverbanks and make the passage across the river as easy as possible for the thousands of infantrymen, cavalry, artillery and supply troops that would have to cross its winding course.

The sound of bugles and drums reached Jack's hillock. The French army was stirring into life far away on the right flank of the allied force. Once again, it appeared that the French were ready to fight while their British allies still laboured in their preparations. Jack watched the first French brigades start their advance towards the steep cliffs that protected the Russian general's left flank. Perhaps the French commander, Saint-Arnaud, was as tired of waiting for the British generals as their own army was.

The movement seemed to spur the British high command to life. A fresh flurry of staff officers left the clump of generals at the heart of the British formation and raced their horses through the massed ranks of the army, a new urgency in their hurried passage. As Jack watched through his field glasses, the massive columns of infantrymen slowly rose to their feet, and the small clusters of officers broke up and returned to their commands.

It was now mid-morning but at last the British army was about to advance.

CHAPTER
TWENTY-SEVEN

The Alma was a river in name only. In most places, the local Tartar children could happily splash across from bank to bank, their passage barely troubled by the shallow water. In places, the river bent and twisted back on itself, forming deeper, more forbidding eddies and dark pools but even the laziest of peasants could divert around them with little effort. What minor inconvenience the river created could be avoided altogether via a single stone bridge that had stood for centuries. The old post road it carried made its way through the centre of the valley, heading, in a roundabout way, towards the great naval base at Sevastopol. The local Tartars only bothered to use the bridge when they needed to transport the harvest in their rickety arabas carts to the larger towns.

Two small villages called the river valley home. The inhabitants of Burliuk and Almatamack spent most of their lives within the confines of the valley, the only visitor to their remote homes the local mullah who taught the children the stories of the Koran, and who fought to save their parents' souls from the few temptations of the flesh that could be found in such remote villages.

Away from the river, the ground was barren, the wide expanse of grasslands left uncultivated, good for little more than grazing for the Tartars' flocks of sheep and herds of cattle. Scattered across the vast grassland stood ancient piles of stones. Local legend spoke of hidden treasure buried under the carefully constructed piles yet no villager had ever summoned enough courage to disturb the work of their ancestors. A terrible black horse was said to guard the treasure, keeping it safe through the centuries.

The legend of the black horse could not keep the valley safe from the violation of war. The bridge and shallow river were of enough strategic value to tempt the Russian army away from the secure defences of Sevastopol, thrusting thousands of soldiers into the lives of the local Tartars. They found themselves evicted from their villages, their herds requisitioned to feed the gargantuan host, their vineyards and orchards plundered. The lives of a few hundred Tartar peasants were of no consequence in the mighty struggle to secure victory over the invading armies of the British, French and Turkish governments.

For Prince Menshikov, the Russian commander, the terrain around the Alma River was a defender's paradise. To the west, where the land met the sea, huge cliffs soared up from the coast, one hundred and fifty feet high and thought to be impassable to the invading army and most especially to their cumbersome artillery. These massive natural buttresses gave way to a long ridge that stretched inland for many miles along the southern bank of the Alma before it abruptly terminated in a high pinnacle that jutted out into the open plains to the east.

The ridge's rugged slopes led down to the southern bank of the Alma. Here the riverbank was at its highest and most formidable, in many places several feet above the slow-moving water. The natural folds in the ground along the slope formed a succession of natural terraces which were perfect for positioning defensive infantry and artillery.

Opposite, on the north side of the river, the ground was open and sloped gently down to the Alma. It offered no shelter and no cover. It was an attacker's nightmare.

Menshikov would not, however, rely on the terrain alone to win him victory. The allied army might have been allowed to land on Rusian soil unmolested, but their slow advance had given the Russian general ample time in which to pick his ground and strengthen the position he had chosen. The two villages were cleared, the houses and mud walls demolished, denying the attackers cover. Huge bundles of straw were positioned in the ruins, ready to be fired to hamper any troops advancing through the debris. All cover near the riverbanks was uprooted or burnt, the many trees cut down and taken away. The enemy was to be given nowhere to hide, no place where they could shelter from the lethal storm that Menshikov intended to bring down against them.

Artillery officers paced the distances and measured ranges. They laid down markers for the gunners, calculated overlapping fields of fire to maximise the power of the massed artillery batteries. The Russians applied the rules of mathematics and physics to the business of administering death. Nothing would be left to chance.

Two great earthworks were constructed on the heights on the Russians' side of the river. The largest, the great redoubt, had a breastwork four feet high fashioned from huge tree trunks. Hundreds of sandbags and wide wicker gabions packed full of earth would protect the defenders from the enemy's fire. Crude embrasures had been hacked out of the southern face, creating openings for a dozen guns which could be brought to bear on any attacker coming across the river. Further to the east, a second redoubt was constructed to protect the open flank, with another battery of guns sited behind its protective barricade.

Menshikov's chosen position ran for six miles from the coast to the smaller redoubt. Forty thousand Russian soldiers, hundreds of pieces of artillery and thousands of cavalry waited for the invading army to arrive. Menshikov was confident. The invaders could send wave after wave of men to try to breach his mighty defences. None would get through. The British, French and Turkish soldiers would be massacred.

Menshikov boasted to all who would listen that he could not be defeated. Such was his confidence that the people of Sevastopol journeyed along the coast to watch the might of Britain and France waste its strength against Menshikov's defences. The invasion was reduced to entertainment, a pleasing diversion for the good ladies and gentlemen of Sevastopol to observe in safety.

"Good Lord, now why are we stopping?"

"The good Lord is the best person to ask, Mr Digby-Brown. Perhaps Raglan thinks we are too fatigued to continue. The man is a damn fool!" Jack growled in frustration as the fusiliers were ordered to come to yet another maddening halt.

"Sir!"

Jack laughed at Digby-Brown's reaction. "I apologise. I really should learn to moderate my language."

"Thank you, sir."

"But even you, Mr Digby-Brown, must admit that this is yet another total balls-up!"

"Yes, sir."

Jack smiled and clapped his subaltern on the shoulder. "Good fellow. We'll make a radical of you yet."

"I hope not, sir."

Lieutenant Thomas made his way over to join them. All along the column bad-tempered officers gathered to discuss this latest infuriating delay. The King's Royal Fusiliers marched in the centre of the Light Division's column, too far from the front to benefit from the clean breeze that swept across open plain from the sea only a few miles to the west. Instead, they were forced to march in the midst of the choking cloud of dust that was kicked up by the boots of those further ahead. Their throats were clogged with dust, they were thirsty and their tempers were fraying at the exasperating regularity with which the column came to a halt.

The King's Royal Fusiliers served the 1st Fusilier Brigade alongside the 7th Royal Fusiliers and the 23rd Royal Welsh Fusiliers. The brigade was commanded by Major General William Codrington, and it was one of the two brigades that formed the Light Division. Raglan's plan was simple. Four divisions would attack the Russian position. They would cross the river directly in front of the huge Russian army, precisely where they were strongest. The divisions would form up in two long lines stretching from west to east. The Light Division would fight on the left of the front line, with the 2nd Division under Major General de Lacy Evans on the right. The 1st Division, commanded by the queen's cousin, the Duke of Cambridge, would follow the Light Division, while the 3rd Division, commanded by Sir Richard England, would be behind the 2nd Division.

Four Divisions. Twenty-five battalions. Nigh on twenty thousand redcoats.

The Light Company's three officers stood together in companionable silence as each contemplated the enemy force. The fusiliers had been ordered to halt yet again on a low-crested rise two miles short of the Alma River. The raised ground gave them a clear view of the Russian position. It stretched for miles across the higher ground to the south of the Alma. Even from such a distance the difficulties facing the attackers were obvious. The redcoats would be marching into a corridor of death.

"I must say, there does seem to be an awful lot of them." Lieutenant Thomas broke the silence, his face pale, his voice cracking as he spoke, the squeak of adolescence betraying his youth.

Jack looked at his junior officer's wan expression and wondered what kind of country took their young boys from school and sent them to fight thousands of miles from home.

"Don't concern yourself about them, Thomas. Our job is to look after the men. Let the generals worry about the enemy."

"Besides, we outnumber them," Digby-Brown sought to add to his captain's reassurance. "We have to share those Russkis with the French and the Turks. I hope there are enough to go round."

Jack turned away from the formidable Russian host so that he was facing his two subalterns. "Today is not about fulfilling any childish dreams you may have of chasing glory. I want you to concentrate on bringing as many of our men out of here as possible. And whatever we face, we face it together. As a company. Do you understand?"

"Yes, sir," both subalterns replied firmly and in unison.

"Good. I'm glad you have learnt not to mumble, Mr Thomas. It's nice to see you making progress at last."

The sound of artillery opening fire echoed along the valley. Far away on the right flank puffs of smoke rose into the still air. The French army had begun its attack in front of the cliffs that formed Menshikov's left flank. The cliffs were a formidable obstacle and Menshikov had decided that only a thin screen of soldiers was needed to keep the allies from turning the flank. The bulk of the Russian artillery and infantry was in the centre and on the right flank, where the British infantry waited to begin their own assault.

Lieutenant Flowers walked his horse over to join the Light Company officers. As one of the battalion's field officers, Flowers was required to be mounted, a rather dubious honour since it made him an ideal target for Russian sharpshooters.

Flowers sat his horse well but the bony nag he was riding rather spoiled his fine appearance. The horse stood several hands too small to suit the adjutant's tall frame, its threadbare coat and prominent ribs testifying to its poor condition.

"Goodness me, I'm glad the French are attacking those cliffs and not us," Flowers observed. "That they think they can get up there astonishes me."

Jack was pleased to see the adjutant. His two subalterns needed distraction. "It wouldn't surprise me if the damn Frogs believe they can win the battle all on their own," he said.

"Still, attacking the flanks, however pointless it may appear, suggests strategy. That perhaps their general has actually thought up a plan." Flowers tugged at the reins of his horse which had lowered its head to crop at the tufts of grass around its hooves.

"Are you implying that Lord Raglan has no plan?" Jack replied. "That his decision to commit us to a

218

frontal attack against prepared defences after advancing over nearly a mile of open, coverless terrain is somehow lacking in forethought?"

Flowers yanked hard on the reins of his recalcitrant steed. The horse was determined to feast on the moist grass. "I'm sure his thorough reconnaissance led him to conclude there was no other course of action open to him."

"His reconnaissance?" Jack raised his eyebrows. "I must have missed that. Did either of you two happen to notice any cavalrymen out in front?"

"No, sir."

An uncomfortable silence followed. In Wellington's time, the British exploring officers had been lauded throughout the army. The intelligence they provided had been vital to the duke's preparations. For Raglan to have chosen not to send out similar outriders was an appalling indictment of his ability as a general.

Flowers tried to lighten the sombre mood. "Well, I think I can say my duty to spread gloom and despair is complete. Should you need any more of my encouraging words then please do not hesitate to summon me."

"I think we've had all of the encouragement we can stomach for the moment." Jack smiled despite the censure in his words, and he was glad to see his two subalterns relax a little.

Flowers turned his head towards the distant sounds of battle which had increased in tempo. "Perhaps, as you suggested, the French will win the day without our help."

"Well, that would be nice." As Jack replied, the bugles sounded and the drums rattled. "But I rather fancy Raglan has other ideas."

All along the British line, the redcoats stirred into life once again. The battalions were ordered to form line. Staff officers swarmed around the column as it slowly broke up, and in the measured step of the parade ground the men moved into the new formation to the beat of the drums. The order came to jettison knapsacks, final confirmation that the wait was nearly over.

An uneasy lull fell over the troops. The bugles and drums fell silent. The shouts of the sergeants and corporals ceased now that the men stood in line, their spacings regular, the files ordered. The staff officers rode back to their commanders, their orders delivered.

The King's Royal Fusiliers stood in the centre of the Light Division, the 23rd Royal Welch to their left, the 7th Fusiliers to their right.

"King's Royal Fusiliers! Prepare to load!" thundered the battalion sergeant major's voice, dispelling the temporary hush.

"Load!"

The waiting was over.

CHAPTER
TWENTY-EIGHT

"King's Royal Fusiliers! Battalion will advance! Advance!"

It was a few minutes past noon.

To their intense disappointment, the Light Company had been ordered to fight in the main battalion line, behind the Greenjackets of the 95th Rifles. The Light Company were the trained skirmishers in the battalion, used to fighting on their own, strung out in extended order in front of the battalion, screening the dense ranks from the withering fire of the enemy's skirmishers. But instead of advancing with the Greenjackets, the Light Company were expected to fire the disciplined volleys of a regular company, adding their rifles to the power of the massed battalion ranks. Jack would have revelled in the opportunity to lead his company forward on its own but for reasons he could not fathom the generals had decided otherwise.

The long red line moved forward at the command, each man's heart beating a little faster. In the centre of the battalion line, the drummer boys beat out the time of the march, the young boys barely big enough to carry the huge instruments that hung heavily from the leather bands that held them pressed against their stomachs. To the front of the drummers marched the battalion colours, two huge squares of coloured silk which embodied the battalion's honour and pride.

A pair of colour sergeants armed with fearsome halberds, a weapon that harked back to the days when all fighting was done hand-to-hand, guarded each colour. The sergeants were there to protect the colours at all costs; they would use their formidable weapons to hack and gut any enemy who tried to steal them. Two young ensigns carried the heavy colours with pride. To be chosen was a distinction, one that would be long remembered and cherished — if they survived. The honour came with a price, for the gaudy squares of silk were certain to draw the fire of enemy sharpshooters.

One ensign carried the Queen's colour, an enormous Union Jack proudly emblazoned with the regimental crest in its centre. The second held aloft the battalion's regimental colour of vibrant blue, with the crossed fusils of the regiment's badge picked out in gold thread. The regiment's battle honours were sewn in the same gold thread, in two columns, one either side of the badge. Each place name was highlighted by a rectangle of blood-red silk, in honour of the fusiliers who had gone before, who had fought and died under the same twin flags. The battle honours read like a chronicle of the British army. Deig. Corunna. Nive. Peninsula. Waterloo. The names resonated with history, and the six hundred fusiliers marching towards the massed ranks of the Russian army were about to take their place in it.

★ ★ ★

"For the love of God!" Fusilier Dawson exclaimed, echoing the sentiments of all the company as the enemy artillery opened fire.

"Silence in the ranks! The next person to speak will find themselves the proud owner of a new arsehole." Sergeant Baker made his presence felt from his position behind the rear rank. His eyes roved over the company, ready to pounce on any lack of discipline.

From his place in the centre of the front rank, Slater laughed at the sergeant's coarse words. He ignored the looks of disgust his fellow redcoats shot his way. He fed on their hatred, nurturing it, savouring it, adding it to the bitterness that burned inside him.

He felt no trace of fear as the company marched obediently into the barrage of fire but he was no fool, he knew the danger he faced. Fate was a fickle goddess but he trusted to her to keep him alive to deliver the justice he craved.

He had vowed that Jack Lark would meet his own fate today. Lark had dared to cheat his destiny, stealing a life and a place in the world far removed from that allotted to him. He would not cheat death.

High in the sky two black dots emerged from the cloud of smoke that enveloped the lines of Russian cannon. Every fusilier watched anxiously as the shot flew through the air towards them, covering the distance in a heartbeat. The roundshot smashed into the ground in front of the battalion, gouging a thick channel out of the earth before bouncing back high into the air and over the heads of the men.

A ragged cheer erupted from the redcoats, the men finding the breath to hoot their derision. Without breaking step, the redcoats treated the first artillery fire they had ever experienced with gleeful disdain.

"Fusilier Trotter!" Jack singled out one of his men who marched close to Slater. "I thought you were the battalion's wicketkeeper. Why didn't you take that one?"

"Too much pace on it, sir. I thought I'd leave it for the long stops in the guards!"

It was not much of a joke but the company laughed as if the finest comedian from the Palladium was among them.

The fusiliers marched on, advancing as only the British advanced — devoid of fanfare, stoic and steady. The line moving forward with deadly purpose.

"Open the ranks!" Jack yelled, tracking the pencil-thin trace that marked the path of incoming roundshot. The Russian batteries were sending their fire into the advancing red line from all along the enemy's position and one black dot was heading straight for his company. Jack screamed at his men to move, his heart in his mouth as he prayed they were quick enough to get out of its way.

The fusiliers in its path scattered. Like an express train roaring through a station, the shot sped through the opening, its horrifying passage startling in its violence. It smashed into the ground behind the company before flying over the heads of the Scots fusiliers who marched directly behind them in the ranks of the 1st Division.

The Scottish troops greeted the fusiliers' desperate antics with loud whoops and catcalls of derision, gleefully mocking the undignified display.

Sergeant Shepherd manhandled the men back into the ordered ranks which had continued to move purposefully forward even as their fellows dodged the deadly missile. Jack scanned the sky, ever vigilant for danger aimed at the Light Company.

"King's Royal Fusiliers! Prepare to halt! Halt!"

The men had advanced close enough to the burning village of Burliuk to feel the heat. Dirty grey smoke swirled around the ruined houses. There was no cover for the redcoats but the smoke screened their movements from the Russian gunners and prevented the use of their range markers so that they were forced to shoot blind. But the British troops were simply too numerous to miss completely.

Captain Devine's 3rd Company was hit, the roundshot ploughing through a file of redcoats in a gory shower of bone and blood. The fusiliers stood silent and still, stoic as two of their fellows were reduced to pathetic, twisted corpses in the blink of an eye.

Colonel Morris left his place in the centre of the battalion, urging his huge black horse forward. "Lie down! Lie down!" He rode along the front of the fusiliers' line, waving his hat over his head to emphasise the urgent order.

"Good fellows! It won't be long now. Well done, my boys." Morris turned his horse when he reached the battalion's left flank, nodding a friendly greeting to Jack as he did so. He trotted easily back along the front of his battalion, repeating words of comfort, showing himself to his men, letting them see that he shared their danger.

The men lay on the ground, the heat from the sun and the burning village making them sweat in their thick red jackets. Their officers remained on their feet, stoically standing in their allotted positions, setting an example to their men despite the terror fluttering in their bellies.

It was impossible for the redcoats to avoid the enemy fire now they were lying down but it was also harder for the Russian gunners to hit them. Most of the roundshot bounced harmlessly over the prostrate soldiers, wasting their power on the clammy soil which erupted in spectacular fountains of earth.

Volley after volley hammered across the plain. The British soldiers lay on the ground beneath the cannonade and endured as best they could, many seeking solace in their God, their lips moving in silent prayers for deliverance.

There was nothing else to be done.

CHAPTER
TWENTY-NINE

A roundshot struck the very centre of McCulloch's company, decapitating one fusilier and taking the arm from another. Jack tore his gaze from the awful sight and tried to stand as still as possible. Despite his best efforts, he could not help flinching at every deadly projectile that rushed by. One came so close to his head that he felt the powerful rush of air as it flew past.

His terror was like a caged beast that prowled and fought for escape from deep inside him. Time crawled by, every second seeming like a minute, every minute like an hour. The barrage tossed and churned the ground around the company, the dark soil like spilt blood across the bright green grass. It was enough to drive a man to madness. Yet the redcoats endured the trial. They lay in their ranks and held their terror at bay, waiting for the order to move.

To Jack's horror a roundshot struck one of his men. In front of his sickened eyes, it smashed down straight into Fusilier Trotter, ripping his arm from his body and sending a fountain of bright red blood into the air. Trotter screamed, a single, shrill cry that rang loudly in the ears of his fellow redcoats before he fell mercifully silent.

"On your feet!" Jack echoed the order he heard shouted somewhere to his right. "Lively now!"

The fusiliers pulled themselves to their feet, relieved to be moving yet terrified to be advancing.

"Fix bayonets!"

This was it, the final preparation before the men closed with the enemy. The fusiliers pulled their long bayonets from their belts, locking them into place on their already loaded rifles. The officers drew their swords and pulled revolvers from their pouches. The bugles sounded the advance and the long red line jerked into motion, leaving their dead behind them.

The fusiliers marched towards the river where the 95th were already engaging the enemy. The far riverbank was crowded with Russian skirmishers who sniped at the advancing red line. Puffs of smoke erupted from the barrels of the Greenjackets' rifles as the British skirmishers returned fire. They moved in extended order, fighting in pairs, like grasshoppers performing an intricate dance. One man from each pair dropped to one knee to fire at the Russian sharpshooters while the other moved forward, covering his partner until he was loaded and ready to move. Officers and sergeants choreographed the movement with shouts and whistles, ensuring their men fought with ruthless efficiency.

Jack watched the Greenjackets at work, impressed by their skill. The line of redcoats marched steadily forward, forcing the riflemen to move quickly to screen the progress of the battalions. Jack was convinced his company would have performed as well, his fusiliers at

228

least the equal of the grasshoppers. The thought that, had he had his way, he would already be in action sent an icy wave of fear flushing through his veins. He had never expected to be so terrified.

He led his men forward into the shattered remains of a vineyard. Long lines of vines lay twisted underfoot, decades of careful tending and growth trampled under the careless boots of the advancing redcoats. A handful of vines survived and the fusiliers snatched bunches of ripe grapes as they passed by, gorging on the juicy fruit even as they marched into the storm of fire.

A fusilier from the left flank of McCulloch's company fell to the Russian fire, his face a mask of blood that spilled over the grapes still in his mouth. He toppled silently to the ground, his death ignored by the men either side of him. The closest sergeant ordered the ranks to close up. There was no time for compassion, sympathy or grief. The advance could not falter.

Rifle bullets fluttered through the vineyard, flicking the branches and buzzing past the ears of the fusiliers, as if the crop was under attack from a plague of deadly insects. The Russian fire was heavy; it was worse, far worse, than Jack could ever have imagined. It seemed inevitable that all the redcoats must surely be struck down. Yet by some miracle only a man here and there fell to the enemy fire. The redcoats continued to advance.

Then Jack was shot.

A solid object thumped hard against his body, a stab of pain flaring in the very centre of his chest. His free hand clutched at the pain, his shaking fingers feeling for the tattered flesh that would reveal a horrific wound.

His fingers closed over a solid lump that rested against his ribs. With a shaking hand, Jack pulled the musket ball from where it had lodged in his jacket. Fired at long range the bullet had not had the force to pierce his flesh, its power already spent. Apart from a neat hole in his coat, it had done no damage.

Shaking with a heady mix of fear and relief, Jack hurled the musket ball away. If the Russians had been armed with Minié rifles, Jack knew he would now be dead. It was a sobering thought and he silently offered his grateful thanks to a beneficent God that had denied the majority of the Russian army modern weaponry.

The Russian infantry on the slopes to the south of the Alma were wasting their powder; their ancient muskets lacked the power to inflict much damage at such a distance. Fusiliers gasped and swore as the spent bullets struck them, the stinging blow was painful but it did little except shred the men's uniforms and their already strained nerves. But the Russian skirmishers were armed with modern rifles. They were starting to exact a high toll on the line that snaked towards the Alma. Sergeant Shepherd fell, his shoulder smashed and two more fusiliers from the Light Company went down under the withering fire.

The British wounded were abandoned to their fate. Some picked themselves up, bravely rushing forward to catch up with their company, cursing at the pain, staunching their wounds as best they could. Others walked, crawled or pulled themselves to the rear, desperate to get out of the line of fire.

The continual order to close the ranks was all that marked the passing of the fallen.

"Come on!" Jack roared, urging his men forward. He sensed the pace of the advance begin to falter. The men were still moving forward but the steady, rhythmic pace of the march was gone. The long red chain was breaking up. The men were moving towards the river in small groups or on their own, their instinct to find cover becoming ever more powerful as more of their mates fell to the enemy fire.

"Leave him!" Two fusiliers had paused to help one of their mates who had taken a bullet in the thigh, the blood pulsing over the fingers he clasped desperately to the gaping hole in his leg. "Come on! Move!"

"Move, you sluggards! Get moving!" Digby-Brown, too, was driving the men forward, physically pushing any fusilier who hesitated. The young lieutenant mimicked his captain, grabbing any who stopped to help a wounded man and sought to use the charitable act as an excuse to stop advancing into the merciless fire.

Step by faltering step the redcoats edged to the far side of the vineyard. The bank of the Alma River was now just a few short yards ahead.

At the edge of the vineyard, the fusiliers staggered to a halt. They stared in fear at the open ground that led down the gentle slope to the riverbank. The dozen yards taunted them, daring them to leave the meagre sanctuary of the shattered vineyard. The enemy fire seemed to redouble as they stood there, refusing to advance despite the roars of the officers.

Jack screamed at his men to advance, thumping his fists against the backs of the terrified fusiliers. He could see their fear in their faces, and the flashes of anger as he tried to drive them into the horrific fire that flensed the open ground in front of them.

"Fusiliers!" Jack's voice was huge. "Advance, damn you! Move! Move!"

But the fear of the enemy fire was too strong. The British advance had stopped.

CHAPTER
THIRTY

Colonel Morris looked on in horror as his battalion went to ground. He was at the centre of the fusiliers' ranks, not that the line truly existed any more. Behind him the young faces of the ensigns carrying the colours were ashen-white, terror bright in their eyes.

Bodies lay on the ground, the twisted corpses of men who had been under his command abandoned amidst the ruin of the vineyard. He saw the tremor in the fusiliers' ranks as they began to shuffle backwards.

Morris refused to let his battalion retreat. Even if it led to their destruction, the fusiliers would advance.

"King's Royal Fusiliers will advance!" he screamed, demanding his men respond. They ignored him.

"King's Royal Fusiliers!" Morris stood tall in his stirrups. Fear twisted inside him as he made himself an obvious target. "Advance!"

Colonel Morris stared at his men, unable to believe they were stubbornly refusing to obey. The shame of retreat was more than he could stand. He felt tears of impotence prick at his eyelids. Then a single officer broke from the tattered ranks.

Captain Sloames, the commander of the Light Company, burst from the midst of his fusiliers. His mouth was wide open, bellowing for his men to follow but Morris was too far away to hear the words. He watched mesmerised as Sloames turned on the open ground to face the cowering redcoats and berate them. Morris could see the fear on the officer's face, saw him flinch as bullets whipped past. Then he raced across the open ground and into the river.

And the fusiliers followed.

They stormed from the pathetic remains of the vineyard, charging like a huge red herd. Morris felt a surge of pride as he watched his men follow the example set by the insane bravery of one officer.

Dozens were struck, their bodies thrown violently to the ground. The enemy fire simply could not miss. But the redcoats ignored their casualties and kept going.

Morris urged his horse forward to join the pack of redcoats churning the riverbank into a muddy slick. He tried to shout across to Captain Sloames but his words were lost in the noise of the melee. He wanted to convey his thanks but his view of the Light Company's commander was blocked by another mounted figure who was pushing his way through the muddled ranks of redcoats to reach the shelf screening the men from the worst of the enemy fire.

"Good show, Morris! Let's get on with it, shall we?" General Codrington spurred past him. Quite what his brigade commander hoped to achieve in the midst of the broken ranks was beyond Morris's comprehension but he urged his own horse forward and followed his general.

The redcoats greeted the appearance of their brigade commander with a huge cheer. Codrington let his willing horse pick its way up the far bank before he turned in the saddle, sweeping his old-fashioned bicorn hat from his head in a grand theatrical gesture.

"Come on, Fusiliers! Advance!"

The redcoats bellowed their approval. They stormed out of the shelter of the Alma, scrambling up the greasy riverbank so they could begin the advance up the pristine slope that led to the great redoubt.

To the right of Morris's battalion, the 7th Fusiliers scrambled out of the river, led by Colonel Lacy Yea.

"Never mind forming up!" he yelled, waving his sword. "Come on, men! Come on!" His fusiliers responded.

The battalions of Codrington's brigade left the river and followed their officers up the slope towards the heart of the Russian position.

Jack elbowed his way towards the front of his company, ignoring the loud protests of the men he shoved out of the way. His feet squelched in his boots, his lower body was wet and chilled but the petty discomfort was easily ignored. Nothing was of any consequence aside from his determination to lead his company from the front.

He was close to breaking free from the crowd of fusiliers when the redcoat directly in front of him was hit. The power of the bullet's impact knocked the fusilier backwards, his hands clutching at the ruin of his face. Jack recoiled as the soldier reeled back against him, the redcoat's body twisted in agony, his scream of

235

anguish cut off with a sickening gurgle as a wash of blood filled his throat. In his horror, Jack shoved the wounded man cruelly to one side, and he fell to the ground. The advance pressed on. The unfeeling boots of the wounded man's fellow redcoats thumped into his body, their oaths and curses at the obstacle the last sounds the dying redcoat would ever hear.

The air was alive with rifle bullets. At the head of his company Jack flinched uncontrollably as the shot flickered past him, his ears full of the cries of pain that followed the sickening sound of the bullets hitting living flesh. He kept his eyes fixed on the wooden walls of the great redoubt, trying to shut out the horror that was all around him, his body quivering with barely controlled terror.

In front of the battalion, Jack could see Colonel Morris urging his powerful horse up the slope. Morris was close to fifty yards ahead of the fusiliers, when he suddenly rose up in his stirrups. At first, Jack thought the colonel was standing tall in the saddle to cheer his men on. To his horror, Morris kept moving, arching backwards before tumbling out of the saddle.

When Jack reached him the colonel was lying stretched out on the ground, his body twisted like a rag doll. In front of Jack's horrified gaze Morris's body twitched where it lay, jerking like a landed fish as more Russian bullets slammed mercilessly into his prostrate body. Jack did not need to look at the blood pooling around the body to know the colonel was dead.

Far up the slope, the Russian skirmishers fired for a final time before they withdrew, disappearing out of sight over the crest of the slope. The air was suddenly still and Jack tore his gaze from his colonel's lifeless body to stare in bewilderment at the Russians' sudden withdrawal. The ridge was clear of enemy soldiers, the path to the great redoubt inviting and open. The fusilier behind Jack pushed him hard in his back, impatient at his dawdling, unceremoniously thumping his officer forward. The jarring blow to his back sent a spasm of pain surging up his spine but it brought him to his senses.

The time to mourn Colonel Morris's passing would come later. Right now, those officers left standing had to lead the men forward, to inspire them to victory.

CHAPTER
THIRTY-ONE

The pace of the advance quickened now that the withering fire of the Russian skirmishers had ended. No other enemy soldiers appeared to contest the redcoats' passage. The fusiliers surged up the slope, all order forgotten. In some places the line had broken completely and one or two men were advancing on their own. Every step took them closer to the enemy artillery which stayed ominously silent, hidden behind the high face of the redoubt. The open slope invited the advance, as welcoming as the splayed legs of a whore.

General Codrington curbed his skittish young horse, slowing its pace as he scanned the open ground. Codrington fretted. He simply could not credit that the Russian general had left his flank wide open. The entrenched battery of artillery was a menacing threat yet no cannon, however well positioned, could hope to resist a determined attack alone. Codrington knew there had to be more enemy infantry close by but, frustratingly, he could not see where they waited. And what he could not see, he could not fight.

He did not doubt that the brigade had to press home the attack. They must be bold and trust to quick, direct action. But the disordered redcoats were vulnerable. On the left of Codrington's men, the Light Division's second brigade, commanded by General Buller, were forming up. Two of its three battalions, the 77th and the 88th, had moved to the side to form into square, something an infantry battalion usually only did if threatened by enemy cavalry. The third, the 19th, had joined Codrington's brigade, further evidence that the Light Division's ordered plan of attack was in total disarray.

Codrington knew he had every reason to order the advance to halt and give his officers the time they needed to re-form the ranks. It was the sensible course of action, the pragmatic thing to do, but any delay gave the Russian general more time to move up fresh troops, to reinforce the great redoubt and secure the exposed flank. Delay, and the opening would be slammed shut.

Codrington dug his spurs into the flanks of his mount, urging the young horse up the slope. He damned caution and threw prudence to the wind. The fusilier brigade would attack as it was.

Ahead of the fusiliers, the Greenjackets of the 95th still screened their progress, the loose chain of skirmishers leading the way up the slope. Then, without warning, they stopped. They dropped to one knee and hurriedly opened fire. Jack tried to see what they were firing at but it was impossible to see past the Greenjackets.

Jack heard the threat before he saw it. It sounded like a distant freight train thundering up the line. But this was no machine. It was the rhythmic drumming of hundreds of boots hitting the ground in unison.

Through a gap in the skirmish line, Jack finally caught sight of the source of the pounding. A column of hundreds of Russian infantrymen, two battalions of the Kazansky Regiment, was aimed like an immense fist at the redcoats.

There was no subtlety in the attack. No deft manoeuvre. This was war by numbers, the column an overwhelming force sent to smother the attackers.

The 95th Rifles fired and fired again at the huge column. Each shot claimed a victim but they could no more stop the Russian advance than a child could stop the rising tide by flinging pebbles into the sea.

The officers of the 95th bowed to the inevitable and blew their whistles, ordering the skirmishers to move to the flanks of the British battalions. They had done all they could.

The Russian column flowed down the slope to the east of the great redoubt, aiming at the left flank of the Fusilier Brigade's advance.

Two battalions stood in its path. One, the 19th Regiment of Foot, should not have been there. It was part of General Buller's command and should have been with the other two battalions that made up the second brigade and were currently formed in a square to the right of Codrington's men. Alongside the 19th stood the 23rd Royal Welch Fusiliers.

Both battalions were badly disordered, their companies hopelessly intertwined and with their sergeants and officers far from their allotted positions. Even the most inexperienced ensign saw the danger the unformed ranks faced. Yet there was no panic. In calm, measured tones, the officers brought the disordered advance to a halt and started to re-form the ranks, organising the men who were closest to them, irrespective of their proper station. A line two men deep emerged. It was uneven, bulging and then thinning out, but it was the best the officers could do in the time available.

The line was longer than the width of the advancing column and so the officers on the flanks ordered their men a few paces forward until the British line resembled a flat U. With both ends of the line inclining forward, every rifle could be brought to bear on the Russian column.

In the packed ranks of the Russian column, only the men at the very front could fire, its own clumsy bulk obstructing the majority from bringing their weapons to bear. The drums in the centre drove it onwards, hundreds of conscripts carried along by the mesmeric beat of the drums and the glory of the moment.

"Present!"

Two British battalions raised the muzzles of their rifles. The redcoats were not overawed by the huge column bearing down upon them. They had been brought up on stories of the Peninsula and of the famous victory at Waterloo, tales that told of the thin British lines that had stood with dogged determination in the face of Napoleon's veterans, beating back the best troops that the Emperor could throw against them.

"At one hundred yards, volley fire!"

The redcoats aimed down their sights at the massed Russian ranks, bracing themselves for the powerful kick of their Minié rifles.

"Fire!"

The two battalions fired within moments of each other. Each volley wrought a dreadful destruction. It was as if the head of the column had marched into the maws of a mincing machine. The high-powered Minié bullets gutted men in the fourth, fifth and even the sixth rank. The Russian conscripts were literally torn to pieces, their limbs smashed, huge holes ripped in their flesh.

"For God's sake! Where is Major Peacock?" Jack screamed in frustration.

The noise of the battlefield was immense, overwhelming his brain with its dreadful cacophony. His cry was lost in the volleys of rifle fire that the 19th and the 23rd were pouring into the Russian column to his left. Smoke drifted across the ground, screening events that were unfolding a matter of yards away from where he stood. The Light Company had lost contact with the 23rd during the pell-mell advance up the slope. Away on his right the 7th under Colonel Lacy Yea were surging in a disordered scramble up the slope. Jack heard the Russians to his left return fire but he could not even see the enemy.

He looked around for orders. With Colonel Morris lying dead on the slopes behind the battalion, command had fallen to Major Peacock. Yet there was no sign of him. He should have been on foot with the colour party in the centre of the battalion. With Peacock nowhere in sight, the battalion was leaderless.

242

"Sir! Sir!" Digby-Brown forced his way through the ranks, flushed with sweat. "We must advance!"

"I know. Jesus Christ!" A glance along the stalled line showed that he was not alone in looking around for command. The captains of the other companies had pushed their way to the front of the line, their heads turning this way and that as they tried to find who was commanding the battalion.

"Where the hell is Peacock?" Digby-Brown had to shout to be heard over the sound of the Russian column returning fire.

"Blow me if I know! Jesus Christ! What a fuck-up!"

"Reload!"

As the redcoats brought their rifles down from their shoulders, the Russian column shuddered to a halt. Stunned conscripts who had thought themselves safe deep in the column now found themselves at the front of the attack. The slaughtered front ranks formed a grotesque obstacle, blocking the way forward. Their officers' commands to advance were ignored; not one Russian conscript was willing to clamber over the bodies of their comrades and move closer to the red line that had delivered such an appalling storm of violence. They raised their muskets and returned the British fire from where they stood.

The smoke billowing around the redcoats' line twitched and flickered as the Russian musket balls penetrated the cloud but the volley did little damage. It picked at the redcoats, taking a man here and a man there, but it was nothing compared to the carnage inflicted by the Minié rifles. The British sergeants closed the ranks where the dead and the dying left gaps in the line, the redcoats shuffling together even as they reloaded their rifles.

The second volley tore into the stalled Russian column. Their torn ranks valiantly returned fire, picking off more redcoats. Despite the terrible destruction wrought upon them, the Russians still vastly outnumbered their attackers. They could absorb the terrible casualties and still have enough men to win through — if they could summon the courage to advance.

The redcoats ignored their casualties, always shuffling together, closing the ranks and presenting an unbroken front to the enemy.

The British line fired for a third time.

The dead and the dying covered the ground where the front dozen ranks of Russians had stood. It was a charnel house. The Russian conscripts started to inch backwards. No soldiers in the world could stand against such dreadful destruction. Their ranks were gutted and hundreds of their fellows lay bleeding and torn in front of them. The Russians broke.

History had been repeated. The line had turned the column.

While the 19th and the 23rd were engaging the first and second battalions of the Kazansky Regiment, a second Russian column moved obliquely across the undulating slope of the valley. It was made up of the third and fourth battalions of the Kazansky Regiment

244

and it was aimed at the exposed right flank of the attacking redcoats.

It marched unnoticed. The noise of its advance was lost in the dreadful din of the volleys that were being poured into the first column, and its packed ranks were hidden by the natural folds in the land.

A cloud of skirmishers surrounded the head of the column as thickly as flies on a dung heap. They broadened the point of its attack, and greatly increased its firepower. At its heart, the drummers beat out the staccato rhythm of the march. The ceaseless tempo drove it forward, every step taking it closer towards the flank of the unsuspecting enemy troops.

The 7th Fusiliers stood on the right flank of Codrington's brigade, the last battalion in the line. Colonel Lacy Yea had spurred up the slope far ahead of his men, only slowing his charger as he came up against the rear of the Greenjackets whose skirmish line was strung across the slope in front of his battalion.

Impatiently Lacy Yea twisted in his saddle, his quick temper rising at the slow progress of his men. He had followed Codrington's lead, rushing his men forward, trading the battalion's cohesion for speed. The sight of his men advancing in what could only be described as a mob raised a grimace of distaste on his proud features. This was certainly not the glorious assault he had envisaged, the likes of which were depicted in so many of the pictures on the walls of his family's estate.

"Damn you, sluggards! Advance the Seventh! Press on, men! Press on!"

Lacy Yea had to pull hard to turn the head of his horse round. Despite his impatience, he had to let his men catch up. Colonels were not supposed to charge alone.

As he sought to curb his skittish young horse, he thought he saw movement on the right flank of the brigade's advance. With both hands on the reins, he peered through the smoke, his eyes straining.

The cloud of powder smoke cleared and the head of the second Russian column loomed into view.

Lacy Yea stared in astonishment as the column marched across the slope towards the right flank of his disordered battalion.

He was staring at defeat, at the near certain destruction of his battalion.

The colonel dug in his spurs and raced back down the slope towards his command.

"Seventh Fusiliers! Form line! Form line!"

There was no time for anything but a desperate defence. His only option was to throw his battalion across the front of the Russian advance and risk everything on his men's willingness to stand toe to toe with the enemy horde.

Of the four battalions that had followed Codrington in his advance towards the great redoubt, the third was about to become heavily engaged with the enemy. That left just one to carry on the assault.

The King's Royal Fusiliers would have to capture the great redoubt on their own.

CHAPTER
THIRTY-TWO

"Fusiliers! Fusiliers!" General Codrington galloped across the slope, his grey Arab pony lathered in sweat. The brigade commander had seen the advance grind to a halt as three battalions traded volleys with two massive Russian columns. Only the King's Royal Fusiliers were unengaged but that battalion had stopped advancing and now stood impotently halfway up the slope towards the great redoubt.

Codrington would not let the attack falter. Standing tall in his stirrups, he waved his old-fashioned bicorn hat, bellowing for the fusiliers' attention. "Fusiliers! King's Royal Fusiliers! Advance! Advance!"

Lieutenant Flowers was the first to respond.

"Come on! Follow the general!" he yelled and spurred his tired horse up the slope. "Advance!"

Codrington rammed the decrepit bicorn back on to his head. With his right hand now free, he drew his sword, all the while shouting his encouragement over the din of battle.

The fusiliers responded and once again surged up the slope, led by their general and their adjutant. They cheered as they advanced. It was a ragged cry, barely more than a growl, but it released some of their fear.

Ahead, the great redoubt was ominously silent. The redcoats could see the muzzles of the Russian cannon pointing down the slope. They braced themselves for the twelve Russian guns to fire, a terrible fear building as they got closer to the redoubt. The tension was dreadful. Twelve pieces of artillery would deliver a storm of canister and roundshot that would shred the advancing line, snatching dozens of the fusiliers into oblivion and leaving countless more twitching and bleeding in its wake.

Yet still the redcoats marched forward, their desperate courage and sheer bloody-mindedness pushing them onwards. They marched as if into the face of a violent storm, leaning forward as if battered by a fierce wind, their muscles straining. Their chests heaved with the exertion of the advance, and the pitiless heat of the sun baked them in their thick red jackets.

With four hundred yards to go, a young drummer boy in the centre of the battalion stumbled and fell, his body tumbling over the large drum tethered to his front. The terrified youngster remained on the ground, curling round the broken instrument, hugging it close as he lay weeping and trembling with overwhelming fear.

At three hundred and fifty yards, a fusilier in McCulloch's company let his rifle slip from his sweating hands. The redcoat marched on regardless, leaving his weapon, terror driving him forward, all rational thought forced from his brain. The discarded rifle lay abandoned, trampled and broken under the heedless boots of the fusiliers that marched behind.

With three hundred yards left to go, the Russian battery fired.

The power of the volley was terrible. The solid roundshot cut through the British ranks, each missile killing several men, the red-hot iron balls passing through successive bodies. Large gaps were blown in the ranks.

The screaming began.

Despite their horrendous casualties, the British line continued forward, heedless of those left behind, stepping over the dead and the dying, callously ignoring the shrieks of agony and the pleas for aid.

The first Russian volley released the tension. The redcoats' terror was still bright but now the agony of anticipation was over. There was nothing left but to close with the enemy and exact a bitter revenge on the merciless Russian gunners.

The Russian gunners swabbed out the red-hot barrels of their guns, producing hissing clouds of steam, then they frantically rammed and reloaded them. They knew their survival depended on tearing the attacking line to shreds, on slaughtering enough of the British so that the survivors broke and ran rather than face certain death from the guns. If the redcoats got into the battery their revenge would be dreadful. The terrible steel bayonets that glinted so brightly in the sunshine would hack and gouge at the men who had laid down the barrage of fire with such ruthless precision.

The Russian gunners switched to loading canister, a tin can packed full of musket balls that would explode as it emerged from the muzzle of the cannon. It was a brutal weapon, a close-range killing machine.

The Russian guns fired again.

Jack whimpered in terror as the blast of canister tore through the Light Company. Sergeant Adams took a load full in the face. His head exploded before Jack's horrified eyes, splattering the men around him with blood, brains and scraps of flesh. His body lurched forward like a grotesque headless puppet for another pace before it fell to the ground, blood pouring from the tattered stump of his neck.

More fusiliers had fallen to the devastating fire. English Davies lay twisted on the ground behind the advancing line, his stomach ripped open, his guts spilling out of the terrible wound to pulse, bloody and blue, in the bright sunshine. At his side, another fusilier screamed abuse at the Russian gunners whose shot had smashed his legs into a vile pulp.

Some fusiliers took their wounds in silence, pressing on even as their blood dripped from their bodies. Lieutenant Thomas wept as he marched, his left arm hanging loosely against his side, the limb shattered and bleeding profusely from a deep wound above the elbow. The subaltern's tears carved thin channels through his dirt-encrusted face before the young officer smeared them away with his sleeve, more concerned that the men should not see him cry than he was about the severity of the wound.

Fusilier O'Callaghan, one of the company's new recruits, calmly bent to the ground and retrieved his severed arm, ignoring the blood that spurted from the tattered remnant of flesh that had once been his elbow. He turned serenely to begin the long march to the rear, the detached limb cradled carefully in the crook of his surviving arm.

Another volley blasted down the slope. Soldiers littered the ground, corpses tripping the living. Wounded redcoats plucked at the coat tails of those still standing, begging for aid, for water or for a bullet to end their agony.

Jack turned away from the horror being wrought on his men, his stomach churning in revulsion. His company was being destroyed before his eyes and he was powerless to stop it. He meant nothing against such destruction. All his ambition and all his hopes washed away in the sea of blood.

The Fusiliers had no choice but to advance. If they stopped then they would be slaughtered where they stood. Instinctively they bunched together, unwittingly making the gunners' work easier. Jack forced himself forward. He wanted to lead from the centre of the battalion line. He knew it was a pathetic gesture but it was one he was determined to make. As he moved, he cast a glance along the ranks, ever hopeful that Slater would have been struck down by the terrible storm.

Slater noticed Jack's look and he met his eyes with a cold flat stare. He was covered in blood but it was not his own; the gore belonged to a nearby fusilier who had been torn apart by a burst of canister. Slater spat in derision and Jack looked away, trying to suppress the dread that flared in his soul.

CHAPTER
THIRTY-THREE

Step by bloody step, the fusiliers forced themselves up the slope. Lieutenant Flowers led them forward, his resilient horse overtaking Codrington's tiring young Arab. The young adjutant was determined to be first into the redoubt, to follow his colonel's example by leading the battalion from the front.

As the distance closed, he gathered his reins in one hand and with the other gripped and regripped the handle of his sword. Horse and rider tensed as they readied to take a wild leap over the wall of the redoubt, as if it was a hedge in a fox hunt. Behind him, the fusiliers picked up the pace, desperate to cover the last few yards before the Russian gunners could fire again.

The front hooves of Flowers' horse had already left the ground to leap over the wall when the Russian battery fired again. The adjutant was so close to the muzzle of a Russian cannon that he and his horse were touched by the blast of flame that leapt out of its mouth. A heartbeat later and both ceased to exist, a single blast of canister striking them in mid-air, instantly reducing man and beast to nothing more than a gory tangle of blood and offal.

The British line staggered under the volley. At such close range each load of canister cut a fan-shaped wedge of death through the already badly mauled redcoats. Jack screamed as the guns fired, a shriek of complete terror that was lost in the massive explosion. Instinctively, he crossed his arms to protect his face from the blast. The smoke from the volley choked him, the stink of rotten eggs filled his nostrils. The canister obliterated the leading ranks but somehow he remained whole.

He made for the wall of the redoubt. He saw General Codrington leap the four-foot-high wall seconds before he reached it himself. He planted one foot in the gap between the two tree trunks that had been laid horizontally to form the base of the wall and propelled himself up and over it. Sharp splinters tore at his hands, the sudden sharp pain nearly causing him to drop the sword that he held tightly in his right hand. His men piled over after him. As their boots thumped down hard on the Russians' side of the redoubt, Jack expected a volley of musketry or thrusting bayonets to greet them but no enemy infantry contested their arrival. They had abandoned the Russian gunners, and the gunners themselves were trying to escape. After the final volley they had dragged their guns backwards and were now frantically trying to limber the weapons up to the waiting teams of horses.

Not far from where Jack stood, a Russian officer was using his riding whip to exhort his men to hurry up and finish attaching one cannon to the limber and team of horses that would drag it to safety. Jack saw the colour drain from the Russian's face as he caught sight of the redcoats vaulting over the wall of the redoubt. The officer dropped his whip and drew a thin curved sabre. He swung it hard against the back of one of his men, cursing his slowness.

Fusilier Dodds landed next to Jack and the redcoat screamed his disgust at the Russian gunners' attempts to escape. "Stole away!"

"Dodds, follow me!"

Jack would not let the enemy slip away without a fight. He had watched his men massacred at the hands of these Russian gunners. It was time to exact a revenge for their suffering.

With Dodds screaming incoherently at his side, Jack charged at the Russian gunners. His anger was terrible, a remorseless rage that corrupted his soul. Nothing mattered except for the burning need to bury his blade in the flesh of the Russian gunners. His fear had been banished, the fury that replaced it all-consuming and terrible.

The Russian gunners saw them coming. In a final, desperate bid to escape, the horse team whipped their mounts into motion. The gun train lurched forward, its trail gouging a deep channel in the ground. The gun twisted and for a moment it looked as if it would overturn. Then with a jolt it straightened and the horses surged away from the redcoats. But in their haste the gunners had left two of the traces unbuckled. With a loud snap of breaking lines, the terrified horses tore free of the cannon. They raced away, their sides whipped by their riders who left the cannon and their comrades behind.

Jack focused his attention on the slim Russian officer who had been beating his men. Jack was close enough to see every detail of the Russian's face, from his gaunt, beardless cheeks to the thin moustache on his upper lip. His pinched lips stood out, cherry-red against his white face. The young officer put his right foot forward, smoothly taking the position of a trained swordsman, his thin sabre pointing at Jack, his left hand angled backwards, his weight balanced on the balls of his feet.

The idea of fencing with the Russian officer never entered Jack's mind. He ran at the Russian with wild abandon, a banshee cry of fear and anger bursting from his mouth. He swept his sword forward, slamming the sabre to one side, and crashed into the Russian with a teeth-juddering impact, knocking him on to his back. Jack landed on top of him with such force that he felt ribs breaking in the Russian's chest. Jack pulled his arm back and punched the iron hilt of his sword into the man's unprotected face. Once, twice then a third time, beating the Russian to death.

Armed with swords, handspikes and rammers the Russian gunners charged the fusiliers with hopeless bravery. One gunner made straight for Jack, his mouth pulled back in a snarl of fury. Jack flung his sword up, his knees still pressing down on the corpse of the Russian officer, and deflected the gunner's handspike but the wild parry threw him off balance and he fell off the body on to the ground. The gunner recovered quickly and twisted round, aiming his makeshift weapon straight at Jack's exposed chest.

The flash of a rifle seared over Jack. The bullet drove the gunner backwards, leaving a large hole in his dark blue jacket. The Minié ball had struck him in the left-hand side of the chest, killing him instantly.

"Got the fucker!" Fusilier Dodds hauled his officer to his feet, a ferocious grin on his filthy face. "Come on, sir. No time for a lie-down yet."

Jack grunted his thanks and braced himself for the next attack.

It came from a huge Russian gunner who swung a wooden swab at his head. Drops of water flew from the damp fleece that still covered the last foot of its length. Jack ducked, almost thrusting his face on to the short sword of a second gunner who attacked from the right. The blade flashed by a mere inch from Jack's face, forcing him to twist desperately out of its way.

Fusilier Dodds fought at Jack's side, doing his best to protect his officer from the melee that surged around them. With a vicious snarl, he drove his weapon into the stomach of the gunner who collapsed over the blade, his fingers instinctively grabbing hold of it. Dodds pulled his bayonet back, mercilessly slicing through the dying Russian's grasping fingers. Stamping his right foot forward, Dodds repeatedly stabbed his weapon forward in short efficient thrusts, the seventeen-inch bayonet deadly in the close quarters scrimmage.

Dodds's action gave Jack the crucial few moments' respite he needed to snatch his handgun from its holster. It was a five-shot, percussion, double-action revolver made by Dean and Adams, the best that money could buy. Jack pulled the trigger five times in rapid succession, a merciless close-range barrage that threw three Russian gunners to the ground.

It was too much for the other terrified gunners, they dropped their improvised weapons and ran. Other fusiliers who had made it over the wall raised their rifles to their shoulders and fired at the fleeing Russians. Not one made it more than a dozen yards. In their thirst for revenge, the fusiliers kept firing, riddling the corpses of the Russian gunners where they lay.

"Cease fire! Cease fire, damn it!"

Jack screamed at his men to stop wasting their ammunition, using his sword to batter one man's rifle upwards so that it fired impotently into the sky.

"Cease fire, damn you."

The rifle fire died out as Jack regained control of his men. The Russian gunners had been massacred. The fusiliers had exacted their revenge.

They had taken the Great Redoubt.

CHAPTER
THIRTY-FOUR

There was no joy at what they had achieved. No cheers of celebration. No shouts of victory. The fusiliers had paid too high a price. The officers re-formed their companies, the reduced ranks and missing faces a reminder of the men who had fallen.

The terraced slope that ran down to the Alma River was covered with redcoated corpses. On the right flank, the 7th Fusiliers under Lacy Yea were still engaged in a dreadful war of attrition with the second Russian column, which was slowly grinding the British ranks into oblivion. The other two battalions, the 19th and the 23rd, were picking their way up the slope towards the redoubt.

For the moment, the King's Royal Fusiliers were alone. The respite would not last for long; the Russian general was sure to try to recapture the redoubt. He could ill afford to leave such a strategic strongpoint in the hands of the enemy.

The remnants of Codrington's Brigade would have to defend what they had won.

"Sir." Digby-Brown thrust a scrap of paper towards his captain.

Jack was scratching the battalion's initials into the barrel of the cannon that had so nearly escaped.

"What's this?" he asked.

"Butcher's bill, sir. As best as I can tell, we're down to forty-nine effectives. We lost Sergeants Shepherd and Adams." Digby-Brown's voice was tight with tension.

"Thank you."

"Did you see the colonel go down, sir?"

"I did."

"And Flowers?"

"I did."

Digby-Brown closed his eyes to shut out the tears. With a visible effort, he composed himself, his captain's calm and measured tones helping to steady him. "Mr Thomas is wounded, sir. He refuses to retire and go to the surgeons. Perhaps you would have a word with him."

"Perhaps he has earned the right to decide for himself."

Digby-Brown opened his mouth to argue but stopped himself. His captain was right. "Yes, sir."

"Thank you, Mr Digby-Brown."

"What for, sir?"

"For agreeing with me." Jack smiled wearily.

"At least it sounds like the French are still attacking." Digby-Brown pointed towards the west where banks of powder smoke rolled across the battlefield.

"Don't worry about the French." Jack kneaded the small of his back. "They can look after themselves. I'm more worried about us. We appear to have been abandoned. I don't see the guards or any of those Scots bastards, do you?"

Digby-Brown looked anxiously towards the Alma River. The Duke of Cambridge commanded the 1st Division, which was made up of the Highland Brigade and the Guards Brigade. The two brigades should have been advancing hard on the Light Division's heels, ready to support their attack as soon as it ran out of momentum or secured its objectives. Instead, they had been halted on the far side of the Alma where they were enduring heavy artillery fire.

"Oh God. They were meant to be right behind us."

"They were indeed, Mr Digby-Brown. Perhaps someone forgot to tell them that. Nothing would surprise me. I suggest you make the most of the peace and quiet. Tell Sergeant Baker to check weapons and ammunition and see to the wounded as best you can. I expect it will get pretty noisy around here soon."

"Yes, sir." Digby-Brown hurried off, glad to turn his mind to practical matters.

To the south, the vast bulk of the unengaged Russian army was preparing to fight. Twelve battalions of infantry were forming into more huge columns. The Russian general's conscript army knew no other way to fight. Three thousand cavalry could be seen away to the south-east. The Russians' second prepared position, the lesser redoubt, lay untouched on the Russian general's far right flank, a battery of artillery in place. The fusiliers may have seized the larger of the two earthworks but vast numbers of the Russian force were still waiting to be committed to the battle, their men fresh and eager.

Codrington's brigade was dangerously exposed. They had to hold fast until reinforcements could arrive. If the Russians recaptured the great redoubt, the whole bloody assault would have to be repeated and the sacrifice the redcoats had already made would count for nothing.

"We made it, sir."

Jack looked up at his orderly, unable to summon the energy to greet him with more than a thin smile. Smith had lost his shako in the assault but otherwise appeared to have survived unscathed.

Smith reached forward and prised Jack's sword from his grasp. He bent down to clean the bloody blade on the jacket of a dead Russian gunner. "Those Russians were lousy shots. Somehow they managed to miss Slater's hulking great arse."

"The bastard can't be so lucky all day."

"He won't be if I have anything to do with it. I'll worry about Slater; you concentrate on looking after yourself. You charged those bleeding Russki gunners like a madman."

"Don't worry about me. I lead a charmed life."

"Fucking foolish thinking, that is. Now give me your revolver. I'll bet you've forgotten to reload it."

Jack meekly handed over his revolver and its pouch of ammunition, and took back his hastily cleaned sword. Slater was almost as much of a threat to his survival as the Russians, it would take a miracle to survive the day.

"Stand to! The bastards are coming!"

The handful of piquets that Codrington had thrown forward hastened to rejoin their battalions.

To the south-west a fresh Russian column was making its way across the sloping high ground towards the great redoubt. The column was enormous, much bigger than the one beaten back by the 19th and 23rd. The period of peace had been short and the fusiliers had been given little time to reorganise.

The three battered battalions formed a single long line. The King's Royal Fusiliers were on the right, closest to the column. They would be the first to open fire.

Major Peacock had emerged from wherever he had been hiding. Someone had managed to secure Colonel Morris's massive black charger and Peacock rode forward on it to stand in front of the fusiliers and address them. The horse fought the major's unfamiliar control and he had to pull sharply on the reins.

Jack swore under his breath. The thought of Peacock being in charge of the battalion was galling. He was spared from listening to whatever poppycock Peacock believed would stir the men to fight because he could not hear what he said through the rattle of French and Russian musket fire to the west. Mercifully, the major's speech did not last long. If he had expected a rousing cheer for his efforts then he was disappointed. The fusiliers greeted his words with stony silence, instead busying themselves with the last-minute preparations of men about to fight. They checked and rechecked their rifles and their ammunition, fidgeted with their pouches and adjusted their uniforms.

"Battalion! At two hundred yards, volley fire! Ready!"

The fusiliers lifted their rifles and sighted the muzzles on the enormous mass that rumbled across the slope towards them. There were enough men in the column to outnumber the brigade three or four times over, more men than had been in the whole of the Light Division when it had first formed up that morning. The pulsating mass of Russian conscripts cheered wildly as the drums drove them forward with their hypnotic rhythm.

Boom-boom. Boom-boom. Boom-boom-boom.
Boom-boom. Boom-boom. Boom-boom-boom.
Boom-boom. Boom-boom. Boom-boom-boom.

The fingers of hundreds of fusiliers tightened on their triggers. Men drew in a breath, releasing half to steady their aim, their muscles quivering with expectation, the slightest increase in pressure on the trigger all that was needed to send the Minié bullet spinning towards the massed ranks.

"Don't fire! Don't fire!"

The panicked shout came from Jack's right, from somewhere towards the centre of the long line. The fusiliers lifted their eyes from their sights and looked at each other in consternation.

"Don't fire! For God's sake, don't fire! It's the French!" Major Peacock spurred his charger forward as he shrieked at the battalion, waving his hat to attract their attention. The buglers picked up the command and the call to cease fire was repeated.

The huge column moved steadily closer, oblivious to the confusion in the redcoats' ranks.

Jack squinted at the advancing column. Every instinct in him screamed that it could not be the French. It simply did not make any sense that a French column would be advancing towards the redoubt from that direction. As Jack stared at the column, his eyes watering with the strain, sunlight glinted off the pointed metal helmets that the approaching men were wearing. Only one army wore the spiked helmet. The column was Russian.

CHAPTER
THIRTY-FIVE

Captain Brewer raised his sword. His Grenadier Company had been hard hit that day. Not much more than half his men were still able to fight. But Brewer was confident the brigade still had enough fight in it to see off the Russian column. After all, they had all witnessed the way the battalion volleys had repelled the first Russian column. The bigger the column, the bigger the mess it would leave on the ground.

At first, Brewer did not hear Major Peacock's panicked shouts. The noise coming from the advancing column assaulted his senses, the rhythmic pounding of the drums filling his eardrums. He only became aware that something was awry when his covering sergeant tugged urgently at his arm and pointed towards the major's frantic activity.

"What the blazes?" Brewer could barely credit Peacock's flustered warning. "They're not French! The fool! Grenadiers, ignore him! Ignore him, I say. The man is deranged! Present!"

Brewer's grenadiers hesitated. Peacock continued to scream at the battalion, his warning spreading uncertainty throughout the ranks. Other companies were lowering their rifles, their captains standing open-mouthed in astonishment, bewildered by the rapid change of events.

"Take aim, damn your eyes. Those bastards are Russian! Take aim!" Brewer exhorted his command.

Towards the centre of the battalion, puzzled fusilier officers were stepping forward to peer through telescopes or field glasses to confirm the identity of the soldiers. Powder smoke still billowed across the battlefield, obscuring portions of the column.

Brewer looked at it again, doubt beginning to eat at him. Maybe his eyes had deceived him. But no, he was certain the column was Russian.

Brewer swallowed the knot of fear that formed in his throat. If he was wrong then he was on the point of causing a terrible catastrophe. But to let the enemy close unchallenged would bring about even greater disaster.

"Fire! Fire!" Brewer abandoned the usual pattern of orders, desperate to get his men firing at the enemy. He frantically pulled his revolver from its holster and fired in the general direction of the column. "Fire!"

The column was far out of the revolver's range and the single shot would not even reach the closest ranks, but it was not wasted. Its loud report secured his men's attention and confirmed his orders.

"Fire, damn you!" Brewer fired his revolver a second time and the grenadiers responded.

They might as well have saved their powder for all the effect their volley had. A handful of men in the foremost rank of the ponderous column staggered and fell but the following ranks flowed over the fallen, their pace unfaltering. It would take more than one battered company to have any impact on the immense column.

"You fool, Brewer!" Peacock yanked at the reins of Morris's charger which fought him at every turn. The horse was barely under Peacock's control as it pranced towards the grenadier company on the battalion's right flank. "They are the French, I tell you! The French! Don't fire!"

Brewer glanced at his major and for a second he saw the panic in his eyes. He looked away in disgust and screamed at his men to reload faster.

Peacock was astonished at the look of contempt and fury in Brewer's expression. He pulled the charger's head back, bringing the horse to an abrupt halt, his bowels loosening with a terrible feeling of dread. He looked again at the massive column. It was close now. Dangerously close. And the identity of the soldiers was obvious. Peacock could see the individual faces of the men in the first rank. He could make out details of their uniforms. Thousands of Russian infantry were bearing down on the redcoats' depleted formation.

"Retreat! Retreat!" Peacock's panic was complete. His disastrous error overwhelmed what little sanity remained in his terrified mind. "Sound the retreat! Save yourselves! Retreat!" Peacock was raging, his voice shrieking in panic. The huge horse beneath him responded to its rider's terror. It reared back on to its hind feet, its huge hooves lashing furiously at the air. Peacock was thrown from the saddle and hit the ground hard. The violent impact silenced his terrified screams.

But the men had already started to respond, obeying the order without hesitation. The battalion's buglers had changed their call, replacing the order to cease fire with the order to pull back.

The right-hand third of the British line dissolved. The panic was infectious; men elbowed and pushed at each other in their haste to get away.

On the left, the remaining two battalions of Codrington's command watched in horror as the King's Royal Fusiliers ran in panic. One-third of the line was in full retreat. The regular battalion volleys, which should already have been flensing the compacted ranks of the Russian column, had been replaced by an uncontrolled rout. It left Codrington and the commanders of the 19th and the 23rd little choice. Within moments of the first fusiliers breaking, the rest of the brigade ordered their own buglers to sound the call to retire.

The British line disintegrated and the remnants of Codrington's brigade gave up the great redoubt which had been captured at such a terrible price.

Jack watched appalled as the rest of the battalion broke and ran. The Russians were being allowed to recapture the vital strongpoint without a fight. Jack would not let that happen, even if it meant the Light Company facing the Russian column alone.

"Stay where you are! Don't any bastard move!"

The Light Company froze, heeding their captain without question. The men's faces betrayed their confusion and their fear. Yet they stayed in their ranks.

"Sloames! What's happening?" Captain McCulloch ran towards the Light Company. His men were still in place but they were wavering. It would take only one man to join the mad rush and the rest of the company would be certain to follow.

"Those are Russians!" Jack waved his arm frantically at the monstrous column.

McCulloch understood in an instant. "Second Company, form line! Form line! Stay with me!"

It would take precious seconds for McCulloch to get his men back under full control. Jack knew he could not wait.

"Light Company!" His mouth felt terribly dry, his tongue cleaving to the roof of his mouth as he tried to shout. "Fire!"

His men heard him. As one, they pulled their triggers. The heavy Minié bullets wrought a horrible destruction on the unfortunate souls who were unlucky enough to be hit but it was no more than a pinprick on the immense body of approaching men.

"Reload! Reload!" Jack screamed at his men. His voice was drowned out by a volley from McCulloch's company, sharply followed by one from Brewer's Grenadier Company.

Three battered companies were all that remained of the battalion. Just over one hundred men standing against thousands, a boulder in the torrent of a flooding river.

Alone they were never going to have enough firepower to stop the Russian column. They were attempting to achieve the impossible. It was brave. It was magnificent. It was also foolish.

As the Light Company fired a second volley, the leading ranks of the Russian column raised their muskets. Only the first two ranks could bring their weapons to bear but that still meant hundreds of muskets were aimed at the three companies of redcoats.

"Dear God! For what we are about to receive —" Fusilier Dodds never completed his sentence, his words drowned out by the thunderclap of the Russians' volley.

Dozens of men fell to the ground, their screams of agony loud in the ears of the redcoats left standing. Their line was torn into fragments by the single volley. To stand in the face of such might was futile.

To his amazement, Jack was unharmed. The musket balls had whipped past his head with a terrifying crack but somehow, his luck was still holding out. He knew he now had no choice but to retreat and save as many of his men as he could.

"Fusiliers! Follow me!" Jack roared at his men, pulling at those closest to him. "This way, boys! It's time to go."

Slowly the fusiliers understood. Jack pushed and shoved them towards the security of a fold in the ground three hundred yards to the north-west. The path Jack had chosen would take his men away from the rest of the British army but at least it would get them out of the path of the Russian column, and at that moment that was all that mattered.

"McCulloch! This way!" Jack yelled at his fellow captain. The two companies were now hopelessly mixed together, cohesion forgotten in the rush to get away.

Captain McCulloch elbowed his way over to Jack. McCulloch's uniform bore witness to just how close the enemy's fire had come to injuring him. One epaulet hung by a thread where a bullet had scored the shoulder of his scarlet coat and a single round hole had been punched through the centre of his shako, smack in the middle of the battalion's brass badge.

"Which way, Sloames?"

Jack pointed to the shallow depression he hoped would offer the battered fusiliers some sanctuary.

"Do you see it? The fold in the ground. Take the men there. I'll bring up the rear."

McCulloch nodded. "Right. Fusiliers, follow me!"

McCulloch pushed through the crush of men, shouting at them to follow him and windmilling his arm to signal the direction. The men closest to him followed immediately, while Jack stayed where he was, pushing and shoving any who hesitated or dawdled.

Dodds came past, a fleeting grin acknowledging his captain. With him came Dawson, Taylor and Welsh Davies, followed by the resolute form of Sergeant Baker who still looked as crisp as if it was time for morning parade. Jack was delighted to see so many familiar faces still present.

Lieutenant Digby-Brown staggered past, blood trickling from a thin wound across his forehead. He was hatless, grimy, bloodied and bedraggled but alive. There was no sign of Lieutenant Thomas, or of Tommy Smith. Jack had to force his fears for their safety from his mind. His sole concern had to be for the fusiliers who had made it.

There was no sign of Brewer or any of his grenadiers and Jack hoped to God they had been able to get away. Of the rest of the battalion, there was no sign. The two companies had been abandoned.

When the last of his men had passed him, Jack turned to make his own way to the fold in the ground.

He never saw the rifle butt that smashed into the back of his head. He was unconscious before his body hit the ground.

CHAPTER
THIRTY-SIX

Jack fought against the layers of suffocating darkness that dragged him ever deeper into their dreadful embrace, smothering his will to live. He struggled against their icy grasp, refusing to submit to their clutches, striving to reach the glimmer of light that hovered above him.

Gingerly he opened his eyes.

The point of a razor-sharp bayonet glinted less than an inch above his face.

"Lie still, you dirty little fucker, or I'll stick you now."

Slater was on top of Jack's body, his huge frame pinning him to the ground.

Jack could feel blood running down the back of his neck into the collar of his uniform coat. His vision misted over with the pain in his head. He gritted his teeth and fought to stay conscious, terrified that passing out would be the last thing he ever did.

"Good boy. I'm pleased you woke up. I would've hated sticking you without you knowing it." Slater's face was so close that his moustache scratched Jack's cheek. The noxious stench of his foetid breath filled Jack's nostrils.

Slater eased the bayonet downwards, inching it steadily lower. Jack could smell the oil on the weapon, the sharp metal tang of the honed edge. Slater brought the blade down until its wickedly sharp point was pressed against the soft underside of Jack's chin.

The bayonet pierced his skin. Jack felt Slater's muscles tense as he readied himself to slide the bayonet up through Jack's jaw and into his brain.

The swing of a black regulation-issue British boot caught Slater above his left temple and knocked him sideways. The breath rushed back into Jack's lungs as Slater's huge weight left his chest, followed by a bright flash of pain as the bayonet scored the underside of his chin.

"Get up, sir!"

Jack's saviour leapt across his prostrate body, aiming another vicious kick at Slater's head. With reflexes that belied his size, Slater thrust his right arm upwards, taking the kick on his forearm, a hissed oath betraying the pain it inflicted.

"Jack! Get up!"

Jack's hands had instinctively gone to his throat where Slater's bayonet had drawn blood, convinced his throat had been cut. To his relief, his probing revealed nothing more than a scratch. He was not going to die. Not yet.

Using his elbows as props, Jack lifted his shoulders from the ground. His vision swam and his head protested at the movement. Through his blurred sight, Jack saw Slater roll on to his knees before throwing himself forward, smacking with bone-crunching force into the body of Tommy Smith.

Jack had not seen his orderly in the mad scramble for safety. Yet, even in the confusion and chaos of the retreat, Smith had been keeping watch over his friend.

The two bodies crashed to the ground, wrapped in a violent embrace. Fists flew as the two men writhed in the dirt, punching grabbing and scratching to get the upper hand.

Smith fought hard, at least twice landing a blow on Slater's head that would have floored an ordinary man. But Slater was as strong as an ox and shook off the blows. Never before had Smith fought against such strength. He knew he could not take much more of the punishment Slater's huge fists were dishing out.

He threw his weight forward, ignoring the fists that were aimed with such power, risking everything in a final, reckless effort. For a second he thought the sudden lunge had caught Slater off balance and he pushed with all his might, grasping each of Slater's forearms in a desperate bid to topple him. But Slater pushed back, returning the pressure, first matching it then overpowering it, so that it was Smith who was forced backwards.

Slater seized on the opening. He thrust Smith hard into the ground then straddled his body, pulling one arm free from the fallen man's grasp and delivering a single massive blow to the now unprotected face. Smith's head lolled backwards, blood streaming from both nostrils. Slater followed the first vicious punch with another, then another. Smith raised his arms to shield his face, relinquishing his hold on Slater's other arm in his desperation to ward off the succession of vicious punches. With both arms free, Slater went wild, smashing down blow after blow coming away smothered in blood.

"Stop it!"

The voice sounded to Smith as if it was far away but mercifully Slater's fists stopped their brutal assault.

"Get up. Easy now or I'll blow your damn brains out."

Slater's weight eased off Smith's chest. Gingerly Smith opened his eyes and saw the muzzle of a revolver pressed hard against Slater's temple.

"You took your bleeding time!" Smith wiped the sleeve of his tunic over his bloody nose and mouth.

"I thought you had the measure of him. I didn't want to spoil your fun." Jack's voice cracked with pain. He was covered in his own blood, the hair on the back of his head was matted and wet, and the dark-blue collar of his jacket was black with it.

"I'd have killed him if you hadn't been lying in the fucking way." Smith wearily levered himself to his feet and picked up his rifle. The pain was bad but there was no time to dwell on it. Not with Slater still breathing.

Smith glanced around. The men from the Light and 2nd Companies had almost all made it to the dead ground Jack had spotted, only a few stragglers were still in sight. The great redoubt was swarming with Russian infantry, and to the south he could see more Russian gun teams heading towards the earthwork.

The Russian general was reinforcing his flank, bringing fresh artillery forward.

The three men were dangerously close to the enemy. Russian skirmishers were moving towards them to cover the flanks of the redoubt and clear the last ragtag groups of redcoats that were all that was left of the desperate assault on the redoubt. They would soon be in range. Slater had to be dealt with quickly.

"Quick, Jack. Shoot the bastard now."

"Shoot him?" Jack sounded genuinely surprised at the idea.

"What, do you want to dance with him? Of course shoot him. Before those Russian buggers do it for you."

Jack was struggling to think clearly. His mind felt as if it had turned to porridge, so laboured and turgid was his thinking. Slater was licking his lips nervously and his eyes kept swivelling to the side to keep sight of the revolver pressing against his temple. Jack knew Slater would not hesitate to blow his own brains out if the roles were reversed. But to kill a man in cold blood, even one as deserving of death as Slater, was something he could not make himself do. He had seen too much death already today.

"Shoot him, Jack, for God's sake!"

Still Jack did not pull the trigger. The danger from the Russian skirmishers increased with every second he delayed.

"Oh, you stupid bastard. I'll fucking do it!" Smith raised his rifle, pulling the heavy lock back.

"No!" Jack bellowed as Smith's finger curled round the trigger of his rifle.

A rifle fired, its sharp, barking cough distinctive, but the sound was too distant have come from Smith's weapon.

The crack of a bullet whipping past his head ended any confusion in Jack's mind. The first rifle to fire was swiftly followed by another and then another. He had delayed too long. The Russian skirmishers had them in their sights.

It was the second bullet fired by the Russian sharpshooters that did all the damage. It hit Tommy Smith on the left cheek, the side of his face that was angled towards the enemy skirmishers.

The bullet ripped through skin and bone as if it was not there, tearing away the lower portion of Smith's face; mouth, lips, nose and chin, all were smashed in a nauseating explosion of blood and flesh.

Smith swayed but stayed on his feet. For one haunting moment, his eyes locked with Jack's, the gaze betraying the appalling shock of the terrible wound. Then he fell, his hands grasping for the lower half of his face, which was no longer there. He hit the ground and writhed in agony, still alive but unable to scream, his blood gushing from the grotesque wound.

Jack ran.

Bullets cracked and fizzed past him. He spared no thought for Slater, or for the direction he took. He ran to escape the look of horrified anguish in his orderly's eyes.

Time slowed. Jack felt as if he were wading through a lake of treacle. Bullets snapped through the air around him but no matter how hard he tried to run, the ground moved with stubborn slowness beneath his feet.

A huge fountain of earth exploded in front of him. The shockwave was tremendous, it snatched Jack from his feet as if he was a mere leaf blown in a gale. Fragments of the exploding shell ripped into his body, lacerating his arms and legs and burning like red-hot pokers. Then he hit the ground with a force that jarred every bone in his body.

With the last scraps of his strength, Jack curled into a ball, his legs pulled right into his stomach, his head buried against his knees. He wrapped himself round his pain and wept.

CHAPTER
THIRTY-SEVEN

"Mr Sloames! Mr Sloames, wake up!"

Jack was dimly aware of somebody shaking his shoulder but he ignored it. He lay curled on the ground, his eyes open and staring yet seeing nothing. His tears were spent, the only evidence of their passing the thin tracks they had cut into the blood and grime that covered his face.

"Mr Sloames! We need you! Mr Sloames, can you stand? Are you hurt?"

The questions assaulted his fragile peace, forcing him back into the awful reality of the present.

"What is it?" Jack's voice came out as a croak, the voice of a crotchety old man disturbed from an afternoon sleep.

"Thank God. I thought you were dead. Can you stand, sir?"

Jack's battered mind was slowly coming to life. "Digby-Brown?"

Lieutenant Digby-Brown saw the matted hair on the back of his captain's head for the first time as Jack gingerly lifted it from the ground. "Yes, sir. Goodness me, are you badly hurt?"

Jack ignored the pointless question and waved his arm for assistance. Pain cascaded through his skull as he was hauled upright and dark shadows clouded his vision. Before he could fall, Digby-Brown took a firm grip of his arms.

"Crikey, sir. You look awful."

Jack was trying to take an inventory of his injuries. Every single part of his body was in pain and seemed to be leaking blood but, individually, none of the wounds seemed too severe. By some miracle, his body was still in one piece. The same could not be said of his soul.

His awareness was improving with every second. The blind panic and horror triggered by Tommy Smith's devastated face was receding into the depths of his mind. There it lurked, like some evil monster hidden in the shadows. For the moment it was contained, pushed to one side so that he could start to function again.

"Mr Sloames?"

Jack pressed his hand into the base of his spine, the comforting habit of kneading his aching back instinctive. He spat out a wad of bloody phlegm and wiped a muck-encrusted hand across his face. "Where's the company?"

"Well, sir." Digby-Brown looked closely at his captain. A hint of colour had returned to his cheeks and his eyes seemed focused. Digby-Brown withdrew his supporting arm but kept it outstretched in case Sloames began to sway. "It's all a bit of a mess, sir. I'm not quite sure where the rest of the company went."

"What about Mr McCulloch and the Second Company?"

"The last I saw they were heading back towards the Seventh."

"Jesus Christ!" Jack swore as the pressure of his hand on his spine sent a lance of pain down his legs.

Digby-Brown took this as the captain's verdict on the confusion and disorder. "I brought as many of the men as I could find."

"You did? Why?" Jack's knees were trembling with the effort of keeping him upright.

"Well, to find you, sir."

"To find me?"

"It seemed like a good idea at the time, sir. I remembered seeing you directing us then I turned round and you had disappeared. I was sure you couldn't have gone far."

"And the men came with you?"

"Willingly, sir. They seemed as keen to find you as I was myself."

"Dear God in heaven. What a bloody mess."

"Quite frankly, sir, it's a fucking disaster."

Jack barely noticed Digby-Brown's uncharacteristic language. They had all been changed by the day's bitter events. "So what did you have in mind to do next?"

"I rather hoped you could tell me, sir."

"You are right. I can. We are going over there." Jack painfully drew his sword.

Digby-Brown's eyes widened. His captain was pointing his sword directly at the great redoubt which was now swarming with Russian skirmishers.

The men Digby-Brown had managed to lead out of the confusion gathered around Jack. He watched them closely. Dodds was there. His lean face was splattered with blood but he had the same look of keen determination he had shown when they captured the redoubt. Next to Dodds stood Welsh Davies, Dawson, Taylor and fifteen other fusiliers from the Light Company. Sergeant Baker was the only non-commissioned officer left and Jack nodded in his direction, acknowledging his presence. There was one face Jack did not recognise, a young fusilier with sunken cheeks and a trace of fluff on his upper lip that betrayed his boyish attempts to grow a moustache.

"Who the hell are you?"

"Flanagan, sir. From Fourth Company."

"Fourth Company? What on earth are you doing here?"

"I got lost, sir." The young fusilier looked around him with huge eyes, nervous of being among strange soldiers even if they did come from his own regiment.

"Well, as of now you're in the Light Company. We will need all the help we can get." Jack scanned the faces that looked towards him. The weight of the responsibility was heavy, the look of expectation in the grimy faces unnerving. But he met their stares calmly and with determination. He would not let his men down.

"We're going over there." Jack pointed his sword for a second time towards the great redoubt. The men nervously flicked their eyes at it but not one murmur of dissent was uttered.

"We're going over there because we captured that damn place and I cannot bear to see our efforts wasted. We fought bloody hard to take it and I'll see my soul rot in hell before I give it back to the damn Russians without a proper fight."

Only Flanagan looked aghast, horrified that he seemed to have throw in his lot with a group of lunatics.

Jack fixed him with a grim smile. "You're a lucky man, young Flanagan. Now you get to fight with real soldiers." Jack saw the grins on the grimy faces of his men, just as he had intended. "Right, Light Company. Extended order. Flanagan, you stay with me. Let's move."

What was left of the company shook itself into a skirmish line of barely twenty men.

They were going to attack.

The retreat of the Fusilier Brigade towards the Alma was chaotic. The redcoats careered down the slope, all cohesion lost in the race for safety. The Russian skirmishers who had moved into the great redoubt poured fire into their backs, gunning down dozens and adding fresh impetus to the rout. The redcoats had achieved so much that day. They had fought hard and won a great victory, yet left unsupported and exposed, the remnants of the three battalions had simply had enough, their willingness to stand and fight exhausted.

As they retreated, the 1st Division finally advanced. The Guards Brigade and the Highland Brigade had endured hours under artillery fire, pinned down on the far bank of the Alma. They had chafed at their impotency, so when the order finally came to advance, they seized upon it and quickly formed up. The Highland Brigade made up the left-hand half of the 1st Division. They would march up a slope clear of debris, their route well to the east of the path taken by the Light Division's attack on the redoubt. To the right of the Highlanders marched the Guards Brigade, made up from the most famous of all the regiments in the British army. Resplendent in their huge bearskins and with their colours flying, they looked magnificent. They were the elite of the British army, the Queen's favourites, and they marched with an arrogant pride.

They followed the path the Fusilier Brigade had taken earlier. The route was littered with the dead and the dying but despite this, the ranks of the guards were immaculate, the officers and sergeants ensuring the line remained perfectly in alignment.

Jack was leading his men towards the right flank of one of the battalions of the Guards Brigade, the Scots Fusiliers, aiming to bring his company alongside in time to join in the guardsmen's assault on the redoubt. His stomach churned yet little of his earlier debilitating fears returned at the idea of a second attack on the vital position. Nothing he could yet experience could possibly be more hellish than what he had already witnessed that day. He led his men with an icy calm, his composure and his determination cleaving his soldiers to him, his firm resolution a rock on to which they could tether their souls.

The men of the Light Company were moving fast but their comrades in the Fusilier Brigade ahead of them were retreating faster. The frightened and exhausted rabble bowled towards the steady ranks of the Scots Fusiliers which stood like a breakwater across their path.

"Open the files, you bloody fools!" Jack snarled through gritted teeth. From his vantage point, Jack could see what was about to happen. He pumped his legs as he led his company across the slope, expending strength he did not have in a futile effort to head off the catastrophe that was about to happen.

Even as he watched, the remains of the Fusilier Brigade clattered into the line of guardsmen, a jarring collision that made Jack wince even from a hundred yards away. The routing troops had one thought in their mind, to get to the rear and to safety. Not even a battalion of fresh guardsmen could stop them. The retreating redcoats drove into the ranks of Scots Fusiliers, their elbows and boots working to force a path through the line. The guardsmen's cohesion was gone in seconds. They tried to advance but they could make no headway against the retreat; try as they might, they were like so much flotsam caught in a raging maelstrom.

One of the British army's prime battalions had been taken out of action before it could even be brought into play.

CHAPTER
THIRTY-EIGHT

Jack halted his men well short of the confusion. They sank to their knees, their chests heaving with exertion, and watched the chaos in silence and growing dismay. Redcoats were pushing, punching and battering each other when they should have been fighting the enemy.

Jack was exhausted and stood doubled over, his hands on his knees, panting like a hound following a long chase after the fox. Finally, he got enough breath into his tortured lungs to allow him to stand up.

The retreating men from the Fusilier Brigade were clawing their way clear. More and more won through, while officers, both on foot and mounted, tried to re-establish control, their bellowed orders adding to the pandemonium.

Like a rock stuck in the middle of a river in flood, the colour party from the Scots Fusiliers stood firm. The routing redcoats were sensible enough to keep a safe distance from the fearsome halberds wielded by the sergeants who guarded the battalion's colours, defending them even from men from their own side. The colours had become a rallying point for the guardsmen and pockets of men made their way towards the twin flags that flew with pride in the heart of the battalion.

"OK, let's go," Jack ordered his men. He had no option but to make for the one part of the Scots Fusiliers that still had some integrity. "Make for the colours."

The easiest route was to move up the slope before turning back to follow the last of the retreating Fusilier Brigade down the incline.

Flanagan loped along beside Jack like an overgrown puppy. As they ran, Jack was forced to keep twisting his neck, trying to keep the colour party in sight while also keeping a sharp watch on the Russians in the redoubt lest they take it into their heads to take advantage of the confusion and push down the slope.

Jack feared a Russian advance. If the Russians moved fast, they could hit the unformed guardsmen and sweep them back over the Alma with all the ease of a Tartar peasant woman cleaning the dirt from her doorstep. The survivors from the Light Company would be caught between the two groups, a morsel certain to be snapped up by the devouring Russian horde.

"Sir! Beware right!"

Dodds's shout made Jack turn his head sharply. Two battalions of the Vladmirsky Regiment had jerked into motion. Jack's fears were about to become reality.

Don't stop! Run, damn you, run!" Jack bellowed at his men, urging them to increase the pace. They were still fifty yards short of the colour party. Jack saw with relief that the Scots Fusiliers were aware of the danger. The guardsmen were forming a line across the path of the Russian advance, their ranks reassuringly steady. But there were pitifully few of them to stand against two fresh Russian battalions. No more than two dozen redcoats and a handful of officers and sergeants remained of the Scots Fusiliers" ordered ranks, far too few to stop the Russians.

Jack's company covered the last few hard yards with their breath coming in tortured gasps. They staggered to a halt in front of a young guards captain who was waving his sword and roaring for more men to rally to the colours. If he was grateful to see Jack and his ragtag company, he did not show it.

"Who the devil are you?"

"Sloames," Jack stammered, his breathing still tortured. "King's Royal Fusiliers."

The captain ran a professional eye over the bedraggled men and Jack's bloodstained and filthy uniform. Whatever he saw must have met with his approval; he reached out a hand and clasped Jack's shoulder in a firm grip that made him wince. "Good fellow. Have your men join the line."

Jack looked anxiously towards the redoubt. The Russian column had been halted while its officers fussily dressed the ranks which had become disordered because of the numerous bodies that littered the ground. The Russian officers' pedantry gave the British a precious few moments to try to organise their own men and allow more redcoats to rally to the colours.

Jack's men took their place in the formation, adding another twenty rifles to the line. Digby-Brown and Sergeant Baker stood behind the Light Company, helping to dress the line, reaching down to grab ammunition or percussion caps from the many corpses that had been dragged unceremoniously out of the way. More men joined and the line slowly extended across the slope. Jack's hopes rose. If the Russians delayed much longer and if more men could be rallied, then there was every chance the British could hold the advance long enough for more fresh troops to be brought forward. There was still a chance to snatch victory from the jaws of defeat.

Major Peacock staggered down the slope among the last of the retreating Fusilier Brigade. His bald head was slick with blood that flowed freely from a deep wound on his crown down into the thin rim of his hair. The fall from Colonel Morris's charger had done little to settle his terrified wits and the fusilier major shouted continuously as he tottered drunkenly down the slope.

"Fusiliers, retire! Retire! Save yourselves!"

Redcoats who had been making for the Scots Fusiliers' colours heard the new order and stopped in their tracks. In the midst of the confusion, there was no voice to countermand Peacock's orders. In the absence of any other instructions, the men did as they were told and moved away from their colours towards the river.

Jack watched in horror. Men desperately needed to block the Russian advance were joining the rout and making their way to the rear.

"Digby-Brown, stay here!"

From somewhere, Jack found the strength to run back up the slope to where Peacock staggered along, his braying voice still urging the men to retreat.

"Sloames!" The single word exploded from Peacock's lips, an astonished squeak of recognition. He must have seen the rage in Jack's eyes, or perhaps the sight of his blood-splattered captain bursting through the retreating mob was too much for his scattered wits. Whatever the cause, Peacock let out a yelp of horror and turned to flee.

Jack flew at the major, hitting his shoulder against Peacock's back with such force that both men were knocked off their feet. Jack's rage drove him on, the pain of the impact barely registering. He flung himself on top of the major's body, flattening him and driving the breath from his body.

"Sloames, no!" Peacock raised his hands in terror. "Please!" he begged. "Don't kill me! I don't want to die! Please!"

Jack slapped the major's hands away in disgust and stood up. It would have given him great satisfaction to beat Peacock to a bleeding pulp. But to do so was to stoop to the level of someone like Slater. Jack had embarked on his long charade to lift himself out of the gutter, to prove that whatever the chance of his birth he was capable of so much more than society allowed. Beating Peacock would condemn him as the brutal ruffian the world expected him to be, the kind of vicious creature he so despised.

Jack reached down and snapped the buckle that held Peacock's holstered revolver around his waist. He picked up the weapon and turned and walked away. He withdrew the revolver from its holster and snapped the gun open. The weapon had not been fired that day and Jack greeted the sight of the fully loaded chambers with a grunt of satisfaction.

He did not look back at Peacock lying on the ground. He thrust the revolver into his own holster replacing the one he had lost when he fled Smith's devastating injury. He made his way back to the line of redcoats, the weight of the revolver against his hip reassuring.

He risked a glance towards the Russian column. He was relieved to see that they were still halted. The Russian officers were running around the flanks of the columns like sheepdogs worrying a flock of sheep. He had time to rejoin his men. The makeshift British line looked desperately feeble in the face of the two Russian columns but Jack's mind was clear. He needed to be with his men, whatever their fate.

The captain from the Scots Fusiliers saw him coming and waved him in, a wry smile on his face.

"Thought you might have left us, old man."

Jack grinned at the plummy voice. It would once have caused him to bite his tongue with anger. Now it did not matter. The guards captain was willingly facing the same grim fate he himself was, his privileged birth no protection against the power of a Russian bullet. Here, at least, two men from vastly different backgrounds were equals.

"Never." Jack smiled, "I wouldn't miss this for the world."

CHAPTER
THIRTY-NINE

The Russian infantry stirred into life and the drummers at the centre of each column settled into the hypnotic rhythm of the march.

"Here they come," Dodds announced.

"Thank you, Dodds." Jack was glad of the chance to speak and break the foreboding silence that had gripped his company. "Aim low, men. Hit the bastards in the guts. Make them hurt."

The officers of the westernmost Russian column, seeing what lay ahead, aligned their attack so that it would swamp the redcoats who bravely but foolishly contested its passage.

The second column, further to the east, bore to the left of the redcoats' flank, ignoring their futile resistance, seeking an easier route to the Alma. It would keep them away from the fight, leaving the redcoats to concentrate their fire on the western column.

Jack prowled up and down the section of the line where the remnants of the Light Company waited for the enemy, offering his few words of advice and encouragement. His feet scuffed against discarded equipment, the detritus of the Light Division's attack littering the ground. Mercifully, the bodies of the dead and wounded had been dragged to one side so at least he was spared having to walk over their torn flesh. The captain of the guards had moved to the left flank of the line, leaving Jack to command the right. The unspoken agreement to share the command left Jack absurdly pleased with himself.

There were less than sixty redcoats in the line, facing more than ten times their number in the Russian column. In the centre of the line the colours of the Scots Fusiliers barely stirred in the light breeze. The two colours added a touch of grandeur that seemed out of place in a scene of such appalling human devastation.

"When they come, stick them with your spikes." Jack was still patrolling the line. "Make those bastards bleed."

To the right, Jack saw Digby-Brown draw his sword. The bright afternoon sunlight flashed from its blade. The lieutenant looked dreadfully young, flecks of dried blood standing out like engorged freckles against his pale face. He offered a tight-lipped smile when he saw his captain looking at him, his young eyes reflecting a world-weary sadness more suited to someone much older than his tender age.

Jack would have liked to go to his lieutenant's side, to offer a word of comfort or to show a shred of compassion. But the advancing Russian column made that impossible. All Jack could do was return Digby-Brown's brave smile with a nod of encouragement.

294

"At one hundred yards, volley fire!" The guards captain's voice was firm, every syllable enunciated with care, as if the officer was aware these could be the last orders he was ever going to give.

"Present!"

The line of rifles steadied as the men braced themselves to fire.

"Fire!"

The volley crashed out, spitting sixty Minié balls into the packed ranks of the Russian column. Many in the front rank crumpled, as did some behind them as the powerful bullets ripped through living flesh and on into succeeding ranks.

"Reload!"

The guards captain called out the orders calmly, as if conducting a company drill rather than a desperate final defence that would likely see his whole command destroyed within minutes. The men obeyed without conscious thought. To Jack's shame he realised that he had not taken the time to find out the captain's name. He would fight this last battle under the command of a stranger.

"Present."

More than one redcoat fumbled his ammunition or dropped his firing caps, exhaustion and haste making his fingers clumsy.

"Fire!"

A second volley exploded across the slope, following by the crackle of tardy shots from the men who had not been ready.

The front of the column had been butchered. Dozens of Russian soldiers had been struck down, their bodies blocking the way of the men behind them.

"Charge! Charge!"

This was the time for the exhausted and bedraggled redcoats to unleash their terror on the stalled enemy. A ragged cheer erupted from their parched throats and they surged forward, sixty men emerging from the cloud of powder smoke to charge six hundred like the very hounds of hell.

Jack drew his sword as he ran, the long steel edge rasping from the scabbard, its balanced weight snug in his hand. The blade felt alive, as if a vital force of energy was flowing into him, filling his aching muscles with a new strength. With his sword held high in his right hand, he tugged Peacock's revolver free from its holster with his left.

The redcoats closed on the Russian ranks, their wild screams freezing the blood of the enemy conscripts. The Russian officers yelled orders, the air full of their foreign words and unintelligible commands. The column jerked into motion once more. The leading ranks hefted their own bayonets and braced themselves for the impact of the charge. Their movements were ponderous, the Russian conscripts clearly terrified of the screaming redcoats.

The redcoats closed the distance quickly and hammered into the leading Russian ranks. The first Russian conscripts died in an instant, wholly unable to deflect the violent assault. The leading redcoats pulled their bayonets out of the flesh of their first victims and

296

moved on to the next, pounding forward, stepping over their victims, stabbing and gutting without pause.

Jack went with his men, his whole body thrilling to the insanity of the charge. There was a wild joy in the madness that he savoured even as the terror and the fear cascaded through his soul. Nothing mattered except the desire to smash his sword into the enemy, to fight and hack at anyone who dared to stand in his way. It was irresistible.

A gap appeared between Dodds and Taylor, the two redcoats fighting directly in front of Jack. He pushed into the opening, thrusting his sword forward eagerly. Its razor-sharp point pierced the flesh of a Russian soldier who had been about to stab an unsuspecting Fusilier Dodds in the side. The Russian's head whipped round with a scream as Jack's blade slid between two of his ribs. Despite the agony of the wound the Russian twisted his hands on the musket so he could bring it round to stab his attacker. The bayonet snagged on the corner of Dodds's jacket, which gave Jack an opening. He raised his left hand and jammed the barrel of his revolver into the face of the wounded Russian.

Without hesitation, Jack pulled the trigger.

The Russian jerked backwards as if an invisible rope had tugged him. The bullet punched his body free of Jack's sword and sent him flailing into the soldiers behind him.

Jack steadied his wrist, changed his point of aim and fired again, repeating the action until all five chambers were empty. The storm of bullets struck home with appalling violence and cleared a space between him and the nearest Russians. Without a second thought, he stepped forward, relishing the opportunity to flay his sword at the enemy, heedless of the risk. As he moved, he threw the now empty revolver into the face of a Russian conscript and swung his blade wildly. To his frustration the sword sliced into the wood of a Russian musket. Jack's arm rang with the impact but he recovered quickly and swept the blade forward once more. This time the tip took the throat of the Russian whose musket had blocked the first wild attack.

The enemy were all around him, his mindless attack had driven him deep into the Russian ranks. Bayonets thrust at him from every angle and it took all his speed to bring his sword round in a desperate, sweeping defence. One bayonet slipped past his blade and tore into the hem of his jacket where it stuck fast. The horrified look in its owner's eyes barely registered in Jack's mind before he swept his sword across the Russian's face, taking the man's sight in a heartbeat.

Jack's men pressed forward and were soon fighting close around him once more.

The redcoats had thrust hard and fast into the Russian ranks but the column was deep and the wedge of redcoats converged into an ever finer point. At its tip, Jack and the men of the Light Company fought like men possessed, dozens of Russian conscripts dying under their dreadful assault. Yet redcoats, too, were falling. Steadily their numbers dwindled and the assault slowly ground to a halt against the sheer number of enemy soldiers.

The Russians moved round the point of the attack, forcing the British soldiers on the flanks to give ground, bending the attacking line back on itself. It was only a matter of time before the redcoats were surrounded.

CHAPTER
FORTY

On the far right of the attacking line, Digby-Brown was desperately trying to stay alive. His left arm bled from where a bayonet had pierced the flesh to the bone and the limb hung uselessly at his side as he fought against the horde of men pressing in on the flank. Many of the redcoats that had stood nearest to him lay dead or dying. The entire right flank was collapsing around him.

Digby-Brown slashed his sword to his left, beating back bayonet after bayonet. He was forced to step backwards, giving yet more ground, compressing the attacking line still further. He had no concept of what was happening elsewhere. He could not risk turning round to see if the other flank was also moving backwards.

He slashed the pitted and notched edge of his sword forward, enjoying a brief surge of joy as he sliced into the neck of a Russian. It was short-lived. He recovered his blade only just in time to beat aside a bayonet that had threatened to slide into his unprotected ribcage.

He took another step back as more bayonets came at him, stabbing at the spot he had just vacated. His quick feet saved him for a moment longer, the sharp points ripping his clothes but stopping short of reaching his flesh. So far he had remained silent but finally a howl of frustration and building terror escaped through his gritted teeth as he swatted aside yet another bayonet and then another. His desire to live was so very strong. He did not want to die. Not here. Not now.

He fought on, beating aside the enemy's bayonets with a desperate strength, his duty tying him to his position as firmly as any physical tether. The nothingness of death terrified him. The tears coursed down his cheeks as he fought. Digby-Brown faced his death but he refused to accept its approach.

A Russian officer was screaming orders behind the closest conscripts, his frantic gestures summoning more men from the body of the column, bringing even more numbers to bear on the creaking flank. Digby-Brown was forced to give ground again, his faltering defence barely keeping the countless thrusting bayonets at bay.

The heel of his right boot caught on the body of a fusilier. It was a corpse from the Light Division's first assault on the great redoubt. It still lay where it had fallen, a great hole torn in the dead man's stomach, eviscerated by a Russian shell.

Digby-Brown was thrown off balance and he fell on to his back across the dead fusilier, his shoulders and back lying on blood-soaked ground and spilt intestines.

The bayonets were reaching for him before he even hit the ground. The blades met no resistance as the first two slipped into Digby-Brown's flesh. There was no pain as the bayonets pierced his body, no searing agony as the Russians leant down on their blades, driving them into his torso so that the tips emerged through his back.

But his terror bubbled through, the horror of knowing he was to about to die forcing a scream from his lips.

He still held his sword and he thrust the blade upwards into the ribs of one of his assailants. The Russian let go of his rifle and grabbed Digby-Brown's sword with both hands, tearing the blade from his weakening grip.

It was Digby-Brown's last act of defiance.

Another bayonet stabbed into his thigh, immediately followed by many more, the sharp blades rammed home with enthusiasm. The pain came now, a terrible wave of agony that flared and built until mercifully he lost consciousness. Digby-Brown died, unaware of the last terrible ravages wrought on his body. The Russian conscripts vented their fear in a frenzy of stabbing and hacking, the young officer's body torn to bloody shreds in their rage.

Jack fought with wild abandon. He had no idea what was happening around him. He saw nothing but the next blow, sought nothing but more victims for his blade, its edge now blunted by countless blows that had landed against muskets or bayonets that blocked it from finding its way into Russian flesh.

The men at his side fought with ruthless efficiency and a merciless professionalism that had the Russian conscripts backing away rather than face them. Jack and his men walked on the bodies of their victims, occasionally ramming their weapons down into the ruined flesh beneath their boots, quenching any last resistance from the men they had struck down. They were surrounded by the dead and the dying, the stench of blood and opened bowels thick in their throats. The very depths of hell were exposed on the Russian plain.

Their arms were leaden, their muscles protested at every movement, yet they fought on, their rage sustaining their bodies far beyond the point of exhaustion. Jack sobbed as he fought, the pain in his battered body an unrelenting agony. Fusilier Dodds still fought at his side, uttering an unceasing stream of obscenities as he killed the men who stood against him, his curses the last sound they would ever hear.

Less than half the redcoats who had formed the makeshift line still lived. The Scots Fusilier captain who had brought them together was dead, his body surrounded by the corpses of the men he had slain. The two lieutenants who carried the colours still lived, protected by the colour sergeants who ferociously beat off any Russian who sought fame and fortune by capturing their enemy's pride.

The surviving redcoats were being pressed ever closer together. The flanks had long since folded and the British were reduced to a desperate huddle, surrounded and alone. The pressure on the small knot of men was unceasing; wave after wave of Russian soldiers rushed forward, urged on by their officers or dragged into the fight by a sergeant.

Jack blocked another bayonet that was thrust at his stomach, punching the hilt of his sword into the attacking Russian's face, bludgeoning the conscript to the ground. A Russian sergeant immediately moved to take the man's place. He thrust his bayonet forward with rapid professional jabs that took all of Jack's wavering strength to counter and left him no opening to counterattack. Jack blocked and blocked, each blow jarring his agonised muscles. The Russian sergeant sensed his superiority and pressed forward relentlessly.

Then everything changed.

The deafening bark of a battalion volley crashed out to the right of the Russian column. Jack heard crisp British voices immediately issuing orders to reload, their clipped tones more suited to the parade square than this sordid butcher's yard of a battle.

Russian soldiers on the right of the column fell to the ground, scythed down like stalks of wheat cut by a threshing machine. The dense Russian formation shuddered, and then emitted a dreadful groan, like an enormous wild animal fatally wounded by a hunter's well-aimed shot. The shudder became a spasm as the Russian conscripts were thrown into confusion. A second British volley shattered any vestiges of cohesion as the shocked conscripts clawed at each other in their sudden haste to escape.

The pressure on the small knot of redcoats eased instantly.

The Russian sergeant facing Jack rammed his bayonet forward with one last, half-hearted thrust that Jack easily knocked aside. The two men stared at each

304

"Stay here. Don't let anyone drag you back into the fight. You've done enough. More than enough."

Jack said nothing else as he left his company for the last time. Ignoring his tortured body, he abandoned his men to Sergeant Baker's care and set off back across the slope. He had one last duty to perform.

CHAPTER
FORTY-ONE

Jack traipsed his way towards the fold in the ground where he had hoped to hide the Light Company when Peacock's terrible error caused the fusiliers to break. His abused body laboured to keep moving and it took all of his dwindling willpower to force it to struggle onwards.

The ground was strewn with the detritus of battle. His feet stumbled against discarded equipment. The bodies of the dead were everywhere. Jack had to force himself to ignore the mangled flesh, each twisted body a tragedy in its own right. The accumulation of death on such an unimaginable scale enough to soil a soul for all eternity.

The wounded pleaded for his aid. Voices wracked with pain begged for help, for water, for their mothers, or simply for a bullet to end their suffering. Jack walked carefully past their ruined bodies, careful not to jar his heavy boots against their tortured flesh, deaf to the pitiful pleas that accosted him, his stony expression betraying none of the sorrow that the sight of such suffering caused him.

As he walked, he thought of his men, the ones still living and the ones who had fallen. He thought of

Colonel Morris, of Lieutenant Flowers and of Digby-Brown.

Finally, he came to the place where the Russian shell had lifted him off his feet. His memory was hazy yet still vivid enough for him to recognise the terrain. He saw the scorch marks on the churned earth where the shell had exploded. He fancied he could even discern the crushed grass that revealed where he had curled on the ground, when the horror had overwhelmed his mind and temporarily displaced his sanity.

With a heavy tread, Jack turned to plod wearily up the shallow incline of the slope, retracing the path along which he had run in such terror. Around him, the sounds of battle still raged yet to his exhausted senses the cacophony of battle sounded muted, as if it was taking place in the far distance instead of only a few hundred yards away. His senses were dulled to such an extent that he felt almost at peace. His battered mind found nothing remarkable in the occasional Russian artillery shells that exploded nearby or attached any consequence to the roundshot that punched through the air within yards of where he walked.

The sight of the torso he was looking for made Jack straighten his shoulders. His weariness fell away. He had no difficulty recognising the familiar figure of his orderly.

He looked down on what remained of Tommy Smith's face. His stomach churned yet he managed to keep the wave of nausea under control. Tommy Smith was dead, his sightless eyes stared up at the clear blue sky. It was what Jack had trudged all this way to discover; the idea that his orderly might still be alive with such a terrible wound was more than Jack could bear.

"He's a dead 'un."

Jack was not surprised to hear that voice again. Part of him had known that coming to find Tommy Smith would result in having to face Slater one last time.

"And I reckon you should join him, don't you?"

Jack stayed still, his gaze fixed on Smith's staring blue eyes.

"You were a fool not to drill me when you had the chance. But then you always was a soft little turd." Slater paused to spit out of wad of phlegm. "I reckon you even started to believe you actually was an officer."

From deep inside Jack summoned the energy to turn round and face Slater. The former colour sergeant was standing a few paces away. The revolver he was aiming at Jack looked like a child's toy in his meaty hand.

"You're a fool, Lark. You were born a fool and you'll damn well die a fool."

The unfamiliar revolver was clumsy in Slater's hands as he cocked the weapon and curled his finger round the trigger.

Jack recognised the gun as his own. The barrel pointed straight at his heart. He looked up and stared

310

into the pit of hatred in Slater's merciless eyes and saw death.

Jack threw his body forward, diving on to the ground. He moved like an old man, his abused body as supple as a brick. He was slow, so very slow.

The cough of the revolver blasted into Jack's ears a fraction of a second after the bullet punched into his body. The impact of the single bullet twisted his diving body, throwing him backwards so that he landed awkwardly on his side. Pain surged through him, an agony so fierce that his vision faded. He heard the revolver firing again and again as Slater wildly emptied all five chambers. Jack's body tensed, waiting for a second explosion of agony. The air around him was punched with violent force as the bullets flew past but Slater's wild firing and lack of familiarity with the gun had sent the bullets wide.

Slater stood with the smoking revolver cradled in his hands, staring at Jack's twitching body. The fresh blood on the grass confirmed that his aim had been true. His enemy's desperate dive had not saved him from the fate he so richly deserved. Jack's body gave a final jerk and then lay still.

It was over.

Slater savoured the sweet taste of revenge.

Jack felt the cold fingers of death slide over his heart. He sensed the nothingness of oblivion pulling at him, an awful void from which there was no return. Something deep inside him flickered, a final spark of life that rebelled against his fate. Jack Lark would not go so meekly to his death.

He opened his eyes. He saw Slater standing over his prostrate body, gloating. The sight filled Jack with rage, a righteous fury that fuelled his injured body.

He snapped his legs straight, driving the heels of his boots against Slater's knees. The sickening crunch of bones breaking was clearly audible.

Slater crumbled over his shattered kneecaps, the suddenness of Jack's violent attack taking him completely unaware. He hit the ground hard, his two hands reaching down to his mutilated knees, his screams drowning out the sounds of battle that still rippled and crackled through the air.

Jack stumbled to his feet, moving away from Slater, his left hand pressed over the wound on the right side of his body. His blood pulsed through his tightly clenched fingers.

He saw Slater twist on the ground, heard his sobs as the huge man scrabbled towards Smith's rifle which lay discarded on the ground.

Jack reached the rifle just before Slater's meaty paws wrapped round the stock. He snatched it away and ruthlessly crushed the grasping fingers under his boot. Slater bellowed. He reached for Jack's ankle, fighting on.

Jack felt the thick fingers claw at this flesh. Without hesitation he brought the rifle round until the long barrel pressed hard against Slater's temple. For a fleeting instant he thought of Molly. He smiled as he pictured her blowing away the errant curls of hair from her face, the knowing smile on her face as she saw him watching her. The memory fled, leaving just the twisted face of the man who had killed her.

Jack was certain he saw the flare of fear deep in Slater's eyes, the realisation that he was about to die triggering a spasm of horror.

Jack felt nothing as he pulled the trigger. The bullet punched through Slater's skull, killing him instantly in a grotesque shower of blood, brain and bone.

As Jack looked down at Slater's body, a violent storm of emotion shuddered through his pain-wracked body. It scoured his soul and released the passions that he had kept contained for so long.

He screamed at the heavens, a single incoherent shriek of bitter grief.

In the sudden silence that followed, Jack's head sagged forward, all emotion spent, his soul an empty husk.

He staggered back to Smith's corpse. He ignored the wounds to his own body, was hardly aware of the flow of blood that pulsed out of his side with every beat of his racing heart. He did not care about the future, the past did not concern him.

His charade was over.

With the final vestiges of his strength, Jack bent low and started to strip the uniform from Tommy Smith's corpse. He sobbed as he dragged off the heavy red coat that was stiff with dried blood. His fingers felt the cheap cloth of Smith's jacket; the heavy weave was so different from the beautiful scarlet fabric that he had stolen.

He had lived up to his desire to better himself, he had proved that he could lead men in the tumult of battle. He had not let Molly down.

It was time for Captain Sloames to die.

Epilogue

The stench was overpowering. It assaulted Jack's senses, demanding his attention. Its nauseating stink flooded his nostrils, filling his mouth with its foul odour so that he came back to the world of the living retching and coughing.

"Oi, oi. Someone's coming back to us."

Rough hands lifted his head and pressed the cold rim of a tin mug against his lips. The noxious smell of the liquid that was tipped over his sore and swollen lips made him gag, but the hand that held him was unyielding so he could do nothing but swallow the bitter drink.

"There you go, chum. It ain't as good as rum but it's all you're going to get for the moment."

Despite its foul stink, the water at least unglued Jack's mouth and moistened his throat enough for him to question his benefactor.

"Where am I?"

There was a gentle chuckle. "Where are you?" The voice found the question amusing. "Well, chum, you're in hospital. In the shit-hole they call Scutari. You've been raving with the fever the last few days, hollering at the sky. Now rest easy. None of us is going anywhere. Not unless we karks it, that is. And that ain't something we can do a fucking thing about. So take it as it comes."

Jack did as he was told and closed his eyes, hoping for the sanctuary of unconsciousness. All soldiers feared the surgeons, feared being incarcerated in the army hospitals where death was as likely an outcome as life. Jack was in the place all soldiers dreaded and it terrified him. His lips formed the words of a silent prayer, one he had learnt as a child. It had crept into his mind unbidden, eerily apt: "If I should die before I wake, I pray the Lord my soul to take."

Scutari had become infamous in the army even before the battle. It was where the sick were taken to die. Now, after the battle, and overwhelmed by hundreds of injured soldiers, it was rapidly descending into a scene of biblical squalor. Men lay everywhere, their bodies still encrusted in the filth of the battlefield. Nearly two thousand souls had been brought to the hospital which had beds for barely half that number. The handful of orderlies, doctors and surgeons worked tirelessly but they were hopelessly outnumbered by the multitude of broken bodies that begged for their attention.

The beds in which the lucky few were laid were filthy, the floor around them encrusted with ordure. The handful of slop buckets in each dank room overflowed with human waste. The wounded soldiers did not have the comfort of even a single blanket to cover them, their bodies were devoured by lice, they

316

were unwashed and stinking, and they still wore the soiled and reeking rags they had arrived in. The few windows in the rooms were bolted shut, condemning the wounded to lie in the gloom, denied the joy of sunlight or of a breeze that would have eased the stifling, stinking, suffocating heat that tormented their final hours.

The injured soldiers stared at the high, vaulted ceilings and suffered. Their torture had started on the battlefield where they had been left, in some cases for twenty-four long hours before they were carried to the beach for evacuation. From there, if they were still alive, they were taken by ship to the hospital at Scutari three hundred miles away. It sat like a festering sore on the coast of Turkey opposite the splendour and the vibrancy of Constantinople.

The ships struggled to transport the vast number of wounded, who shared the limited space with hundreds of men who had been struck down with fever before the battle had even been joined. The decks were blanketed with the bodies of the sick and wounded; men died in the filth, uncared for and alone. Their bodies were dumped unceremoniously overboard or simply left to rot where they lay. Most ships had just one or two orderlies, or perhaps a single surgeon to cope with the hundreds of men.

The dreadful journey lasted three to five days, each an interminable hell, where minutes crept by like hours and hours felt like days. One ship, the *Shooting Star*, took a dreadful thirteen days to make the trip to Scutari, a period of unimaginable horror for the one hundred and thirty wounded on board. Just under half died in the time it took their vessel to reach its destination.

The hospital at Scutari was a dubious sanctuary for the men whose bodies had been broken in the horror of the fighting. If shock, infection, gangrene or loss of blood did not kill them, then a raft of fatal diseases claimed them — typhus, dysentery, cholera, fevers. Disease stalked the hospital, thriving in the dank and squalid conditions.

Jack gave up counting the bricks in the vaulted ceiling above his head. He had drifted in and out of consciousness for what could have been minutes, or hours, or days. Time had no meaning.

He remembered little of his journey to the hospital save for mere flashes, random memories of being taken to the shore on one of the pitifully few carts the army had available to transport its wounded. Of the short voyage itself, he remembered nothing. He could hazily recollect the pain of his flesh being stitched back together, and the feeling of deft hands binding his wounds, but whether that had been on board the ship or in the hospital, he had no idea.

The memories of battle he locked away in a far corner of his mind and threw away the key. But his dreams betrayed him. They broke down his barriers, replaying the horror so he woke in terror, bathed in sweat, his body trembling with fear. The wounds to his soul ran deep. He tried to remember the past but memories of his childhood or of his early years in the army resisted all his attempts to access them. Even Molly's face remained stubbornly distant; the image of her he carried in his mind was faded, robbed of its vitality, little more than a vague impression.

He lay on his filthy bed and tried to shut out the constant moans, groans, sobs, curses and pleas of the other inmates. Mercifully, the men on either side of him were silent, although they were pressed so close together that Jack's bed vibrated with every movement made by the wounded guardsman in the bed to his right. Barely two inches separated the rows of filthy beds. A narrow gap down the centre of the room gave access to any of the scarce medical staff who dared to venture into the foetid space.

Once, Jack had woken to the sound of a fresh patient being brought in. He had watched with morbid fascination as two orderlies deftly settled the man into the bed, and then bound his wounds with bandages stained with old blood. It did not take long, their practised hands worked swiftly. Neither orderly said a word during the few minutes they were in the room.

Jack knew he faced a choice. He could give in to his despair and let the grief and the guilt and the festering horror claim him, body and soul, or he could once again fend for himself. He could rise from this stinking pit and find a way to live.

"Oi! What's your game?"

Jack started, his battered nerves jangling at the sudden shout. He had been scraping a metal ladle across the bottom of a wooden bucket that should have held enough fresh water for the whole room but which now yielded only a few thimblefuls of dark brown, scabby liquid.

The desire to bark back at the overweight orderly corporal was hard to subdue; his mind was responding as if he were still a captain who would command immediate respect. The corporal's florid face twitched with annoyance. He stood staring at Jack, wiping his bloody hands across an apron that was so encrusted with blood and filth that it stood proud of his body, as stiff as thick card.

"Just getting some water, Corporal."

"Well, if you're recovered enough to be out of bed, you're well enough to be passed fit. What's your name?"

"Smith, Corporal."

"Smith? There's more bleeding Smiths in this here hospital than there are lice in my crotch. You taking me for a ride, sonny Jim?"

"No, Corporal. My name is Smith. Tommy Smith."

"Well then, Tommy Smith. Seeing as you is hail and hearty enough to be up and strolling around, you can give me a hand."

Jack straightened up, wincing as the wound in his side pulled painfully.

The corporal sneered at him. "It's no good acting like you is hurting now. I've got your number. Come over here and grab this dead 'un by his ankles."

Jack did as he was bid, looking dubiously at the body of the man who had lain so silently in the bed immediately next to his own. "Is he dead then?"

"Well, he ain't bleeding dancing, is he, poor sod. Is he dead, indeed! Of course he's bleeding dead on account of the fact that he ain't been bleeding breathing for the last two bleeding days. Now grab hold and shut up."

"Yes, Corporal."

The two men lifted the dead weight of the redcoat from the stinking bed. Jack was forced to tug at the man's legs, which were stuck to the filthy sheet. The smell of the dead man was awful.

"Come on, let's take this poor sod away. Then I reckon there's more work for you to do, young Tommy Smith — if you don't fancy being passed fit for duty, that is."

Jack staggered as he helped carry the dead redcoat from the room, his legs betraying his weakness. There was a sharp tut of disapproval from the corporal. It was a struggle but between them they carried the body outside to a walled yard that was already piled high with corpses.

"Bloody hell!" Jack could not keep back his exclamation of horror. The dead had been dumped without ceremony and lay in all manner of unnatural positions, legs and arms bent at impossible angles. Some lay with their eyes wide open, staring serenely at the clear blue sky, while the faces of others were twisted and terrible, their tongues bulging grotesquely from gaping mouths. The wounds that had killed them were evident on most of them, their bodies missing one or more limbs, or with large holes in what had once been living flesh.

It was a scene straight from a nightmare.

Jack dropped the legs of the fresh corpse he carried and bent double, vomiting out his horror at the dreadful sight.

"Come on, lad. That's enough of that. These poor sods don't care. Not any more." The corporal let go of his end of the body and reached forward to place an unexpectedly soothing hand on Jack's back, rubbing it in small circles like a parent winding a child.

Jack wiped the saliva that dangled from his mouth on his soiled cuffs and straightened up. The corporal was right. The dead were past caring.

"Good, lad." The corporal turned to lead Jack from the charnel house. "Plenty more to shift," he said over his shoulder. "Officers too. Not that the Jack Puddings get dumped outside. Oh no. We have a special room for the toffs."

The corporal led Jack through a confusing maze of gloomy corridors.

"Here we are. One officer recently expired."

Jack followed the corporal's corpulent figure into a dark side room that contained a single bed. The body of a young man lay peacefully in it, a sheet neatly tucked round it. Somebody had taken the time to undress the unfortunate officer; his uniform lay folded on top of a travelling chest that had been placed to one side of the bed so that it could double as a bedside table.

"He's dead?"

"What is it with you? Yes, he's a dead'un all right."

"What killed him? He looks like he's just asleep."

322

"Fever. He's been here nigh on a fortnight. From before the battle. I was only speaking to him yesterday. He seemed as right as rain. Telling me all about his new commission and everything."

"What do you mean?"

"Well," the corporal perched his oversized backside on the corner of the bed, relishing the opportunity to talk. "His ma and pa died a little while back and he just got his inheritance, you see. Now a clever chap, like you and me, would spend that wisely, on beer or women, or something worthwhile like that. But this young fool blows the whole bleeding lot on a captaincy. And not just that but a captaincy in a regiment stationed in bleeding India of all places. He was going to make his fortune, or so he thought, the daft bugger. Why anyone would want to go to that heathen place is beyond me, like it's beyond him now, poor sod."

Jack looked down at the ill-fated officer who had died just as he had secured the same rank that Jack himself had risked so much to take as his own. "What was his name?"

"His name? Let me think. Danbury, I think it was, yes, that's it. Lieutenant Danbury. Or Captain Danbury, I suppose now."

Jack smiled. "Danbury. That's a good honest name. I like it."

Historical Note

The Battle of the Alma resonates in our history. Many towns boast an Alma Terrace or a pub called The Heights of the Alma and countless little girls have been named after the battle fought over one hundred and fifty years ago. Yet it appears to have disappeared from our national consciousness. Ask people about Waterloo and all will know of the great battle where Wellington defeated Napoleon. Ask about the Alma and you will be greeted with blank looks or given directions to a nearby hostelry.

The tale of battle happens largely as described in *The Scarlet Thief*. The King's Royal Fusiliers have stolen the role of the 33rd Regiment of Foot and for that I humbly apologise to the men who fought on that bloody day in the ranks of that most illustrious regiment. General Raglan did indeed fling his troops against the heart of the Russian position and one has only to look at the enormous casualties those leading regiments took to see what it cost the men ordered to advance towards the massed ranks of the Russian army. Raglan rightly received harsh criticism in the national press, much of it written by officers so appalled that they broke the gentleman's code of not "croaking" by writing to the newspaper in droves.

Raglan and Codrington existed, as did the charismatic Colonel Lacy Yea who did indeed order his battalion to "*Never mind forming! Come on, men! Come on, anyhow.*" Otherwise the characters are from my own imagination, yet I hope they convey something of the men who had the mettle to fight in that most terrible of battles.

Anyone wishing to study the battle in more detail will find a wealth of resources available. I would not hesitate to recommend *The Battle of the Alma* by Ian Fletcher and Natalia Ishchenko for a wonderful account of the battle from both a Russian as well as a British perspective. For more detail on the life of the redcoat I cannot speak highly enough of *Redcoat* by the unsurpassed Richard Holmes, a book that is never far from my side.

Jack Lark will soldier on. Somehow he will find the strength to put Molly's death and his memory of the bitter fighting behind him. His adventures will take him far and wide and without a tie to a regiment or even to a name he will venture across a British Empire that was at its very peak in the middle of the nineteenth century.

Acknowledgments

This book was started on a train after a long, tiring day at work. It has only seen the light of day thanks to the efforts of many wonderful people.

I owe a great deal to David Headley, my agent, who saw something in my decidedly dodgy submission that inspired him to read the first draft of this story. His perseverance made this book what it is today and his unwavering support and boundless enthusiasm have been the driving force behind this project.

The team at Headline have worked tirelessly to shape and tidy the story and I must thank them all for their efforts. I am deeply indebted to my editor, Martin Fletcher, for his advice and insight.

My colleagues at work have endured my endless wittering about this novel and I must thank them for their patience. The last few years have seen us put through the wringer in so many ways and their great humour and companionship, even in the bleakest of times, have made coming into the office a genuine pleasure.

My parents have always offered me every support and I would like to take this opportunity to thank them for everything they have done for me.

Finally I must thank my wonderful family. Debbie, my wife, and my three children, Lily, William and Emily, are truly the centre of my universe and they have my love and gratitude for always.

APL		CCS	
Cen		Ear	
Mcb		Cou	
ALL		Job	
WIL		CHS	
Ald		Bel	
Fin	3/2014	Fol	
Can		STO	
TIL		HCL	